a novel

LEPER TANGO

DAVID MacKINNON

ESSENTIAL PROSE SERIES 95

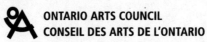

Canada Council   Conseil des Arts
for the Arts   du Canada

ONTARIO ARTS COUNCIL
CONSEIL DES ARTS DE L'ONTARIO

Guernica Editions Inc. acknowledges the support of the Canada Council
for the Arts and the Ontario Arts Council.
The Ontario Arts Council is an agency of the Government of Ontario.

a novel

LEPER
TANGO

DAVID MacKINNON

GUERNICA
TORONTO • BUFFALO • BERKELEY• LANCASTER (U.K.)
2012

Copyright © 2012, David MacKinnon and Guernica Editions Inc.
All rights reserved. The use of any part of this publication,
reproduced, transmitted in any form or by any means, electronic,
mechanical, photocopying, recording or otherwise stored in a
retrieval system, without the prior consent of the publisher is an
infringement of the copyright law.

Michael Mirolla, general editor
David Moratto, book designer
Guernica Editions Inc.
P.O. Box 117, Station P, Toronto (ON), Canada M5S 2S6
2250 Military Road, Tonawanda, N.Y. 14150-6000 U.S.A.

Distributors:
University of Toronto Press Distribution,
5201 Dufferin Street, Toronto (ON), Canada M3H 5T8
Gazelle Book Services, White Cross Mills, High Town,
Lancaster LA1 4XS U.K.
Small Press Distribution, 1341 Seventh St., Berkeley,
CA 94710-1409 U.S.A.

First edition.
Printed in Canada.

Legal Deposit — First Quarter
Library of Congress Catalog Card Number: 2012932925
Library and Archives Canada Cataloguing in Publication
MacKinnon, David (David J.)
Leper tango / David MacKinnon.

(Essential prose series ; 95)
Issued also in electronic format.
ISBN 978-1-55071-367-1

I. Title. II. Series: Essential prose series ; 95.

PS8625.K5535L46 2012   C813'.6   C2012-901199-1

To S, L & C
who make all things possible.

THE LAST WILL AND TESTAMENT OF FRANCK HUDNER ROBINSON, ESQUIRE

I, Franck Hudner Robinson, residing in *Hotel du Quai Voltaire*, Paris, France, being of sound and disposing mind and memory, do make, publish and declare this as and for my last will and testament, hereby revoking all letters or instruments of a testamentary character by me heretofore executed.

FIRST: Allahu Akhbar and praise the Lord, due to a dissolute life, I have virtually nothing to my name.

SECOND: I direct my Executor, Mr Hervé Bourque, Solicitor, to pay all of my just debts, funeral expenses and testamentary charges as soon after my death as can conveniently be done, and to dispose of my remains in the manner set forth hereafter in the event such procedure is not undertaken by Ms. Sheba Rosenstein, as more fully detailed at Section the FIFTH hereof.

THIRD: I direct that all succession, estate or inheritance taxes which may be levied against my estate and/or against any legacies and/or devises hereinafter set forth shall be paid out of my residuary estate.

FOURTH:
    (a) I give and bequeath to Alena Poinconneuse, *whore*, should she survive me, the sum of $10,000.00.
    (b) I give and bequeath to MILLIE REIS, *whore*, should she survive me, the sum of $10,000.00.
    (c) I give and bequeath to Mr and Mrs Tranh Nguyen Thu, or to the survivor of them, or if Mr Nguyen Thu should predecease me, then to his

wife, Anastasia Nguyen Thu, the sum of $5,000.00, it being my wish that such sum be used towards an all-expense weekend at the Krasnopolsky Hotel, Amsterdam prior to Ms Nguyen Thu's final treatment in the Amsterdam Zuid euthanasia clinic.

(d) I give and bequeath all of my personal effects and clothing to Sheba Rosenstein, or if she should predecease me, then my Executor hereinafter named, shall dispose thereof, in his sole discretion.

FIFTH: I hereby confirm that Ms. Sheba Rosenstein shall be sole beneficiary of my Lloyds of London Insurance Policy Number AG2099-6777, provided however that receipt of proceeds under the policy shall be subject to fulfilment of the following condition precedent, namely, that she shall personally amputate my penis and genitalia, and have the emasculated remains of my manhood crushed into powder. Furthermore, in order to receive the proceeds, half of the powder shall be dropped into the Canal St-Martin, Paris France, and the other half buried in Plot 17-E of the canine cemetery operated by the *Cimetière de l'Association pour l'Inhumation décente des Animaux,* Narbonne 66000.

SIXTH: I give and bequeath to my Trustee, hereinafter named, the sum of $100,000.00, in Trust, for the following uses and purposes:

(a) To hold, manage, invest and reinvest the said property and to receive and collect the income therefrom.

(b) To pay the net income therefrom, together with such amounts of principal as shall be necessary to provide $5,000.00 per annum, in equal quarterly installments, for the maintenance and support of Francine Bennaton, *whore,* during her lifetime.

(c) To pay the net income therefrom, together with such amounts of principal as shall be necessary to provide $2,500.00 per annum, in equal quarterly installments, for the maintenance and support of Mme Claude Ducastin-Chanel, *retired whore*, during the remainder of her lifetime.

(d) Upon the death of the survivor between Millie Reis, Francine Bennaton, and Mme Claude Ducastin-Chanel, to pay over the principal remaining in the Trust, together with any accumulated income, to DR. EMILY GROENTZWIG, to be used towards research into deranged and demented lawyers.

SIXTH: All the rest, residue and remainder of my estate, both real and personal, of whatsoever nature and wheresoever situate, of which I shall die seized or possessed or to which I shall be in any way entitled, or over which I shall possess any power of appointment by Will at the time of my death, including any lapsed legacies, I give, devise and bequeath as follows:

(a) to Spike Nussbaum, one Canadian dollar, provided he can produce proper personal identification,

(b) To Margaret Tillman, Head of the Investigations Branch, *Barreau du Québec*, four dollars, and my law degrees.

(c) To Collette Mesrine, *the oldest whore in Paris*, the remainder of my estate, and a return travel package to Niagara Falls, Canada with the tour operator of her choice.

SEVENTH: I nominate, constitute and appoint Hervé Bourque, Executor and Trustee of this my Last Will and

Testament. In the event that he should die or fail to qualify, or resign or for any other reason be unable to act, I nominate, constitute and appoint Tranh Nguyen Thu in his place and stead.

—Franck Robinson Esquire

SIGNED, SEALED, PUBLISHED and DECLARED by Franck Robinson, the Testatrix above named, as and for his Last Will and Testament, in the City of Paris, France, in our presence and we, at his request and in his presence and in the presence of each other, have hereunto subscribed our names as witnesses this 14th day of January, One Thousand Nine Hundred Ninety Nine.

Laraine Sandusky, businesswoman, residing at 10 West 86th St. NYC
Hanna Van Trotta, executive secretary, residing at 709 E. 56 St., New York, NY

PART I

Hotel du Quai Voltaire — Chambre 52.

Dear Hervé,

A French prison is no place for a white man, Hervé. About the only thing in its favour, is that it gives you a little time to review matters, if you're so inclined. It's strange the thoughts you cling to in order to survive such places. There was an image that returned to me. I was seventeen years old and managed to find myself in Amsterdam, wandering through the Dam Square area, terrain you know only too well, my friend. Found myself in front of one of those store-front windows, staring at a middle-aged hooker. Her finger curled, as she observed me watching her through the looking glass, beckoning. I couldn't walk away, couldn't even move as a matter of fact. As if my whole future was contained in that finger drawing me towards the diseased of the world. I mark that moment as my passage into the decayed compromise of adulthood.

A brief *obiter dictum* on the sub-species to which I belong. The much despised, the deservedly despicable *john*. Oddly enough, we johns firmly cling to the ill-conceived myth that we are adventurous rogues defying the powers that be, prowling the streets to create a new saga with an unknown woman. In fact, nothing could be further from the truth. The john craves repetition, then more repetition. Then he tries to repeat the experience. Somewhere in the seedy recesses of his mind, he is looking for the same piece of silky underwear, the same thwack of a bare hand on his ass, the same stretch of rope tying him to a bedpost. And not only does he hunt relentlessly for that same viral reminder of whatever he has on the brain, he knows he will never find it. And he doesn't care. Any whore worth her epsom salts understands this perfectly, and never really provides the goods, while artfully implying that the unnamed, unspeakable pleasure is just around the corner. This approach is not in the least offensive to the john, who couldn't care less about *caveat emptor*. On the contrary, the risk of fraudulent misrepresentation even adds on value, as the diamond is contained within the promise itself. Fulfillment is nothing compared to the anticipation. Knowing you are in a room with someone, and here it doesn't really matter what she looks like, who understands that you must, in order to have meaning to your life, act out certain scenarios which appear absurd to the normal eye.

My fetish was Sheba. In conventional terms, I suppose one could argue that our lives were monuments of banality, but to us, nothing within the human realm could approach our own self-created drama. Just offhand, I recall a day, like any other, but somehow it remains embedded in the memory banks. Our morning agenda called for fucking, followed by Dunhill cigarettes and lazy conversation. We picked up and left off topics, locations and people with equal indifference. Not even money held our attention for long, other than to calculate ways of procuring it with the least possible effort. She had just emerged from the washroom where she had spent several hours preparing herself for the day's theatrics. Her skills in the art of makeup alone put my pedigree to shame. I only had a profession, a few diplomas and, at least for a while yet, cash to spare. I had read thousands of books. She had sucked thousands of cocks. I could recite Supreme Court obiter dicta *extempore*. She had a case load of her own: tales of her victims, a trail of broken men, now horizontal in hospitals, asylums and cemeteries. But we both trafficked in human disappointment and, for both of us, a deal wasn't a deal unless somebody got burned.

She wore a pearl-coloured brassiere and thong, panty hose, and a garter belt that artfully exposed her rust-coloured cunt hair. The cunt itself seemed to be propped up, as if on a storefront demo shelf, as her vertical posture was unnaturally accentuated by her stiletto heels. Pastel was the leitmotif of the day. It suited her well against the backdrop of sand being wind-swept across a dismal stretch of Rochelais beach and the Atlantic taupe-grey sky. Sheba was describing someone she truly admired, a madame who ran a number of bordellos in Paris back in the sixties.

"An extraordinary woman," she pronounced, her glance half-withering, half-inquisitive, as she gauged the effect of each of her soliloquoys. *Classe*, she summarized. Everything was *classe* with her. Or *nickel*. Or *clean*. Do you know, she added, pirouetting around me mockingly, "if you would only listen to me, you will never work another day in your life."

She crouched onto the floor, arched her back like a panther and sprang at me, reaching for my cock, her mouth opening like a question mark or a vacant room. Looking back, an unequal contest, right from the start.

Why does one man cross the Atlantic, and another play *pétanque* and never move beyond the confines of his neighbourhood? These inclinations have far more to do with the pull of magnetic North than morality. All attraction and repulsion, Hervé. The laws that govern us are far more impersonal and terrifying than we dare admit. The clearest proof of this is what is called love. Two complementary voids or fields of emptiness, ions and protons matching each other, negative to positive. If the love is perfect, there is mutual extinguishment, and we call the phenomenon death. When in fact, it is nothing more than a form of chemical reaction.

I

Early morning, *rue Montmartre*. A man insistently flogging a newsletter for the poor. C'mon, it's only ten francs. Ten francs too much, my friend. Spare change? No such thing. Cigarette? Get a job. No jobs left, *monsieur*. Fuck off. *Va te faire mettre.* Have a nice day, *monsieur*. A lime-green garbage truck rolled past. Two Africans behind, one spraying *rue Réaumur* sputum and debris into the gutters with a hose, the other whisking languidly at residual shit with a metal-pronged broom. Six thousand francs a month and free medical benefits. Heaven for an African. Hell for a white man. The echo of her laugh pulling me back from reality. I pulled out my cellphone and dialled.

"*Allô?*"

"Where the hell are you, Sheba?"

"I'm on my cellphone, Franck."

Two forces boring in, sucking on the pituitary gland. Her voice, *ottava soprana*, ligating me to her wound.

"Where the fuck are you, Sheba?"

Her voice reverberating, twisting my loins.

"Do you remember the cemetery, Franck? Père Lachaise ..."

"Just tell me where you are."

"I'm in the land of forgetting, Franck. The land of the distant past."

The dismal spectre of St-Eustache church casting its shadow over the quarter. A Hindi man, wearing a shabby, pin-striped suit, standing at the South entrance door, his palm extended outwards. *Whatever you can spare, sir.* I pushed past him through the South exit doors. The church empty, but for a few geriatric penitents sitting in the pews before the main altar, lifeless as blow-up dolls. I moved past the crypt and a hemicycle of tombs and the remnants of immortalised ministers, harlequins, jugglers, slaughterhouse owners and whores.

A bald, gaunt Sulpician priest entered the confessional, his robes swirling behind him. A red light lit up over the confessional box. How many red lights up in Pigalle? *The Lucky Club. Bar Huit. Le Frou-Frou. Maryelove.* Couldn't be any harder than sneaking into a bordello. I edged towards the box, slipped inside, waited in the dark for a second until my eyes adjusted, then knelt down. After a minute or so, a foot-square, sliding wooden apparatus opened, exposing a screen. Behind the screen, I could just make out the bald silhouette of the priest. I mentally rehearsed the lines I had retrieved from www.confessional.com.

"Bless me father, for I have sinned."

"How long has it been since your last confession?"

"Are you Père Montagnard?"

"Yes."

"A woman named Sheba comes by occasionally to confess. Have you heard from her lately?"

"*Pardon?*"

"Look, I know this is an unusual request, but this is an emergency. I have to get in touch with her."

His head jolted forward slightly.

"I must ask you to leave. Immediately."

"Listen, friend. I know a thing or two about privilege. I'm a solicitor. I don't blame you for being a little uneasy. Tell you what. Just nod your head if she still lives in the quarter."

He wasn't saying anything much, so I tried another tack. More along the lines of betting on an inside straight.

"She told me about you. The altar boys. Your seminary adventures. Everything."

"If you do not depart immediately, I shall contact the police!"

I exited the confessional, ambled past the crypt then out the same door I had entered. Same Indian beggar parked at the door. Same shabby pin-stripe suit. Same makeshift crutch. Same right eye bugged out in fierce entreaty.

"Sir, I can see you are a gentleman. I too was once a gentleman. Truly."

That word. *Gentleman.* I stopped and examined him. He was middle-aged. Thick, wavy black hair, but for a white streak running incongruously down the centre of his cranium. As if he'd fallen into a pit unexpectedly. Boo!

"Once a gentleman, always a gentleman," I uttered towards the remains of the sub-continent.

"No, sir, no, not at all, not at all, if you only knew how false this is. I was to be married; she was so lovely, you should see the girls of Bombay, they are remarkable. I was coming here for a weekend. A weekend, can you understand?! And then I threw everything away.

Everything! And it led me here. To this! No, I can tell you sir, you are only a gentleman if the world says you are a gentleman. Can you understand this, sir? Can you understand?"

I flipped him a few francs, returned to *rue Montorgueil*, and stopped in to purchase a local daily at a kiosque, entered a café. On the *faits divers* page, an article concerning a woman who poured acid over her husband's face while he slept. Nothing unusual in that. Not anymore. Or even the fact that he had been tied to the four bedposts. Page 17 material. Hell of a way to celebrate a honeymoon. Particularly in the Ritz-Carlton Hotel on the Place Vendôme. Not enough to conclude, but plenty enough to keep me reading. The accused's court records had disappeared into the ether. The *Tribunal de Grande Instance* suspected an inside job, but had no choice but to dismiss the case. What the French call a *non-lieu*. It had never taken place.

A couple of days after my return, I had answered a newspaper ad for a flat in the second *arrondissement, rue de Mulhouse*, a one block street in the Sentier textiles district which starts on *rue Cléry* at the *Société Parisienne de Boutons*, and ends seventy-eight metres up the road at a gutted out merguez palace on the *rue des jeuneurs*. The street of fasters. The location suited me well enough. *Rue Cléry* was a direct pipeline leading to Saint-Denis from the rear. During the day, the quarter resembled a Tamul rebel outpost, but the terrorists were armed with off-the-rack fall fashions.

The first two floors of Number 2 housed illegal textile operations. The police were never far. Just as many were on the take in the Sentier as in Saint-Denis, but the racket here was illegal immigrant workers. I had to climb six flights of hardwood stairs to reach my flat, located just over the residence of Bazin, my landlord. Bazin was a pharmacist, and a homosexual of the old school. The kind who shined his oxfords twice a day, and showed up at the door in initialed terrytowel bathrobes at three in the afternoon. Next door was Lafontaine, the resident onanist, and across the way an old rack of a lady, who used the Turkish toilet as a multi-function unit to wash her clothes, urinate, brush her teeth. She also wore her bathrobe twenty hours out of the day. But hers wasn't the same brand as Bazin's, or, if it was, it was forty-five years older and had devolved into a ratty, lime-coloured shred of terrytowel. A mad, compulsive cheer-fulness possessed her.

I had never seen her descend to the ground floor. Every night at seven sharp, a Vietnamese delivery man in his early sixties arrived on the sixth floor landing, carrying a plastic container with steamed rice and spring rolls. The only other person I saw regularly was De Vec-chi, a heavy-set balding Italian who sluffed up and down from the third floor landing twice a day, dragging an arthritic german shepherd he refused to have put down. De Vecchi claimed he had boxed Jake La Motta before La Motta won the championship belt.

"I had him down for a count of eight. Lost on a split decision, but it was a fix from the start. Then, some of LaMotta's handlers visited me one night. Smashed every joint in my hands with a crowbar. Then a few over the head. Look."

He peeled back a few remaining strands of hair from his skull, baring a scar laterally traversing his cranium. As if a makeshift railway track had been hastily embed-ded into his skull.

"None of that matters. They're all dead. LaMotta. Sugar Ray Robinson. Tunney. Marciano. Cerdan. You seen the current crop? Bunch a goddam ballerinas. Never heard of a boxer getting his hair done in the old days. Ballerinas, I'm tellin' ya. Bunch a goddam ballerinas."

My descent into the catacombs of St-Denis started by way of *Place du Chatelet*, pushing through the Friday night shoppers until the wide square narrowed into a tubular stretch between *Pas du Grand Cerf* and *Aboukir*, where the commerce of whoring began in earnest, and continued through to its North end at the *Porte St-Denis*. No sign of the arid spheres of Paris society. The well-bred gallantries of better quarters yielding to a buttery river of sperm, blood, skin and vomit gushing upstream towards Montmartre, where St-Denis himself was decapitated, prior to walking across the city carrying his detached head in his hands.

I caught sight of her as I rounded onto Boulevard Sebastopol. She looked all right. Knew how to strike a pose. Casual, swinging a purse, smoking a cigarette. Something mundane and day-to-day in it. A veteran Parisian whore. I'm out doing my job. Nothing more, nothing less. Just a cunt for sale.

I offered her a cigarette. What's your name? Francine, she cooed, culling out of her mental catalogue. What's yours? Oh, Franck, I answered out of my own brochure of duplicity, and bang, the contract was sealed. Francine and Franck. Just a nice couple having a chat on a Parisian *trottoir*. How's your cunt, Francine? Just fine, Franck. I've let fourteen men stick their dick in it this morning, and I've sucked twenty-six cocks. Are you available still? Of course. But, do you have special requests, she said, with a side glance to see whether I had a hard on or not. Judging from the knife scar down her left cheek, she had good reason to be a little careful.

"*Tu as l'air correct*," she concluded.

We moved up *rue Réaumur* together, Francine half a step ahead. She had ink-black hair which flowed to her shoulders in rivulets. I imagined her dancing tango in an obscure, ill-lit private club, somewhere on the Iberian peninsula, then being expelled for performing fellatio on the instructor as his wife walked through the door. At St-Denis, she turned North, me following in tow, until we arrived at an entrance located at 143 bis, which led into a narrow outside corridor. We continued five or six more paces, her buttocks swivelling between two musty walls. Then, a showcase window, blocked by venetian blinds. A red neon sign advertised Thai massages, blow-up dolls, aphrodisiacs.

"Here. In here."

She drew back a curtain in the doorway, and we entered a long room set up as a film theatre, with a dozen fold-up chairs arranged into a haphazard semblance of rows. The screen at the opposite end was an off-white bedsheet nailed to a sheet of plywood. As we sat down, the bicycle chain tackety tack of a thirty year old sixteen mm projector announced the showing. At first, nothing but light, which briefly exposed two long yellow streaks across the middle of the screen before the film began.

"Très *kitsch*," she said, but the tone of *kitsch* implied it was perched near the apex of her pyramid of values. I caught sight of an old man in the far corner, his pants at his ankles, jacking off. The film was in black-and-white, an ancient silent movie, other than the player piano jangling in the background. A long dead porno idol dressed in white lingerie sat in a chair of a far West saloon, her breasts partially exposed over a half-cup bra. A second woman entered the saloon, dressed in the Charleston style, smiled, then, a propos of nothing in particular, bent over the knees of the first woman, who began thwacking her on the ass with a wooden ping-pong paddle. The projector briefly sputtered, then shifted into another scene. The same feminine duo, now clad as Austrian frauleins, on all fours, being walked on hunting grounds by a thick-necked moustachioed man wearing a green leather jacket, peasant hunting cap, carrying a boar spear.

Meanwhile, Francine had crawled to her knees and was now facing me. She leaned over, stuck her hand inside her purse, pulled out a condom and a small plastic glass.

"What's that for?"

"Something special."

She pushed her index finger and thumb inside her mouth around her upper gums. A clicking sound like a suction pump pulling on the roof of her mouth. A full set of dentures popped out of her mouth and into the glass.

"*Sthpethial,*" she lisped, wrapping her gums around my cock. Lifting three fingers upwards. I slipped three hundred franc notes between her index and forefinger. Glanced over at the old man, still industriously jacking off in the front rows of the makeshift theatre. A look of ragged intent on his face, as if summoning the troops for one last charge into the German lines on the Marne river. His trenchcoat rising and falling. A tent in a nor'wester gale, flushing shit and mud across a no man's land. *Dulce et decorum est, pro patria mori.*

"*Ca va?*"

"Sure. Go for it."

Later, she asked me whether I had access to a computer. As a matter of fact I do, Francine. Here, then take this. She pulled a floppy disk out of her purse and slipped it into my jacket pocket. Goodbye, Franck. Enjoy. Then evaporated. The way they all did. I drifted down *rue Aboukir*, my mind nowhere, until I fell on Cléry and the now familiar nocturnal spectre of the *Société Parisienne des Boutons*. De Vecchi was entering his apartment on the third floor, wearing nothing but a sweat-stained undershirt over grey jogging pants, the exposed portion of his torso protected by enough hair to turn an orangutang green with envy. The door closed behind him.

As I passed by Ducastin-Chanel's door on the sixth floor, I could hear her cajoling her cat.

"*Descend, descend,*" she squawked, "*combien de fois je t'ai déjà dit, minou?* Come and see madame Claude."

I entered the flat, reached for one of the four bottles of *Côte du Rhône* perched on the tile counter, poured out a glass, drained it. I repeated the process three times. I flipped open the laptop, pushed in the diskette and opened the file. The screen burst into a pyrotechnic display of a garbage dump. This was succeeded by a panoramic shot of screeching seagulls unleashing shit pellets onto the shell of a giant Galápagos tortoise. Then a flash onto a clip of another spanking scene. Then a shot of Hitler being appeased by an obsequious, arse-bending crew of Iron-cross bearing senile generals. Suddenly, an eclipse. Followed by a whore jacking off a donkey. All shot with a hand-held camera by someone suffering from a nervous disorder.

I lit a cigarette, walked to the window overlooking the *Société Parisienne des Boutons*. Across the way, all the textile operations closed for the evening. On the third floor, one room alight. A forty-ish man, shoulder-length hair, skinny as a rockstar, reptilian features, swatting a girl. Her head was bowed, in complete submission to him. He was toady, pock-marked. Whatever had happened to him had been used as barter material to acquire his air of authority. As much as anyone could own anything, he owned the girl. She had given up her liberty. Whatever. I turned out the light, lay on my cot and lit a cigarette.

After a while, thoughts once again channelling through ducts and micro-vessels in a chaotic harmony that suited me. *Déjà vus.* The usual thoughts aborted by short circuiting of the cerebral vectors. Memories of whores. Nothing but whores. The whole planet crawling with cunt for sale, or cunts selling shit, or shitheads looking for cunt, and me only one john in a buyers' market, and unable to meet the supply, unable to satisfy all the cocksuckers in the world who just wanted my jism and my cash, and wanted to suck it out of me as soon as possible.

The rain was falling again, splashes pinging off the aluminum roof, bouncing off so loudly that I recalled a similar time, in the St-Regis Hotel, San Francisco, after being dumped by my first wife, Donna, and was just getting ready to take a mental elevator up seventy-five floors, fuelled by some high-octane blotter acid. Four hours, I was married to a whore named Donna. After a four-hour engagement. Then it was over.

I was awoken by the Portuguese concierge who had come to collect the rent. Yes, she added, as an afterthought, this also came for you. It was postmarked from Bourque, concerning a character reference for my disbarment hearing. He was quite matter of fact about the whole thing, seemed more interested in knowing whether I was still frequenting that lovely *nymphette* he had once seen with me in the old port. Followed by a brief codicil, congratulating me on my return to the city:

"I remember my years in Paris were constantly plagued by the imminent prospect of financial difficulty. But, to my mind, the price was trifling. Paris is its own reward, Robinson. Just hang in there and ENJOY EVERY MINUTE. Daily life can appear banal occasionally, but don't let that happen. All those flirtatious glances in the gutters of Pigalle — Jesus, I'd concede disbarment three times over just to leer one last time into the eyes of those shameless tarts ..."

Bourque, my seventy year old mentor, handing down his last piece of nostalgia from the annals of his own depravity, still salivating at the prospect of an ultimate, mind, body or soul-wracking experience.

But, I was too far away, another anonymous john in a whore of a city. Whore writ large in every nook and cranny. You could see the whore in the most erudite comments of the oldest member of the *Académie Française*. You could hear it in every discourse pronounced by the politicians, judges, clergy and the journalists. It looked to me like everybody was on the take, one way or another, which eased the pressure considerably.

Not that I was in better shape just because I had a clear read on things. I was a john, which by definition meant I would empty my wallet when my prick was standing on end. I could see the confidence trick, *deconstruct it* as my contemporaries would put it, but I far preferred to believe the whore when she claimed it was all about beauty, when I knew damn well it was and always had been about cash up front.

They were lined up in their usual postures in *le paradis* club on *rue des Martyrs*. Six tiny broads perched on stools. All wearing miniskirts, all between johns, all of them indistinguishable. Fungible goods. Girls from the 18th *arrondissement* or from the provinces. Girls who just didn't have the hand-eye coordination or the drive to become Monoprix cashiers. Cleopatra bartender. An awning of indigo bangs hanging over her forehead. Scarlet lipstick burnishing a ghoulish complexion.

Despite being twice the size of anyone in the place, I managed to fit in after a while. That was easy enough. Order a beer. Light a cigarette. Say nothing. Tip the girls. Become listless. Do nothing. After a week, I fit right in with the ersatz Rodin sculptures and the velvet table tops.

I had taken to carrying a book of Hieronymus Bosch paintings during my wandering. A detail of the left wing of the Garden of Earthly Delights peered out from page 73. The painting depicts a bird-headed monster devouring damned souls, then defecating them into a chamber pot, after which they fall into a foul pit. The seven deadly sins hover obsequiously around the monster. The slothful man visited in his bed by demons. The glutton forced to vomit into the pit. Vanity viewing her reflection in the backside of the devil.

After an hour or so, I waved one of them towards a curtained doorway. She led me through, up a set of stairs, then along a hallway to one of the rear bedrooms. She opened the door with an old skeleton key. Two counter-clockwise revolutions, then inside. What's your pleasure, sir? What's your name? Zazie. That's not a name. What's your real name? Alena. What's your pleasure, sir? My pleasure is another room. That's impossible. Next time, I want a room looking out over the street. You have to ask Yannick. Who is Yannick? The guy at the door. He's not a client? A client? Ha! *Pauvre con.*

Then, more impatiently, as if expecting Yannick to kick the door down, what do you want? *Une pipe?* Get to the point, *m'sieur.* I don't have all night.

"There was a Sheba who worked here once."

She laughed.

"*Oh, ça alors.* Look, I have to go back to work."

"When's the last time you spoke to her?"

"Listen, you want something special, something you've never tried, two thousand francs. *Sinon, faites pas chier le monde, OK?*"

II

I was back in the city for my own reasons, but those reasons would take care of themselves in good time. Meanwhile, the cafés were there, and you could remain inside for as long or as little as you liked, no questions asked. The café denizens acted like they were members of Masonic orders, or provided unnamed but extremely essential services, or were in on the latest conspiracy to end civilizations. At the same time, there was a certain humility to their arrogance. Which is to say, none of them spent their time telling you they were going to reinvent the wheel or change the world. It's pretty hard to take it personally if someone brags about seven generations of his family cleaning sewers or pouring béchamel into *Croque Monsieur* sandwiches.

I followed a default nocturnal trajectory which took me through the sleazier ends of the St-Denis and Montmartre quarters. Down the stairs of N° 2 *rue de Mulhouse*, out the thick *porte cochère* horsegate door, onto the *rue des jeuneurs*, which I followed up to *boulevard Mont-*

martre. Ten million people in the city, and never more than two or three desolate figures on the street of fasters.

The pure desolation of the street, its name, the grime of the couscous palace at the end of the road, provided me with the backdrop I required to review a set of apparently random facts which had accumulated in my mind. The facts were simple, when placed one in front of the other. They added up to my life. But, taken together, they lost all meaning, became more indecipherable than Boolean algebra.

My thoughts by now had carried me well into the backwash of the 9th *arrondissement,* and into a twenty-four hour café in the *Faubourg Montmartre* called *Le Bled,* owned by a Marseillais second-tier mafia racketeer known as *Coco Lunettes.* Ghassim, a hundred and thirty kilo gorilla from Chad, surveyed proceedings from the entrance. A group of Africans were jamming franc pieces into illegal slot machines near the bar.

I parked myself at the counter beside a grey-haired paunchy man wearing a tweed cap.

He held a large goblet of Leffe beer in his right hand, and was staring fiercely at his companion, a middle-aged Asian gentleman. His listener looked to be Vietnamese. Thick-lensed glasses. Dressed Camus existential. Camus existential had always been a big look for the Asian crowd. A halfway ground between inscrutability and pessimism as a fashion statement.

"Meteor, Khaled," I ordered.

"Good evening, Mr Robinson."

The old man at the counter beside me struck me right away as one of those sour lefties from the sixties who figured they were Picasso or Che Guevara for whatever reason, and rained their bitterness on the world.

"Diderot was right, *mon cher ami. 'L'art est au fond des testicules'.*"

He turned and snarled in my direction: "What do you have to say about that, *monsieur l'américain*?"

"You've pretty well covered the topic."

The Asian man waved him silent.

"Allez, du calme. Roger, this gentleman is not responsible for whatever ails you."

He extended his hand in my direction.

"Allow me to introduce myself. Victor Tranh. Chairman of the unofficial ninth arrondissement club of reprobates and degenerates. *Merde de la merde. Santé.* And your name?"

"Franck Robinson. Reprobate."

He raised his glass as a toast.

"Do you know who I am?"

"Sure. Victor Tranh. Chairman of the reprobates."

"No, Franck Robinson. I am the son of Vo Nguyen Giap, the man responsible for the defeat of the French at Dien Bien Phu in 1954."

"And only a *Phu* people remember who your father is?"

Victor Tranh laughed. Like mice in an attic. Unexpected and irritating.

"Hee, hee. That is very funny, Robinson. So, you have a sense of humour. Excellent, for I am convinced that your life is a disaster."

He scrutinised me for a moment.

"You've done time, haven't you?"

"You ask a lot of questions."

"Let me offer you a beer."

"Sure."

Roger the leftie had drifted towards the exit door of Le Bled, where he was banging angrily at the flippers of a vintage pinball machine called *Bon Voyage.*

For a minute or two, Victor Tranh directed his clinical gaze at Roger the leftie while tossing back his Leffe, then turned towards me.

"You ever feel loneliness, Robinson?"

"Sure, we're all alone in the end. That's lonely enough."

"Loneliness is a funny thing. It has nothing to do with being physically alone. It's realizing that, no matter what you do, nobody even comes from the same planet. It can get lonely at times. Sometimes, the loneliness gets so intense, you become attached to it. In a perverse way. Then, when it lessens, it becomes hard again. Beer?"

"Beer."

"What brings you to Paris?"

"Just passing through."

"What's her name?"

He wiped the beer off his mouth with the sleeve of his trenchcoat.

"No one just passes through the Faubourg Montmartre. This place is for people who fall off the planet. Maybe you should share your story. *With a friend.*"

It was the way people talked nowadays. *Share your story.* No story to share. I had taken up with a whore named Sheba, then did the rest of what followed. Sheba. A lifer. Someone who really believed in it as both art and craft. You never read about people who answer a calling anymore. One hundred and forty-three titles on billiards listed in <u>Books in Print</u>. The perfect carem. The champion players. The crowds. The best tournaments. Nothing on whores. Who gives the best head. The oldest whore in the world. The managers and agents. No customer surveys. No instruction manuals. In a spoon-fed universe, whoring was the last refuge of the autodidact.

"Why do you think people talk like that these days?"

"Like what?"

"You know. *Share your story.*"

"You don't want to share your story?"

Victor Tranh now turned to the remainder of the six drunken clients in the bar.

"*Il s'appelle Franck Robinson.* He has no story to share!!"

I'd spent enough time in Southeast Asia to know the place was as good at producing lunatics as any other part of the planet. Tranh's laugh now a rodential flood of scavengers racing into a cellar after a block of Roquefort.

"It's a woman. Only a woman can do this. You have been ruined by a Cunt, capital C, and you are ashamed before the world, and think it a tragedy. You know, I met a Welshman once. He said, cheer up, you *bastahd*! I suppose you want to kill yourself now."

The man named Tranh turned back to the counter, ordered two more Leffe beers, and quaffed both down in front of me. When he turned back, his eyes had reddened. In the alcohol tolerance zone, I was a racial profiler, and I'd rarely met a chinaman who could make it past four or five drinks in an evening.

"When I am attempting to seduce a woman, Mr Robinson, I always ask her whether she has ever tasted dog meat."

Tranh had crossed from over-the-top courteous effeteness to slobbering dog meat marketer within seconds. My theory was intact.

"If a woman stays with you after you have confessed to eating dog meat, you can do anything with her. I recall an evening at the Opera Garnier. *Giselle* was playing, danced by Nureyev. The performance was exquisite, and I took advantage of the moment to invite my escort to the *Café de la Paix* for Veuve Cliquot. While she sipped contentedly, I leaned over and whispered 'cocker spaniel', then sat back and watched. She was a very spoiled woman, obsessed with herself, and a self-described animal activist. Her smile, even *a priori*, was a sentimental, kitsch shield to mask her utter lack of taste. '*Pourquoi dites-vous cocker*, Egmond,' she hummed. She insisted on calling me Egmond. 'Because I eat them.' When did Western women embark on this dog saving crusade, Egmond?"

All that to say we decided, or not so much decided, as ended up drinking a good portion of the night away in each others' company, while we addressed each other as Egmond. And, for a little Viet, it turned out that he could toss back more than a few Meteor beer. He seemed to have a dozen zones of imbibing, plunging first into temporary inebriation marked by a comment on dog meat, followed by a retreat into clearly articulated thoughts on the state of the world, another drink, and a plunge into the next phase of his drunkenness. He'd developed some kind of sui generis style. Later, at a hole in the wall in the 9th, there was a legionnaire, old guy, and he knew Tranh. There was no love lost between them, so he could have been telling the truth. The legionnaire looked like he would know the answers to certain questions. As for the rest of the night, it was pretty vague. At one point, he mentioned something about his wife having MS. Those things are traded off with casual disinterest in certain establishments of the second *arrondissement* of the city of Paris. We agreed to meet a week later in a café called *Le Tambour*, which Tranh referred to as a "temple of absurdity".

Tranh had grown up in Cambodia and Laos in the seventies, and I had run a few scams Wanchai way after the Tiananmen fiasco, which was more than enough to keep us going, and we both wanted to kill time. Later in the evening, the owner of *Le Tambour*, a moustachioed hulk named Maurice, joined in on the conversation. Just prior to daybreak, he locked up the bistro, and ordered his chef to cook food for the three of us.

There's a point in the night in Paris, where if you're with the right people and mix the right drinks, you start waking up again. Nothing really happened that evening, other than the fact that I decided to tell these rogue gentlemen my story. A David Byrne song, "I Love America," playing over the speakers. Maurice had opened up another bottle of *Gigondas Seigneurie de Fontanges*, a few years old, and his cook had prepared a Navarin lamb stew, and Maurice was relating a few tales about his time in Algeria in the late fifties, and how sometimes you have to leave a man in a cell for three weeks without sleep, before you even began interrogating him.

It turned out that all three of us had had contracts put out on us at various times, although mine was the only one still outstanding. We were discussing basically, when is the person serious and when are they not, that type of thing. There was no doubt that, sooner or later, if you wrote your own rule book, some people wouldn't like it, and among those people, one or two might utter a few threats, and then there was the case of the person who had nothing better to do, and more or less set about making killing you a high priority item. So, of course, you had to deal with these people.

And, the conclusion was, you're never a hundred per cent sure, but there's an equation, more or less, the less experience with firearms, the more the person had to be desperate. So somebody who killed people for a living, if there wasn't money involved they wouldn't do you in, unless there was a really good reason.

"In Algeria, we were not perfect. We broke rules. But, we knew what the rules were. We had codes of our own. Look, see this tattoo? *1er régiment de chasseurs paras.* And, the other night, a couple of kids, *sauvageons*, tried to rob me at gunpoint. I put them both in the hospital."

He shook his head.

"No respect."

That word, *respect*, obviously meant something to these people. It was a word with consequences.

Tranh's skin flushed red. He gained in exuberance as he drank. One of those alcoholics who have the gift of uttering truths during states of intoxication, then erasing it from their memories.

"Gentlemen, I am going to articulate the content of our agreement. Maurice, you only know me as a client. This *Egmond* comes from America, so his truths are not ours. But, I put to you the following tripartite proposition. Point One. Virtually all men cannot see what is right in front of their eyes. Point Two. What is right there to be seen is not very pleasant. Point Three. If you can see it, you are best to keep your silence anyways."

We nodded agreement. It was the drink, but it also sounded true, and perhaps the loss of the world is that perfect strangers cannot meet anymore and say what is in front of their eyes. That the world is an absurd, hypocritical lie, and that the thing they call love is the biggest lie of all.

The soup arrived in wide, brown *soupe à l'oignon* ceramic bowls, emitting a thick stench of parsley, sage, thyme, garlic, tomatoes. Tranh sucked its vapours into his nostrils.

"This soup, gentlemen, was created in honour of the Franco-English victory over the Turkish-Egyptian fleet in 1827, during the Greek war of Independence. There are evenings like this which must be seized upon, evenings like this when I feel that our tales must be told, that we must get to the bottom of things! And, just the three of us, burrowed into the sewers of Paris, with nothing to do but tell our tales. I am telling you, Egmond, this is fate."

Tranh poured out the wine.

"At the age of six, I was caught in a rocket attack launched by the Americans in Vietnam. The attack killed my mother. I lost my memory for a week, and the blast deafened me for four years. For that period, I was in a state similar to autism, but my condition had not affected one ability, that of playing chess. It also gave me an intensity which unsettled all of my opponents. My mere glance was enough to defeat many. At the 1966 Leiden invitational, at the age of 16, I came up against the rising star of the Asian chess world, Ivan Sakharov. A Russian, of course. It was a game held in the AULA in Amsterdam, a 15th century auditorium constructed during the golden era.

"Sakharov was my only true rival. Being my father's son, I set out not only to beat Sakharov, but to destroy him. He was pumped up with pride, came from a bourgeois family of St-Petersburg. He was intelligent, but he lacked imagination. His openings were considered to be novel, but invariably, he fell back into a classical mid-game, played out from the Queen's side, almost without fail. After allowing him to win the first game in order to test my theory, I responded to an opening: an East Indian gambit as I recall, and then announced that I would write down his next eight moves. Impossible, he responded. Nevertheless, I shall do it, I said. What will you wager on it. Anything you like. Then it shall be your life against mine...

"This boy pronounced me insane after my proposition, but his vanity and greed were elements I knew I could count on. I laid it out for him. If I am wrong, I shall end my life, and no one will stand between you and ultimate glory. *And, if I lose*, he responded, showing his fear. And, if you lose, I stated, deliberately offhand, you shall know me the superior player, and your life will no longer have any meaning."

It was a good story, and it might even have been true. Also, I felt free to tell my little tale and, for the first time I could remember, I started thinking back on where I came from, and how I had ended up in a Paris bar with murder on my mind, a price on my head, and still some things to be played out. It was a form of luck, in a way. It would end badly, but, within it all, there was luck, to be here with two other men who understood the way things really are.

The marquee attraction the following evening at *Le Tambour* — "Rhanya and Gaston sing Piaf and Montand" — was announced on a chalkboard on the sidewalk outside the café. Upon entry, we spotted a robust Arab woman, stumbling around in a paisley smock on a make-shift stage near the rear of the bistro. She cursed loudly at a microphone, eventually tossed it to the floor and stamped on it once or twice. A liver-lipped, beet-eyed man — who wore his hair in a tightly tressed Chinaman ponytail, and was stuffed inside an undersized Sergeant Pepper admiral uniform — joined her onstage and on cue, they kicked into an off-key version of *Les Feuilles Mortes*.

The act was macabre and burlesque, proving the Parisians hadn't lost their taste for low-level *music-hall*. Rhanya, the star of the evening, had a head like a rhomboid stump, adorned with a shrub of follicles that looked to have been culled from a subterranean garden. Her face thickly painted with an oily film, smeared unevenly over her pulpy features. A makeshift bandage, wrapped around her head from skull to chin, completed her hybrid lizard lounge/emergency ward look. She was heavily intoxicated, but once she got into her number, she sang an honest, industrial version of the Piaf song *La Vie en Rose*.

An old woman sat at a table nearby the stage, clapping listlessly. Three men stood together at the bar, drinking Pastis. If they lived in America, they would be assistant golf pros or real estate salesmen, or franchise operators. But, this was Paris, so they were just drunk. Two men seated alone at neighbouring tables, their backs to the wall, seemingly unaware of each other. One of the two bore a striking resemblance to Elvis Presley. Thick, pitch-black sideburns bordering a face buried in melancholy. Wearing a black leather vest, no shirt. His forearms covered in tattoos. Elvis II was seated in front of three empty bottles of St Emilion and was busy working his way through the fourth. Behind the King, an oversized map of the Paris Metro, and a message woodburned into the wall:

No British, No *Amerloques*

As Rhanya stepped off the stage, she noticed Tranh, who waved her to join us at the bar.

"Je vais crever, Tranh. This time I am sure I am done for."

One of the three pastis drinkers caught wind of this.

"Allez, Rhanya, vous étiez merveilleuse!"

The second of the three pastis drinkers, a broad-shouldered working stiff, lumbered up and put his arm around her.

"Apollinaire!"

Rhanya burst into tears.

"*Je ne dors plus*! Before, at least, I could sleep. And now, *terminé*. If only I could sleep!"

"Come home with me, Rhanya. I will make love to you. Like a Cossack!"

"Thank you for joining me this evening, Robinson. I am very pleased."

Rhanya sidled up to Tranh.

"If you buy me a Kir, I will suck your Asian cock, Tranh."

Tranh observed her momentarily, amused.

"Mr Robinson, there is nothing new in the human genome project. We have developed our own laboratory of mutant strains, right here in *le Tambour*."

He turned his attention back to Rhanya.

"Have you not heard, Rhanya? The mayor has launched a vast campaign to flush Paris of anything and anyone offending the hygiene and anti-loitering laws. There is a chance you will be flushed out of the city if you are not careful."

"I cannot be stamped out. My stench is Parisian stench, and the mayor is a Corsican *enculé*!"

As Rhanya said this, a trap door opened, and a lift came up, an oversized dumbwaiter, common to Parisian restaurants, used to bring up merchandise.

"Get on the lift, Robinson. Maurice has a special room downstairs. I want to hear more of your tale."

We rode the lift downstairs, into a cellar vault, stacked to the ceiling with wine, beer, Campari, and foodstocks. At the far end of the room, two olive-green doors, barricaded shut. Tranh pushed hard against the doors, forcing them open.

We entered a large room, with half a dozen rickety tables set up for board games. Pairs of men were intently focussed on games of speed chess or Chinese Go. An oval doorway led out of that room into a narrow, damp corridor.

"We are walking over the remains of the old *cimetière des innocents*. Molière is buried beneath us. And, at the exact same spot, La Fontaine. Here we are."

We entered a room at the end of the corridor. Burgundy-red curtains covered the walls and ceiling. Four sets of electric bulbs hung loosely in clusters. There was only one rectangular pine table in the room, dead centre with a bench on either side. Tranh sat down, invited me to join him, clapped his hands. A gruff looking man appeared with a straggly beard, trailing the remains of food and mustard, wearing an open-necked Greek blouse.

"Raki, Dmitri. Rib-eye steaks. Os à moelle. A la Bordelaise. Some cool Touraine wine."

Tranh turned towards me.

"You recall our conversation the night we met. About this Sheba, this boa, this killer woman who is looking for you. Or, is it you looking for her?"

"Vaguely."

"You asked me for some assistance. Something about ridding yourself of her presence."

"Just talk."

"You told me you loved this woman too much to let her live. I can help you, but you must tell me the rest of your tale. There are certain things which escape me. Any woman deserves a man's attention for an evening or two. But, why for so long? I want to hear more about this obsession. I have an idea about this woman. I presume you don't have any scheduled appointments, Robinson. Bear with me, Robinson, I have my own reasons for listening to stories such as these."

III

A few stints doing factory work and waiting tables as a young man taught me quickly enough that you had to find an angle if you wanted to escape a life of drudgery. This meant learning to stand on your own two feet, and selling yourself to the world. My ticket to a palatable life was a law degree, once I realized the lucrative possibilities of being *vested with a public trust*. After a few years representing the scum and dregs of the city of Montreal, I tilled more fertile soil.

At one time or another, I have sold junk bonds, raised funds for First Nations tribes, run immigration scams out of Wanchai during the post-Tiananmen fiasco, acted as front man for venture capital schemes and served as an intermediary between the First World and the Third for rebuilding projects in Beirut and Algiers until the Hezbollah and the Armed Islamic Group brought beheading back into fashion. At one point, I hung out my shingle as a *facilitator*, and spent my time organizing golf dates and bordello visits in the Wanchai for Taiwanese defence ministry types and French arms salesmen with a taste for retro-commissions. With a law degree, you could pretty well do whatever you wanted during the eighties and early nineties. People were selling everything from plutonium to countries. The whole planet was open for business.

I never did business to make a fortune. Getting by was plenty for me, and I was happy enough on the margins. You didn't have to be a genius to figure out that everything would collapse sooner or later. The markets were like a global casino. The conditions were created by a war, and a war or some act of terrorism would bring it to a halt.

Oddly enough, it was during a brief return stint to the practice of law that I hit the jackpot. A colleague, or rather crony, Hervé Bourque, had asked me to take on some of his case load during one of his own sordid sex tours of Bangkok before the politically correct cut out that as a viable option. One of his cases involved a girl named Kimberley Sutherland. She had been honeymooning in the South-West with a man named Spike. Spike suggested they rent an ATV. What's an ATV? asked Kimberley. They're made by Honda, Spike responded, omitting to mention that ATVs run on three wheels, which makes them notoriously easy to flip. When Spike hit the first dune in the Mojave Desert, Kimberley screamed. As he hit the second, Kimberley's butt bounced off the seat. On the third, the ATV flipped, bringing the honeymoon and life, as she had previously known it, to a full stop.

Spike couldn't have known it at the time, but his lunatic driving would also turn my life around a hundred and eighty degrees. Sentimentality aside, a quadraplegic is of no use to anyone, except for a personal injury lawyer. When the victim is on a car manufactured by Honda, and insured by a notoriously solvent insurance company with pockets deeper than the Grand Canyon, everything moves quickly from the courtroom to the corridors. The day after my motion for a jury trial was granted, I settled for 2 million, which left me half a million as a contingency.

If you are planning a long life, half a million really isn't that much. It might buy you a house, where you can set up shop until it's your turn up on the chopping block. On the other hand, if plan A is to overtip a few waiters and spoil a whore or two, it's plenty. I picked up and relocated to Paris with nothing more on my mind than cunt and *blanquette de veau* ...

It was around 2:30 in the morning. Thirty-six hours after my arrival in the city, when I stumbled out of a taxi on boulevard St-Germain and weaved into the *Café de Flore*. She was sitting alone, writing notes at the second table to the right as I entered, her eyes cast skyward in reflection, and a mechanical pencil jammed in her mouth right at the point where my cock would be moored three hours later. Another budding genius. Paris is full of them. Always has been. Some of the budding geniuses are well into their mid-sixties, still waiting for the big break, still raving about their genius. But genius is still very marketable currency as a posture in the city of light, and being able to posture is crucial for survival.

There were five people in the Flore. I recognized three of them, although they didn't me. One was a TV fashion commentator. He stood in the stairwell, his tongue wrapped around the arm of an ochre-tinted set of sunglasses, eyes rolling imploringly, while he tried to placate a clearly dissatisfied dyke comedian with a sour grimace on her face that said Paris didn't measure up to her own virtual realities. A high profile philosopher known for his anti-American jingoism was intently scribbling his next piece of vitriol. That left her and me. The only illustrious unknowns in the place.

We were made for each other. I had been sliding into a posture of indifference for years. Nothing was real to me, except the strong smell of grains in the whisky I drank, or the nicotine stains on my fingers. Those were my faithful companions. They would lead me to premature death, but in the meantime, they allowed me to navigate through my personal mental wasteland of scrub and savanna. I, at least, knew my gaoler, whereas the great mass of humanity had not yet even realized they were in prison. It allowed me clarity, if not liberty.

Anything I did had no meaning, other than as a means of marking time. From one cigarette to the next, or one drink to the next. Or one cunt to the next. The only remaining issue was to see how things played out. Occasionally, I would latch on to the illusion that I could accomplish something useful. Those intervals were short-lived, and led nowhere. A decent poker game would pull me back to reality. Or a month or two with any given woman.

At least that was my state of mind until I spotted Sheba. The second I caught sight of her, I knew I had fallen onto terra incognita. I sat down at the table beside her. Asked her who she was. What brought her there. Her nationality. All of it in a deliberately slow, plodding accent as if I had just wandered in from Cracow or Prague. I had no idea what effect I had on people, didn't really care at that point. It was a weak, clumsy ploy, but tactics were a secondary issue when people didn't really exist. I offered her a drink. Watched her consider giving me the brush-off, then decide she would put up with whatever I had to offer. After some small talk, I could see she was in for a few more, provided I paid. We moved up the street to a rum bar.

When the rum bar shut down, she offered to take me for a spin in her car. We took a fast, rain-slicked drive up the *rue de Seine*, onto *Vaugirard*, and alongside the Luxembourg gardens. For those of you who have never tried it, it's a hell of a lot of fun to whiz along Parisian rain-driven streets at high-speed with a French broad stripped of the usual moral scruples, and not a clue where you're headed. Type of thing that can make you forget you've been up for thirty-six hours. We raced the wrong way up *Soufflot*, higher than kites, thanks to some ecstacy she had stashed in her purse, then did a few 360s around the Pantheon. Not a soul to be seen. The pillars of the austere law faculty staring down at us. The Pantheon, and a slew of famous men's graves — Voltaire, Montaigne and Pascal, the foolish experimenter and conjecturer — Foucault's pendulum, *Ste-Geneviève du Mont*. We were higher than the philosophers, macrocosmic. Nobody could touch us. We had been sprayed with human repellent.

It's pretty difficult to describe your state of mind when you find yourself in these regions. From the outside, it definitely looks like insanity. It's not, though. It's just not caring anymore. Outside of everything else, Sheba had provided me with the perfect excuse to write off humanity once and for all. That's how I felt when we jumped out of the car and entered a bar on *Mouffetard*.

"Bartender, for those in attendance who are interested, one round of cranberry vodka martinis or Black Bush coolers or other poison of their choice."

I must have said something like that as we took our seats. If Western Union had walked through the door just behind us, in that hole in the wall on *Mouffetard* to announce that America had been destroyed by nuclear holocaust, I would have turned my back and ordered another round of cranberry vodka martinis for the house. To celebrate the event. Or more precisely, *to get on with it*. Or just to keep the chaser rinsing my vocal chords between the lines of coke we snorted. Or to underline my *core belief* that all life had now magically been compressed inside the bodies floating within my spongiform cerebral universe. But more than anything because Sheba had become magnetic North, and the sound of that siren voice cooing in my direction just sent me right off whatever was left of my head. But, it was voluntary. Consensual synallagmatic every step of the way.

And not a single redeeming feature to her. Unless you call a cunt like a pocket warmer a redeeming feature. Or a superhuman ability to perform fellatio better than a piccolo player in the *Orchestre Nationale de France* a redeeming feature. Or an assassin's smile, and an attitude to match a redeeming feature. Lucifer's daughter was perched in my lap and I felt the date was long overdue.

"Sheba, you know what I am thinking?"

She was sizing me up, basically as prey, not because she was immoral, or evil or any of those things. It was just in her nature. She was obeying the voice, or as the new-agers would put it, just *following her bliss.*

"What are you thinking, Franck?"

"I'm thinking I'm Faust, and you're Beelzebub."

"No, it's far better than that, Franck. You see, I can be *anything* you want me to be. Anything, Franck."

The next day, Sheba took me for a spin down the *Quai Jemmapes*, which runs alongside the Canal St-Martin. We were more or less drifting, passing a cigarette back and forth between us. She was looking out the car window driver side towards the water slapping against the side of the locks, monitoring something, smiling at some private joke. The soundtrack from *Lift to the Scaffold* was playing on FIP FM, 105.7. I could see Sheba was happy. There was something else, too. But there was happiness. I was already learning to separate it from whatever the other part was.

The city had crawled to its usual Sunday morning halt. It was a grey day, of a kind that only Paris can give you, because even with ten million people in it, the city still knew how to come full stop, shut down and loll like the lazy, self-indulgent whore it was. The Miles Davis track had yielded to the husky reverb of a female voice describing a traffic jam in a tone and cadence that sounded piped direct from a caisson at the bottom of a river.

She turned right, drove onto a curved street, which hugged the edges of the *Buttes Chaumont* and pushed us through Belleville and further South. Once on *boulevard Menilmontant*, she pulled over, then parked just outside the walls of *Père Lachaise* cemetery. The city was grey, overcast.

The street where we parked was a short stretch of alley named *rue du Repos*. We climbed some steps. Walked through the main entrance of the cemetery. A concierge was sitting inside an office at the entrance, blandly leafing through the daily horse-racing form in *le Parisien*. Sheba walked several steps ahead of me towards the lower end of the Eastern divisions of the cemetery, just inside the walls. The cenotaphs and shrines, visible at higher levels of the cemetery like contours of a mountain vineyard, yielded to simple headstones, flat tombs, and a few scattered cairns at the sliver of plots where we now stood. The surrounding lawn was neglected. Many of the stones were partially overgrown with thistles, vines, milkweed, dandelions. I followed her along a narrow path between two rows of marble slabs. She eased past an old man, hunched over, kneeling as he lay a bouquet of *muguets* on a tomb. She wore a thin, gauze-like material as a scarf, over a cream-coloured blouse and a knee-length skirt. Dressed for the role. Woman in a Paris cemetery on another dismal Sunday near the end of the millenium. The sun was creeping through the clouds, casting out thick beams of light.

I watched her buttocks swivel back and forth, taunting death with the projects that still lay ahead. I looked back towards the entrance to see if anyone other than the old man was in the vicinity. A young group of anemic Germans had entered by the main road, looking for Jim Morrison's tomb, or looking for a place to drink. Or just looking. I looked back at her. She was examining me. Everything else, corpses included, were backdrop. There was only her, and her cunt, and the wreckage of her mind.

She bent to her knees, wrenched a sprout of milkweed from the soil. She bit off part of the stem. A lactic fluid oozed out into a rivulet onto her lips, then into an estuary over her chin.

"Look at the area around this *mauvais herbe*, Franck. Nothing alive. Just to live, it has to suck and choke the life of everything within reach."

She held a small bouquet of the weed, as if she were a bridesmaid. She turned around and continued her walk towards a vertical mausoleum in the shape of a balustrade. Both the inside and out were covered with graffiti and ivy. She pulled me inside.

"Look, Franck."

She reached for a stretch of ivy clawing at the wall and pulled it back, revealing an etched inscription on two drawers:

Victor Levy   Estelle Goldstein
Rachel Levy [1950-1970]   "a refuge for men
                                     in need"

There were several swastikas on the wall. One of the
graffiti said: "*Mort aux juifs.*" Another said: "*Juden verboten.*"

She leaned backwards against the wall and pulled her
skirt upwards, showing her rusty cunt hairs draped between the two white straps of her garter belt. Ready for
the matinee performance.

"Now, Franck. Now."

A shaft of sunlight was coming through an open
crack in the wall of the mausoleum. She lifted up her
left leg and wrapped it around my thigh. I pulled her
upwards until both her legs were wrapped around my
waist. Over her shoulder, as I felt my cock penetrate past
her labia and lodge against the spongiform walls of her
vagina, my eyes fell onto the graffiti. *Mort aux juifs.*

After, for what seemed a long moment, I propped my
hands flat against the damp wall, stared at it. She smiled.
Placed her finger in the nucleus of her pursed lips, indicated silence. I peered outside the mausoleum onto the
grounds outside. The old man mourning his wife had
departed. A Maghrebian gardener, pushing a small cart
with a shovel laid flat inside, walked by on the main
pathway leading upwards.

Later, we visited a number of tombs of celebrities.
She seemed to have a pre-set itinerary, and I had the
impression she had done the routine before. Not that it
made any difference, but even then, she didn't strike me
as someone who lost a lot of sleep over others' suffering.
But, the headstones made good props for her performance. When she described Chopin and Balzac as
cuckolds, or cried at Michel Petrucciani's grave, who

she said had been a friend, it was purely a favour for the deceased. Gracing them with her presence so to speak. She stopped in front of the tomb of Abélard and Héloise.

"What should we inscribe on our tomb, Franck?"

"What makes you think we will be buried together?"

She examined me briefly.

"I hope it's not all talk, Franck."

"What?"

"I hope you have what it takes."

The wind was strong, billowing her gauze scarf into bubbled shapes. I felt a sucking pressure pulling on me from my lower torso, as if I had a taut, shredded ligament linking it tentatively to the pituitary gland.

"I want to reveal something to you, Franck."

Even through the wind, the sun burned harshly. We were passing the Monument to the Dead. The road circled upwards, overlooking the Eastern portion of the city. We sat down on a bench on a promontory, near the tomb of Apollinaire. She walked to the edge of the promontory, leaned over a wrought-iron railing, protecting walkers from a twenty metre sheer drop.

I briefly considered the option of pushing her over, and watching her body and head smash onto the pavement below. She turned around, her eyes probing me, as if detecting something she had been looking for. Then walking towards me, the outside contours of her hips undulating, reminding me of another time, a forgotten *déjà vu*.

"Do you believe a woman can be fucked by God, Franck?"

The heat of the sun had become unpleasant. Chafing, abrasive. A vapour emanated from the moss clinging loosely to the Monument of the Dead.

"I don't believe in God."

She looked away from me.

"I have a recurrent dream, Franck. It is so real, I wonder whether it might not have happened in a way. A spiritual way. I see something. A person or a presence. But the contours and individuality of the person are not distinct. Like an angel, Franck. Carrying a burning sceptre of sorts. The tip of the sceptre is red-hot, molten iron. The angel approaches me, and plunges the sceptre right into me. Here, Franck."

She placed both her hands flat on the upper portion of her loins.

"Right into my entrails. The pain, Franck, is absolutely unbearable, yet exquisite. An irresistible force. What do you think it means, Franck?"

"Death."

"You do understand, don't you, Franck? It *is* death."

She paused momentarily.

"Death doesn't seem such a bad place."

When she said it, death seemed like a good place. At least good for the two of us.

"Let's go back," I said.

We walked down to the *rue du Repos* in silence.

IV

A couple of days later, we were exiting the revolving doors of the Hotel Crillon onto the crimson-carpeted steps leading onto *Place de la Concorde*. She was saying something like:

"You have no idea how to treat a woman, Franck Robinson."

And, I was responding with something like:

"Don't get me wrong. It's been a great weekend. But, it's a little early for diamonds, Sheba."

I watched her theatrically wiggle that tantalizing ass of hers past the valet and park it on the front seat, driver-side of her Audi. And, I recall thinking that this was pretty well too good to be true. Absolute top-shelf cunt, spoil her rotten for a weekend, watch her throw a tantrum or two and then *pfft*, gone forever, like a spring breeze. I was finally figuring out a basic equation of life. It was easy, just so long as nobody got inside the inner enclaves. Stick to hotels and whores, Franck, and everything will remain incredibly cool for the duration.

After the Audi spun around the *Place de la Concorde* twice, then evaporated into a cloud of exhaust on the *Quai des Tuileries*, I looked to the left, lit a Marlboro, then scoped out the situation stage right. A CRS type, standing outside his van near the *Palais de l'Elysée*, had observed the whole thing played out. I shrugged my shoulders. He laughed. He'd probably seen the scene played out three or four times that morning. Suddenly, I recalled that I was within walking distance of some old cronies who never ventured further than Wee Willie's Bar up on the *rue des Petits Champs* on Sunday afternoons. Wee Willie only caters to wine traders, *charcutiers* and local restaurateurs. Last time I'd frequented the place, Willie the Wee in person was handing out Louis XIII cognac, and *Hoyo de Monterrey*s gratos to all present. The best way to finish off a Sunday afternoon in my books was a little visit at the Vincennes track, a few *Quinte* and *Quarte* bets, preferably with some short-skirted tart carrying a tray in her left hand filled with *51* or Calvados. In short, the slate was being cleared and, as I crossed the arcade of the Palais Royal, things were looking more than up, and time stretched out into an infinity of low accountability and high-grade sensorial enjoyment.

I was working my way towards the *Galéries Vivienne*, the idea being to pick up some champagne and *Medoc* for the post Wee Willie's phase. I casually reflected that I was within walking distance of the *Madeleine*, a neo-classical temple erected by the French to honour a whore. It was a private joke and I was glad to be alone. Then, I looked up and there she was again. The first thing I noticed were the tears running down her mascaraed eyes.

"Oh, is it really you, Franck?"

"What the hell are you doing here?"

"Me, can't a woman take a stroll in Paris, it's still a free country and, what a coincidence, how did *you* show up here? For all I know, you were following me."

Dab, dab with the handkerchief, she went, paying her dominical respects to the gods of hubris and artifice.

"How could you have hurt me so?"

She stopped short, recalling something. Her tears now yielded to a slight smile, as if there was still slight recompense in a world of injustice and unspeakable pain.

"By the way, I had a little discussion with the *concierge* during our brief separation, Franck. Olivier of course recognized me, he knew you were being unkind to me, so he, at least, was *correct* enough to give me your plane ticket, passport and a few other items. You know, Franck. Bank cards. Mementoes. I think there might have been a few pictures too. You know the ones, Franck. If the law society ever saw them, I wouldn't want to be in your position. All of which, of course, I have stored in a safe place until I decide what to do with them ... Frank, one of these days you must learn how a real *French woman* deserves to be treated."

The anglicism oozed out in a stipply gallic roll, as if she were Kiki of Montparnasse herself stepping onto stage, back in the nineteen tens, pre-American invasion, and not a late millenial whore who spoke a very creditable version of Kensington English whenever she put her mind to it.

One thing you should never do if you've decided to break with the past and devise your own life plan is introduce people from past lives. But, I didn't want her anywhere near Wee Willies. That was sacred territory. On the other hand, I had a dinner date with Laraine Sandusky back in the Flore towards the end of the day. I had fucked Laraine one night in her New York condo while her accountant husband was sleeping upstairs, and felt bad enough about it to avoid her unless absolutely necessary. On the other hand, Laraine always had some scheme up her sleeve which involved easy profits. The agenda was rapidly evolving, and some decisions had to be made. I invited Sheba to come along for the ride, thinking she might be a good deflector if Laraine got any funny ideas on the personal level. Sheba magically produced my wallet, and suddenly the world was a brighter place. Not quite as good as ten minutes previous, but not bad.

As Sheba and I entered the *Flore*, Laraine was creating a made in New York moment, railing at the waiter in her brassiest Manhattan moxy for passing off *Bleu de Gex* for *Fourme de Montbrison*. I recognized the waiter, Cédric, who sodomized by night, and made the general public pay for his excesses during daylight hours. But Laraine had the type picked off on sight, and, either for her own amusement or as a sideshow for us, performed her usual number on him with extra flair, punctuating her moral outrage with a piercing scream until Cédric volte-faced and heeled it back to the kitchen to ricochet Laraine's wrath onto the cheese cutter.

That left the four of us with nothing to do but get to know each other. Laraine, her executive secretary, me and one of Paris' rising whores on the subterranean St-Denis human stock exchange, commodities division, where day-trading in harlotry was booming, in fact one of the few *core businesses* in France which hadn`t yet been submerged, or merged into an American conglomerate, because the *French touch* just had a twist to it that not even the franchisers could figure out. And, now Laraine's semi-quizzical amused glance, as if asking, Franck, what the fuck are you doing with this trollop at your side? She looks like Jeanne Moreau in one of those cheapo *film noir* things you were always plaguing me with while I was recuperating from my last bout of cosmetic surgery in the solarium of my Boca Raton condo. And, what the fuck are those rings doing on your fingers, Franck? Have you really gone wacko this time? And that hat? Are you Alain Delon in *The Samurai*? Are you Peter Coyote in *Bitter Moon*? I am not cutting any more deals with you, Franck, until you come clean and tell me what the fuck is going on here. Her bulging, blue friendly eyes, and straight ahead ruthless New York facelift were all shouting it louder than any *pronunciamento* ever could. But, all that is coming out of her mouth is:

"Delighted to meet you, Ms. Sheba."

She articulated the name as if it were an earthenware tajine being discounted at a *souk*, or the name of a lost toy Pekinese scheduled to premiere in the spring dog show. Sheba smiled.

"I have never encountered an American woman. Of course, I have heard a lot about them. From American men."

"New York, honey. Nowhere further from America on this planet."

They scrutinized each other for a moment.

"Sheba, you may be wondering where Franck and I *fit in*, so to speak. Let me reassure you. It's always been strictly business. Although, for a time, Franck did fuck me in my marital bedroom while my ex romped in the rec room with his new boyfriends. Right, Franck?"

Laraine swivelled a hundred and eighty degrees, stabbed with the memory of something.

"Where the *hell* is my goddam cheese!!"

Sheba emitted a low whistle of appreciation. America one. Gaul zero.

"Now, Franck, if you don't mind me getting to the point."

"Be my guest, Laraine."

"You recall the Channel First people, Franck, don't you?"

"Chanel, chanel, are we talking perfumes and the like here?"

"Speaking of fucking, Franck, you fucked me roundly on that file."

"Correction, Laraine. They asked me what I thought of your accountant."

"Stanley Kirsk is no worse than any other Manhattan Jew, Franck. Or for that matter, any Lebanese Christian, or Amsterdam diamond dealer, or anybody who's any good at business. And, you torpedoed him, Franck. Him, and my own deal. Now, can you assist me on this IPO or not, but make up your mind. And quit harassing me with your goddam conflict of interest. Nobody even knows what it means anymore. By the way, do you mind if I tape this conversation? Just so there's no confusion on the terms of any agreement. We've got the money, but I want this to work this time. Which it can, if you don't go into sabotage mode."

Laraine was Big Apple brassy with a nose for cash and connections, which was common enough, but she enjoyed spreading the wealth, and that made her special enough for me, and good to stay close to. Laraine knew everybody from Trump to Robert Dole to the junk bond dealers, and from the sounds of the preliminary sketches of her *business proposal*, this information had come right from the inner circle. In fact, it had insider scam written all over it. A no-brainer, hit-and-run job on the NASDAQ, and an easy skim of illicit profits before the man in the street got in and lost his hard-earned cash.

The setting was fitting enough. Sunday afternoon in the Flore. Spielberg, Quincy Jones and their wives at the next table. Inès de la Fressange fluttering around. Looking for a new sponsor or a new boyfriend.

Bohringer ostentatiously lounging his feet on the table in front of him. Gainsbourg weaving his way down *St-Germain*, providing ringside seats to a preview of his upcoming funeral. Even from inside the *Flore*, you could see his breath streaking the air like a piece of cheap streamer graffiti. He was carrying a Mexican hairless under his left arm, and escorting a weedy-looking, middle-aged 60s leftover with oversized, capped teeth. But, as far as Laraine was concerned, I was the only celebrity in attendance. She was giving me the twice-over, like a plaintiff's lawyer in an asbestos litigation trial, occasionally tilting her head in Sheba's direction with a convincing "why should being fucked by Franck prevent *us* from being friends" smile, then back to riveting me with relentless, head-shaking cruelty. Sheba stood up.

"Please excuse me, I have to telephone someone."

Laraine ordered more coffee.

"So, fill me in, Laraine. What's the *schtick*?"

She shook her head, stamped out her cigarette.

"Not quite your style, is she Franck?"

"Just to keep in touch. French culture, ear to the ground and all that."

"Aren't you reversing the usual roles here, Franck?"

"Say what, Laraine? You're not serious. You think some little piece of French *poontang* is going to fool old Franck Robinson?"

"You never leave people indifferent, Franck. I'll give you that. There's talk in the city about Franck Robinson."

"Well, it's nice to hear people still remember me."

"The talk is don't go anywhere near Franck Robinson, unless you want the Securities Commission and fraud squad down your throats."

"That's ridiculous. I haven't done more than six IPOs in my life. Excluding immigration files of course."

"Franck, you like risks, but this looks *kamikaze* to me. She looks like dotcoms, circa 1998. Hot as hell and ready to fizzle. A short sell, Franck, and you know it."

"How's Colbert, Laraine? Has he found himself?"

"Fuck off, Franck. You know damn well Cuthbert and I are divorced. I sicked Howard Rosenbaum on him. Cuthbert is a *bottom*, Franck, so I thought I'd get someone to carve him out a second asshole. A going away present. So to speak."

"Must have been a *blow* to him. No pun intended. Divorce always very painful. Many never recover from the experience."

Laraine flashed her post-op facelift smile.

"Don't try and pass that hubris off on me, Robinson. *I'm* more than surviving. I have a low investment-high return gig that the Rothschilds and the Chase Manhattan people are losing sleep over, but take the little piece of cunt, Franck, see what I care. I mean, Franck, I'm *sure* this time will be different. Oh, and here's Sheba, how did your phone call go. Everything settled?"

It was a great meal. The food was good. The Veuve Clicquot cost triple whatever else everyone had. Laraine was making a point of being funny, expansive, gregarious; in other words she obviously hadn't been properly fucked since Cuthbert had crossed the great divide. I made a mental note to send a Chippendale escort up to her apartment. Sheba was charming while she scoped out Laraine for future considerations. Even Laraine's six foot tall dyke of an Austrian secretary with the Nana Mouskouri eyeglasses, the lime-green, feathered hat and the face of an embalmer wore a smirk to go with her smock for the afternoon. And of course I was in attendance. In a manner of speaking. That is, I was physically present, although at the same time, Laraine had read the situation perfectly. I was *history*.

V

It was only a Paris weekend, nothing more, but after my return to Montreal, things started drifting a bit. Not that they'd every been completely on course. After a while, I thought, fuck it, I'm not married anymore, no reason to clean up after myself, so I moved into a hotel near the downtown core, a grey square building named after a governor who ran Quebec while the territory was an English colony. I think the guv' was best known for a plan to exterminate a tribe of Indians with a flu virus. A man two centuries ahead of his time.

But I had picked the hotel for geographical, not historical, reasons. It was close to my office, which I leased on the waterfront in the old part of the city. The quarter hummed during business hours, then vacated at dusk. This suited the rhythms of my new plan. As others' days were coming to an end, mine would begin.

I had been half-heartedly practicing law, while I waited for something to turn up, something in the way of a lottery win or another good quad case in the courts

before I left the racket for good. The office was still necessary, as it would take some time to wind things down,
close files, let people know that I was no longer available.
I fell into the habit of walking down towards the old
port during the early evening, past the abandoned sugar
factories, breweries and textile houses which had made
the city rich a century previous, but which now stood
like sightless beggars, muted by the grinding screech of
freight cars rolling into the container port.

About six months after my return, I found myself
drifting down my usual route along the rue de la Com-
mune during the early evening. Stopped at a liquor store
and picked up a few bottles of wine, then returned to
the hotel. I retrieved a straight-backed wicker rattan
chair, ersatz colonial-style, and placed it in front of a
drafting table. I had purchased the two items from an
architect. He had retired following a nervous break-
down. I placed two of the bottles on the table beside a
writing pad, and a black telephone.

I stared at the phone for a few minutes, flipped
through the yellow pages, looking for an escort service
close by as I glanced at a clock perched outside just over
a video porn shop, flashing a neon triple x from the opposite side of the street. It was just after nine p.m. Don't
ask me why I remember the time. But, it was nine. It
suddenly came to me that I had been rehearsing a mental
choreography for a number of days, possibly weeks, as if
I were somnolent.

I reached into my pocket, retrieving a crumpled up
note. It contained the message she had dropped into my
pocket six months previous. The note had the impression
of a mouth on it, traced by magenta lipstick:

"we can do anything together. If you call me, I will
come ..."

There was a cell phone number beneath the message. I perused the handwriting again. The letters appeared to be rising and falling, beckoning me forward by their slow, undulating curve, reminding me of the way she moved. As if each member of the Roman alphabet occulted a series of secondary hieroglyphic symbols representing mistresses, jackal heads, motions of flight. I still felt pretty well on top of things, but at the same time, her cunt was drawing me closer. Emitting signals from an ocean away.

Nothing new, it had happened before. As if a miniature devil periodically crawled inside my brain and squatted there for the evening before moving on. Earlier in the week, while in a similar state, I had spent a while drinking and more or less examining myself in the mirror, watching sweat rivulets seep right out of my scalp and onto my forehead. But, that was last week, and this was now.

I continued drinking for a time, watching the crimson-bouqueted liquid descend into the glass, then rise upwards to my mouth, then down the gullet to wherever that led. The wine was a Gigondas, a wine so thick and coarse, drinking it was like swallowing dirt. Pleasurable, type of liquid that can make you forget anything. I had purchased it several years previous to commemorate an evening after my ex-wife had announced within the same sentence that she was pregnant and that she was aborting. Something about not being able to bear bringing life onto the planet with my genes.

It was a common enough comment from my ex-wife. But, since I didn't care, the thought would evaporate. I had a general feeling that humanity had been nuked, yet I'd miraculously escaped. A feeling of anesthetized perfection. While mulling over this, I had finished the first bottle of Gigondas, and was working my way steadily through the second. I wrapped my hand around the neck of the bottle, choking it, and slowly poured some of the wine into the cup of my hand. I lifted my hand over my head and allowed the drips of thick liquid to slip through my fingers and leak onto my face. I poured more of the wine into the cup of my palm, and clawed out a suppurating, clotted trail up my forearm with my index and forefinger. I leaned back in the chair, laid my head back, and poured the rest of the bottle into my mouth, steadily, swallowing some, allowing the rest to spill out over the edge of my mouth, recalling the memory of my unborn offspring and knowing that I would never create life. Drinking this Gigondas triggered the issue of completely banal clichés which somehow kept me happy for the evening that I was alone. The current axiom went: a blood pact between men is about loyalty, and a blood pact between a man and a woman is about betrayal.

I was drunk. Again. Time to figure out who to disturb next. My mind was in order, but my body would no longer follow. I stared listlessly at the phone, languishing in a fatalistic stupor, incapable of anything but pouring out another glass of Gigondas. The wine now formed into a pool on the hardwood floor beneath.

I leaned over the phone, picked up the handset, dialed the international exchange. A vocal recording informed me that the telephone exchanges in France had changed. The recorded voice was recent Parisian, with a trace of an accent from the Southwest. Biarritz. Or Toulouse. I hung up, and redialed. After three rings, an answering machine kicked in.

"*Bonsoir. Vous êtes bel et bien dans le domaine de Sheba.*"

The phone fell out of my hands. Like I said, I was pretty drunk. I picked it up. Dial tone.

I started thinking back to the Sunday morning we had spent together in Paris. We were walking down *rue Mouffetard*. The markets were open. An old anarchist was giving a speech to an assembled crowd. We stopped for a moment. He interrupted his speech, beckoned Sheba forward with a show of gallantry and a big bow. Further down the street, we could hear the echoes of accordion, concertina, orgue de Barbarie, bal-musette. We were completely insulated from the world. I was thinking at the time: this is what my life is about. Not life. Just my life. It wasn't a hell of a lot, but nothing much else looked better. I hadn't conquered anything, hadn't saved anybody, but I had stumbled across this first-class whore, and she seemed to actually enjoy spending time with me. That was plenty for me. Nothing mattered. Nobody else existed.

I picked up the phone and dialed.

This time she answered.

"Sheba, this is Franck Robinson. You may not recall me."

She said nothing for a second. I saw no point in apologizing. I had her pretty well pegged as a night hawk.

"... *et alors?*"

"Sheba, do you know the meaning of the word contingency?"

"*Non.*"

"Contingency, bear with me, Sheba, is one of the three ways of accumulating considerable sums of money without working."

"Really, Franck. It's Franck, you said?"

It went on like that. I don't recall the other details. Except that she never hung up. She may have entered into one of her mediaeval inquiries about me being worthy, or whether I was the chosen one. I don't recall. If it were banal or kitsch, I wanted more of it. Or she might have suggested we move into a tent, or under a bridge on the Rhone, or inside a cave somewhere in the Dordogne valley. That might appear absurd to others, but to me it made perfect sense. The details are vague, but she relented, although I'm pretty sure that the word contingency caught her attention.

VI

I spotted her from the upper departures level, gliding through customs, accompanied by two men in business suits who wore flushed schoolboy grins twenty years too old for the wear and tear of their faces. From my angle, I could only make out an oversized, white brimmed fedora and beneath, a pair of spiked heels. By the time she emerged from within the arched walls of immigration on the main floor, the two men had disappeared. She prowled down the drab floor as if it were a YSL catwalk, putting on her own invitation-only performance for an audience of half a dozen Sikhs and three baggage valets sucking on cigarettes. I could now see, from the front, a halter neck dress over a black velvet skirt tied at the waist with a jewelled belt. At some point during her passage through customs, her fedora had disappeared. In its place, she wore a turban, tightly coiled around her head like a boa. She walked towards me, coyly, pouting her magenta lips, playing it up for a couple of baggage handlers and a Punjabi cab driver gawking at her backside. She had no baggage, and a white hand-bag dangled carelessly from her left hand as she wound her way up to me and planted a light kiss on my lips. She retreated two steps, examined me briefly, smiled.

"Hello, Franck."

We turned around, and I escorted her across the floor of the arrivals level, neither of us speaking. It was late April. Montreal was still feeling the wrath of a lingering winter. Snow flurries and sleet storms had been sweeping the city for days. As we neared the exit, she broke away from me and walked towards the wide plate glass windows that surrounded the arrivals level like a welder's mask. She pushed the index of her left hand up against the glass, and drew a vertical line on it, then peered through it at the whiteness outside. She uttered my name, sending a small whiff of vapour into the window.

"Franck."

I approached her from behind and wrapped my arms around her waist. She continued staring out the window, witnessing for the first time the cold winter I had endured for the previous decade. A low, whistling sound accompanied the gusts of snow piling up on the ramp outside and slowing traffic to a crawl. Two burly policemen, wearing raccoon caps, their arms vertical, motioning like air traffic controllers. The traffic inched past and between them, through the whistling silence.

"*Oh-la-la*, Franck, I knew, but this ... Franck, put your coat around me."

She curled up under my arm, and we ran out onto the road, through fifty metres of the driving storm, then into the relative safety of a multi-tiered parking lot. We were under shelter, but I didn't pull my arm away.

Within minutes, I was behind the wheel of my silver Saab 9-3, downshifting the motor into third, and hitting the ramp onto the freeway and the beginning of our life together. The Saab handled well. As good a snow machine as you could expect in a luxury car.

"I met two charming men on the plane," she said.

Unconsciously, I glanced at the odometer. At 120 km, I clicked on the cruise control. I felt a slight pain gnawing at my stomach.

"I know."

"You know?"

"I was watching you as you came through customs. From the upper mezzanine."

Her eyes seemed to flash briefly, then receded into something else. The gnawing pain returned. As if I had been drinking coffee for days. Or that there was something essential that I was ignoring at my own peril.

"They wanted to know everything about me."

"What do you mean, everything?"

"Why someone like me would come to a place like this."

"What did you respond to that?"

"Oh, I told them it was purely business."

I had always more or less felt that I had two or three sectioned off quarters of the brain, each of which conducted operations from an autonomous *état-major*, competing with the other compartments to put their own spin on anything I experienced, much in the way of a sleazy but desperate politician, creating slush funds, conducting dirty tricks campaigns, rigging elections. But, processing none of the information through the usual, legitimate channels.

In anticipation of her arrival, I had moved out of the hotel, and leased a five-level mezzanine loft which had been built on the remains of a Scottish Presbyterian church. The building was located on a dismal stretch of road lined with brick buildings in the midst of a low-end Portuguese-Jewish textiles district. The interior was all art-deco and Alvar Aalto. Sleek brass counters and overhead wineglass racks nailed to thick cedar beams.

The woman who had let us the top floor was a tall, strapping Newfie, the spoiled daughter of a national media baron. From the day I leased the place, she made a point of dropping by to recount her current sexual antics and forays in very graphic detail. She was proud of everything. Proud of her tits. with good reason, and proud of her brassy voice, with less justification, and proud as hell of her feminist ideas which were oxymoronic and cliché to the extreme. But she was most proud of her Haitian fuck-boy whom she towed around with the aplomb of a slave ship bounty hunter.

The Newfie travelled among a group of girlfriends, each of them with boyfriend in tow. They were inseparable. All of them rabid feminists, and none of them capable of even scrambling an egg or holding down a day job. They more or less tolerated me, but the distrust was never far beneath the surface.

After we took possession, her first move was to decorate the flat top-to-bottom with mirrors. Specula, hand mirrors, vanity mirrors, rear view mirrors. She liked the vanity mirror best. I am a tall man, and she was short, even propped up on her four inch stilettos. Taking her from behind allowed the two of us to stare into the oval as if posing for a Las Vegas photo-op, as our faces marked our path into full thrust and onwards into violent orgasm, and back to our usual state. Boredom. While we waited for the next exciting thing to happen, provided it had everything to do with us, and didn't involve what the rest of the world called work.

She wore a mauve body suit. We hadn't left the room since arrival, except to visit the WC, or to retrieve drinks, which involved walking through the kitchen past the gaping, hostile stares of our new stable mates. Small talk or pedestrian courtesies were not an option either Sheba or I was inclined to exercise.

She lay on her back. We had been acting out a number which she had laid out for me the previous day. It involved tying her up, gagging her and raping her. I had tied her up, and was fucking her from the top.

"Stop."

"What's the matter?"

"I want you to hit me."

"Whatever. Where?"

"In the face."

I pushed my left hand into her throat and kept her head rigid. I delivered a solid cuff across the left cheek, then backhanded her across the right. Her face folded into a grimace which I initially mistook for pain.

"I said hit me, *espèce d'imbécile*! As hard as you can."

"Have it your own way."

I wound up this time, a good telephone booth swing. I think I was recalling an old newsclip of Sammy Snead blasting the ball out of the 18th sandtrap at Augusta with his sand wedge. My open hand made a sharp ping as it collided with her face, and left the palm of my hand a scarlet red. The force of it knocked her to the other side of the bed. She righted herself, and lifted her hand up to her mouth. A trickle of blood spurt from the inside of her mouth. Her tongue licked it dry, but the moisture prevented the blood from clotting and it leaked out in a steady trickle.

For a moment, we stared at each other wordlessly, listening to the heavy, thudding steps of the Newfie marching down the hallway towards our room.

"Everything all right in there?"

"T'inquiète pas."

Sheba had not turned her face away, and was still displaying a smile of lurid satisfaction. As if she had found something she had lost for a long time.

"That's better. Now, *play it again, Sam*. But, this time on the other side."

The next afternoon, things deteriorated. The Newfie, whose overtures not a week earlier when she met Sheba had been replete with lesbo-friendly we're all sisters jargon, was pounding on the door so loudly it shook.

"I want to talk to the two of you," called the Newfie.

"Go away," responded Sheba from the other side of the door. "We are busy." She looked at me and placed her index finger over her pursed lips, and pried open the lower lip as if she were shucking an oyster.

"This cannot wait."

Even from the other side of the door, I could sense some apprehension in the Newfie's fury. She had been accustomed to pushing people around, whether men or women, big or small, and her Amazon physique and 38 Triple C tits coupled with a rude, brassy voice and lack of manners had served her bullying ways well in her local society. But, even the Newfie's thick skull could detect through the previous week's renovations, the newly installed mirrors and canapés, the boxes of perfume still arriving by courier, the lavender veils and catwalk fashions and general air of secrecy which had suddenly enveloped the place that, whatever Sheba was, she didn't fall under any definition of the word *sister*.

Sheba stood up and walked across our room to her vanity table. She glanced at me, shrugged, reached inside the top drawer. She pulled out a large wad of bank notes and slipped them inside the lavender, ruffled panties clinging to her cunt as if an alternating current were running through them. As she walked towards the door, I noticed she was making an effort to suppress a smile. She stopped short, and looked at me. Through the glistening eyes and moist lips, she was telegraphing one of her favourite messages, one which I would learn to decipher before long. Act II. Scene III. My next piece of prey. Then, she opened the door. The Newfie opened up festivities with an announcement.

"I am missing five thousand dollars from my safety deposit box."

I had never seen the Newfie lose her footing before, but Sheba had clearly unnerved her, despite being half her size. Sheba stared at her wordlessly for several moments, considering something. Her mouth was slightly parted. She calmly scrutinized the Newfie, whose next phrase was emitted in a higher octave.

"Where is my money?"

The phrase spilled out in a vaudevillian chirp. Again, Sheba paused. She looked back at me, whatever she had been considering now confirmed, then back at the Newfie. Finally, she spoke.

"Wait here."

She walked over to a coffee table, picked up her burgundy-toned pack of Dunhills, her back to the two of us, drew one from the pack and inserted it in her mouth, taking her time about it. A languorous ether permeated the atmosphere, anesthetizing the three of us. Sheba walked back to the door. She lit her cigarette, allowing a small pyre to drift into the Newfie's face. As I watched the drama unfold, it came to me that every breathed insinuation, sideward glance and mocking smile had been stage managed down to its finest detail, and that the performance had nothing to do with money, or with the Newfie. It was meant for me, and me alone.

"You had better be able to back this up. Otherwise I will make you pay. I promise you."

I think that what shook up the Newfie more than anything was not Sheba's icy threat, but the revelation that she had no self-knowledge whatsoever. She knew Sheba had stolen her money, and had no intention of returning it. Sheba's casual stare was ample evidence of that. That bland admission first enraged the Newfie. Then, she came to a grinding halt, as if her inner hard drive had suddenly shut down. The shock and suddenness of her defeat filled her with an unfamiliar, nascent desire which confused her. When she looked at Sheba, she could see that Sheba had detected whatever this perversity inside of her was, even before she had suspected its existence. And somehow, Sheba's seemingly random scenario had triggered it within her.

The Newfie was like a lot of other people we came across, in the sense that I have no idea what happened to her next. Maybe she went into social work.

Later that day, we stopped in at the *Air du Temps*, a jazz bar in the old city. She was leafing through a real estate magazine, and I was having a coffee, mentally replaying the scene earlier that morning, where Sheba had somehow managed to convince the Newfie to write out a cheque for the furniture we had left behind in the other flat.

"Listen to this, Franck. *Luxurious loft, overlooking the old port in the oldest street of North America. Must lease immediately.* It will make a good *pied-à-terre*. While we review our options."

"You're the CEO, baby."

I rang up the number. The voice answered in French and switched over to English immediately.

"What do you do? You are a lawyer? Fine. That's just fine. I have a slot open later this afternoon."

We decided to kill some time walking around the old port. She had been asking me about my sexual fantasies.

"Fantasies arc for people with shitty sex lives. That's never been a problem for me. Actually, come to think of it, Sheba, Franck Robinson is my fantasy."

"No, Franck. That's not sufficient. It must be something that you have kept for yourself. Something dark, which fills you with shame. That, if the world knew of it, you would feel exposed and ruined."

"I don't think I have that kind."

"That's impossible, Franck. Everyone has one thing."

"You have to care about the world for that one thing. That's not really a family trait. The Robinsons have never cared enough."

She stared darkly ahead.

"I know you like beating me, Franck. There was a look in your eyes. As if you were discovering something for the first time."

She watched me for a while, still probing for something, or as she would call it, that one thing.

"Franck, there are desires I have myself. They are so dark. So perverse ... it is hard to describe. It is as if they are controlling me, and I am only following. There are days, Franck, when I wish I had never been born."

"You were born for me. That's enough."

"Let's go to the port, Franck. I want you to show me where you took your walks. Before we were together."

The day's theme colour was peach. Peach-tinted bra, panty hose and garter belt, topped off by nothing more than an olive-hued, knee-length trenchcoat, which left her legs and lingerie visible for anyone who was interested.

"Let me take your arm."

Her eyes were glassy, translucent.

"Je mouille."

We exited the car and crossed the road, which put us on a boardwalk running alongside the river through the

Old Port along the ramparts. It was still early afternoon. The boardwalk was busy. Further on, I noticed an older man approaching us, staring fiercely at Sheba. As we approached, I recognized Bourque, a criminal defence lawyer I had worked for defending drug traffickers and whores until he quit the practice of law to run for public office. As fellow moral relativists, we hooked up periodically for drinks and what-not. Bourque was a silver-haired fox with bushy eyebrows, and a fierce, lascivious look which left no doubt that he was a throwback to an era when politics attracted another sort of man. He managed to get elected, but was forced to resign within the year. His name, a common one in the Montreal area, had been discovered in a hooker's black book. When confronted with it, he denied everything. No one believed him, particularly since the john in question was also a barrister, and a Montrealer. By the time his name was cleared, he had been booked on a drinking and driving charge and he was ruined.

"Oh, hello Franck," he said in that deep resonant voice, and despite all the talk in the papers, you couldn't write off someone who had the moxy to pretend his prostate was still operational. Hervé was a bird-dog from the beginning, and was capable of just about any posture to keep his lecherous eyes feasting on a woman for a few minutes longer.

"Haven't seen you in the courts lately, Franck. Taken a leave of absence, have we? Don't tell me you are doing solicitor's work, Franck. Not a line of work for any counsel worthy of the name, Franck. Piece work, Franck. Assembly line. Might as well work in a coal mine, Franck. And, who might this be, Franck? Sheba? What an intriguing name. And what a thoroughly marvellous ... specimen, Franck."

He eyed her from head to toe.

"You should have told me about this charming young lady. Yes, yes, I can see now. *Novus Actus Interveniens.* Quite understandable, Franck."

It took a good five minutes to move old Bourque along, and his furry eyebrows turned back our way twice, even after taking his leave.

"Let's sit down," she said weakly.

She held tightly to my arm as we walked towards a place on a bench overlooking the port area.

"I am so hot, Franck."

"It's a hot day."

"No, Franck. It was that man. There was something about him. Franck. Hold me, Franck. I want to watch the water for awhile."

We looked out past the terminal at the river, and an island containing remnants of an old world fair.

"It is the reason we are together, Franck."

"The water."

"You see it too, Franck, don't you. It is the water. It is the reason we are together."

The loft lived up to the advance billing. A luxury 3000 square foot loft, balconies on every side, and a solarium overlooking the port on the St. Lawrence. The owner was an Egyptian. We learned later he was skipping town on a tax evasion charge. His wife was Brazilian. She had big, siliconed tits and perfectly tanned legs, which emerged from her tight thousand dollar dresses and made her look like a star member of a Rio cabaret revue. Judging by her clothes and the furniture in the place, and the date of the Egyptian's plane tickets, the tax authority's chances of recovery were not high.

I signed the lease, and handed over twelve post-dated cheques. By the time the Egyptian and I had finished our third beer, the day was coming to a close, and the moving men were being directed by Sheba back and forth in front of us with a king-size brass-rail bed. She eventually settled on dead centre of the loft. The rear wall was systematically lined with antique mirrors, brass lamps and other paraphernalia I had purchased cut-rate from the Egyptian. Within the day, we had gone from hell to heaven again.

The Brazilian woman's name was Zeta. She and Sheba spoke in different accents, but it was the same language. They were both experts in setting up or taking down camp very quickly, and wherever they were they knew they were born to lead the march towards the next great consumer frontier. The Egyptian, now that his cheques were safe in his pocket, was waxing philosophy.

"I knew the fates would intervene. I could not leave this place with just anyone. I have my reputation and my businesses here, of course. Maybe, someday, I will even come back and live here in Canada. But, you know, the taxes are far too high. This, you people must learn to change. Until you do this, you can never become a truly great nation."

Later, I realized that he had left no forwarding number, so I had no way of helping the police and the revenue service when they arrived the next day looking for him.

The loft became our own little temple of sex and pain. The light coming through the windows of the solarium and the balconies were illusory, as there was only one exit to the loft, a thick door with a double deadbolt on it. The bed, a brass four-poster, quickly became the centrepiece of our existence. Right after the noon meal, I fell into the habit of strapping her arms to the top posts, fucking her from behind as her legs wriggled back and forth like two eels, then leaving her chained to the four-poster while I checked things out at the office. Upon my return, she would be crazy as a rabid dog, and only three or four hours of sex would get her as near to normal as someone like her could get. Then, after protracted discussions, she would insist I repeat the process on the following day. All that to say, in her own way, she enjoyed it.

It was a cold winter morning, but the loft was tropical. She was stretched out beneath the sunroof, wearing a mud-coloured bodysuit. Her eyes were half-closed, the evil temporarily assuaged, yielding to the languid pleasures of our day-to-day life, such as it was. I still had money, and while I continued to use it up, things remained at a manageable level. She hadn't moved for awhile, outside of casually leafing through a local cultural newspaper, which filled the front pages with rants against sexual abuse and the back pages with S & M personals.

I was standing at the bar counter which divided the kitchen area from the rest of the loft. A notebook, what appeared to be a journal, was open. A series of handwritten entries in log form:

Carnet.	Coup:
Sans 1 mot	700
Rendez-vous, vieux	3000
Touches parties	1000
Jew	3500
Bishop	5000
Nichons	2000
Le dingot	XX
The singer	5000
Slave	4000

I think it was the first time that I had considered up front that she was a whore. A whore fucks men or fucks them around for a living, so she needs a log book for that. So, she was a whore. I looked up. She was watching me.

"Do you know, Franck, there is a wine in the *arrière-pays* region where I grew up."

"Which *arrière pays* would that be?"

"It is called Biturica vine, I think, a wine first sown by the Plantagenets in the twelfth century. It endures cold, storms, rain. It lasts forever."

"I don't see the connection."

"The connection? I'll give you one if you have to have one, Franck. I am five hundred years old, but I cannot endure the cold."

"Don't sweat it. Montreal is hydro-electric heaven. We'll heat up the loft and buy a cactus."

She continued thumbing through the personals for a minute or two.

"I want to take you back, Franck. My country, it is built on the remains of a volcano. White clays, rusted volcanic tufa, chalky limestone. It is like me, Franck. Stratified."

"I'll think about it."

"There is nothing to think about, Franck. Look at this ad. Single mother of two, enjoys bowling, looking for honest lover. Bowling. Honest lover. There is your America for you."

"This isn't America."

"It's worse, Franck. You are a watered down version. And colder. Franck, you told me the other day that you want to be anonymous. This is your chance. You can live like a Sultan, basking beneath the olive trees, drinking wine, and making love to me. What more could you want? You just have to trust me."

Our lives may have appeared unconventional, but I recall thinking at the time, that I was just getting started, that it was time for the two of us to somehow leave our mark. In our own little way. Obviously, really good sex involved some element of nihilism, and why not continue the dance back in the old country? But, I hadn't answered the question quickly enough, as her monologue had moved onto another tangent.

"*C'est vrai.* It's true, Franck. I can be a little psychotic sometimes. But, be reasonable, Franck."

It was a reasonable statement, one you would expect from a rational actor, and I might even have conceded the point, if she weren't turning up all four heaters on the gas stove, as a little dramatic backdrop. She held two brochette skewers over the flames, watching me as the tips turned charry black, and then red-hot.

"Sometimes I think you are going to completely miss what I am about, Franck."

I watched her, thinking, the threat of imminent violence slows the rhythms down, pushes us into an atavistic headspace which has always been there, but is left temporarily dormant until we bring it back into life.

"You can really be *nul*, at times, Franck. *Moins que rien. Un plouck. Niais.*"

One of her gifts was being able to articulate each word distinctly, yet leave it hanging, coagulating like a thick mortar. I watched her some more. She rotated the skewers as she edged towards me. I was aware of her hands, which only slowed to a halt when she was preparing something a little more explosive. I could thank her for my improved peripheral vision. Sheba had charted the next minutes of the day, and designated them as Dantian.

I looked behind her, at a poster which had appeared on the wall of the kitchen. It was two-tone, emerald green and steel-grey, in the Soviet realism style. The poster was a 1923 public warning against syphilis. It showed a man in the pose of Rodin's *Thinker*, being punctured by an augur boring a hole through his belly. The head on the poster read:

PAILLE DANS L'ACIER
DE LA MACHINE HUMAINE
ABAT L'HOMME LE PLUS FORT

Don't expose yourself to this contagion, said the advice beneath the caption. And beneath the poster itself, I noticed something else for the first time. A series of books on sorcery and incantations. Whatever. Her voice interrupted my survey.

"Your past is over, Franck. Are you ready for the future, Franck?"

Suddenly, she broke into a smile, turned off the stove heats, and let the skewers drop out of her hands onto the undulated portion of the aluminium sink. She walked over to me, dropped to her knees, placed her hands on my thighs, stroked them soothingly.

"Franck, I don't want to hurt you. I've had enough of that. So, don't make me. There are times, Franck, when I love you too much to let you live. But, you evoke something within me. I don't know what it is. Goodbye, Franck."

She stood up and threw her arms around me. I'd already forgotten the previous five minutes. I wanted her too badly.

I was awakened later in the night by the sound of glass breaking and the smell of smoke. I called out for Sheba, but there was no sign of her. I next heard the sound of a loudspeaker, ordering residents out of the building. By the time I hit the street, a high winter gale had created a funnel effect, the flames had blazed out of control, and were well on their way to taking out four neighbouring buildings. The loft survived, but a family next door didn't. Half a dozen firemen had to be treated for smoke inhalation. Police investigators' antennae were tuned to insurance fraud. They were sure it was arson, but the origin or the motives behind it were never determined.

VII

After she left Montreal, I found myself at loose ends again. The loft was empty except for a few pieces of furniture and the mirrors that lined the walls. After a few days, the phone rang. It was Axelle. I invited her over. Axelle had curly thick black hair. She was small-chested, and her ass was rubenesque. Still, there was something about her that made her sexy. It wasn't so much a physical thing, although she did have pouty lips and dreamy eyes. And the eyes conveyed that she just might, even though it wasn`t in her interest at all, she just might throw everything away for a really good afternoon, that is if you were worth it. In other words, she had weaknesses and, being a good urban Montreal girl, she didn't worry too much about exposing them. For her, a man was not attractive unless he was married. This type of character flaw was what bound us together. We each had our compartments of perversity.

After she had had a drink, I asked her if she would try on some of the lingerie Sheba had left behind. No, Franck, I can`t do that. Why can`t you do that? I can`t do *that*, Franck, because you don't attract me. At least not right now. What is it in me that repulses you, Axelle? It`s not so much repulsion, and her way of answering made me temporarily happy that I was at least in the city, where people shamelessly tell you things about themselves and about you, because it's all part of a bigger game, and the game is to keep the essential out of the other's grasp, even if it means mounting an imposture so elaborate that it makes you look like a criminal, or worse.

Franck, no matter how deep you go into your own speleological expeditions of the psyche, there seems something salvageable about you. I see, I responded, realizing that this automatically excluded me as a candidate of any kind for Axelle, who demanded either to destroy or to be destroyed in order to feel she was even halfway alive. Do you think, I asked, this will always be the case. Not necessarily, Franck, she answered, I see signs that you may eventually move up to *priorité 4*.

Axelle left shortly after, leaving me alone with a wardrobe filled with women's lingerie, $80,000 worth of mirrors no one wanted to buy and some time on my hands. I stepped out onto *rue Notre Dame*, and walked towards the Main. It was still early evening. Across the street, fifty metres up, was the Sulpician monastery. A bum was standing just outside the entrance. He was hiding his crutch and sneaking around the corner to have a cigarette.

I turned left and walked past the *Palais de Justice*, at the bottom of the Main. Not eighteen months previous, I had been practicing law, or more precisely cajoling, threatening, sucking up to judges, and bluffing my way into my own version of justice, which meant out-of-court settlement at any price. And now, I had as much in common with my ex-colleagues as a vice-deacon from the Kazakhstan Orthodox Church. I walked down the hill and glanced to the other side. The Montreal Mission for the Homeless. I still hadn't been reduced to that, but now I felt it was no longer outside the realm of possibilities. It could happen. Anything could happen.

Another fifty metres and I was in Chinatown. I stepped into Fong's Saigon Success and ordered a bowl of soup. Across the street, the first few transvestites were setting up for the evening. The bark of the Québecois accent, the cacaphonic Cantonese threaded with Ho Chi Minh city insults and salty pork soup were more nourishing to me than anything the Louvre could offer. This was one of the few places in the world where I could feel right at home. I felt I was on my way somewhere, choosing a path of my own making.

Two buildings further up was the Cleopatra, a night club where boys could be girls, and more than likely were. I would occasionally drop in for a drink towards the end of the night. The Cleopatra was a natural stop-off for me because it was filled with freaks. To me, freaks weren't unhappy people, or unbalanced people. Not when you found them in their own element. Sodomites and pansies could gather unashamedly in the Cleo and wallow in each other's company. Quite a number of conventional looking men were regulars as well. They would ask the girls to dance, and everyone knew that every one of those girls had a cock under her dress, but she was acting like a woman, more than any woman could. The women in these men's lives, i.e. the ones being abandoned for the she-male tramps waltzing around Cleopatra's, preferred parody to actual sex and seduction. It was just a question of taste. One person likes watching members of his own sex create a caricature of what a woman might once have been. Another prefers soap operas and supermarket schlock about rampant incest and sexual abuse in the workplace.

The seasonal posture for the standard replicant woman was ridicule and mockery. So, at least that year, the average magazine-reading female did not consider herself up to scratch unless she engaged in mockery, preferably of any pretentions a male might have to a life. Like with everything, there was cost-benefit. The mockery saved her from all risks, including the risk of being loved by her man and the risk of being subjugated and taken the way only a woman can really enjoy. The john's stance, and basically Cleo patrons were all johns of one sort or another, was evasion. The only risk for the john was getting caught, and the odds were against it. Basically, the equation was simple. Each of them wanted to get fucked on his own terms.

These were the types of thoughts that came to me, partly because, in Sheba's absence, my mind shifted back to the general from the particular, and partly because it was Tuesday night, and I was on my way to watch Lola's striptease act, which usually brought a crowd of outsiders, college kids in gangs, stags, outsiders who wouldn't be caught dead in the place alone. Lola's attraction lay in her breasts, apparently the biggest in the world, 105 cm. Each of them weighed in at three kilos. Everything in her had been pumped up with silicone and hormones.

I first met Lola at four in the morning just after her weekly performance in a diner called Le Caféteria. She was seated alone in a neighbouring booth, contemplating her mammaries, looked up and caught my eye.

"How long can they stay up?"

"Hard to say. Not forever. Inflation always precedes a depression."

"It's not just the tits, honey. Once I got them done, I had the cheekbones, *les pommettes*, the mouth, mini-lift for the eyes. I even had my eyebrows tattooed. Then I started everything all over again. They removed the *arc de cupidon*, rolled back the mucous membranes right up to the nose, and pumped the lips full of silicone. Look at me. I'm a surgery addict. I love going under the knife."

Her mouth was a perfect replica of a vagina. She pushed her lips out into what was more a pulsation than a pout. It throbbed automatically, and it lacked conviction. Like a cat's rectum. Her breasts protruded across the table insolently parking on my placemat. World War I vintage zeppelins landing at the Paris Air Show.

"I am basically a woman transvestite. I have succeeded in creating a completely artificial woman. Barbie to the extreme. You know, I would like to have even bigger breasts. But, not even the black market abortionists will come near me anymore. Look at me. I am a complete freak."

Obviously, she was a freak. What was less obvious was her daily consumption of neuroleptics, anxiolytics, and enough sleeping pills to keep a small druggist in the black on an ongoing basis. When you are in your early twenties, you can still do these things and look all right.

"I can't sleep on my stomach anymore. I have to wear a bra twenty-four hours per day."

As I recalled my meeting with her, I had arrived inside Cleopatra's and ordered a couple of vodka shooters. The pre-act, a stand-up cross-dressing comedian, a throwback to the Rocky Horror Picture Show days, had just pranced onto the stage. The crowd burst into applause. It was superior to television, but the audience didn't require cue cards to applaud.

The androgynous mummy on stage risked being stoned to death just walking down the street during daytime hours, but in Cleopatra's, temple of freaks, she was adulated. The patrons loved her for having the guts to turn herself inside out. Inside the Cleo, thick with artificial Marilyn Monroe clones waltzing, or allowing johns to light their cigarettes, or powdering their recently shaved chins, we were all bound by the same sacred truth to which we clung with the desperation of the fervent believers. Engraved in our talmudic tablets was the knowledge that the really sick ones were out walking the streets, wearing off-the-rack ready to wear, paying their taxes, holding down the day jobs.

While enjoying an after dinner Scotch with Bourque one evening, I asked what it was in me that had pushed my first wife to hire a hit-man to take me out. More of a by-the-way conversation item than anything. We conversed from inside a solarium hatched onto the rear of his twelve-bedroom mansion, which overlooked a glacial lake from its perch up in the Laurentian mountains. It was a pretty spectacular winter panorama, interrupted only by the occasional cameo appearance of his fourth wife who drifted in and out wordlessly during proceedings, clad only in a powder-blue babydoll lingerie, and laced to the eyeballs with Librium. But Bourque scarcely noticed her, and was directing his full attention to a tale I was recounting of my own first marriage, which had been *conventional to the extreme.*

"An interesting phrase. Tell me, Franck, about the day you left her."

Bourque often said I intrigued him, but it was more the fact that he was so far beyond the pale himself that he could only draw enjoyment from other purveyors of the bizarre.

"Actually, I have no recollection why I married her in the first place. No memory of things like love or for that matter, even a long term plan."

Bourque sipped his Glenfiddich, eying me, a smile curving around his beak of a nose.

"But, you were living with this person, Robinson. You were building a life! Surely ..."

"Correct. For a time."

"Even went so far as to have a family."

"We had three children, I believe. Two boys and a girl, as I recall. For a time, I even participated in their upbringing."

"Such as it was."

"Such as it was. One evening, I glanced at her from across our living room, one of those sunken mezzanines that looks like it was retrieved from a John Cassavetes film. She was eating tapioca from a bowl she claimed had been designed by Alvar Aalto, with an undersized burgundy coloured spoon. She was a tapioca fanatic, not above consuming up to six bowls during any given evening, but somehow she never gained weight. On the other hand, her complexion was growing prunish."

"Prunish *to the extreme*, so to speak."

"She was very big on mud masks and sun lamps. On the complexion issue, pretty hard to determine *causa causans*."

I imagined Bourque to be a mutated offspring of a Frenchwoman raped by an oversized bird. I was at least half right. He nodded sympathetically.

"Causation is one of the thornier aspects of the law. That's why I stick to product liability, wherever possible. Res ipsa loquitur and Hedley Byrne principle."

"As she reached the bottom of her bowl, she had a habit of tapping and scraping her spoon against the walls of *that* bowl in a rhythmic, absent-minded manner, which pushed her into a reverie. That particular day, I watched her repeat her ritual, mentally preparing myself for the question which always followed ..."

I stopped, wondering whether I actually had been married, or whether I hadn't imagined the whole saga.

"*Do you love me still, Franck?* It could have been her spin, but the phrase struck me as grammatically flawed and highly ambivalent. I considered how quickly its weak sentimentality would mutate into simmering hatred once I left her. So, it was probably the tapioca that did it. In retrospect."

Whatever kind of bird Bourque was, it was in danger of extinction. Pterodactyl? Albatross?

"*Mon cher Franck*, I don't give a whit about your motives. Just give me the facts—chronologically."

"There aren't any facts. I just up and left her."

"You up and left her!"

A grin found its way onto his dungyard fowl of a head. He shouted the phrase in mock outrage, as I had recounted the story a number of times.

"You can't just up and leave your wife, Robinson!"

"It was early in the morning. I told her I would make breakfast. *Do you love me still, Franck?* Never more than today, honey. I couldn't overplay my hand. Wait here, I said, this morning, I have a surprise for you. *What kind of surprise, Franck*, she gurgled in her usual tapioca tones. Just promise you'll wait for me here. Then, I descended the stairwell, took the keys from the kitchen table, walked out the door, and drove away."

"How did she react?"

"I have no idea. My lawyer took care of matters."

"Did she not even try to approach you, track you down?"

"You, obviously, have never met my lawyer."

"Franck, I will tell you why other men detest you. You do what they all long to do, but lack the courage to execute."

"That's not my problem."

"You lack moral fibre, Franck. You are what we French call a *lâche*. A *faux-jeton*. I confess that there are times when I admire you. But, I cannot think that it will end well for you."

I shrugged my shoulders.

"Does it end well for anybody?"

The next time I was in Cleopatra's, I ran into Lola's husband, a transvestite with a heroin addiction who performed shows at the Love Affair, a booze can located in the rear of the Beijing restaurant. I sat down with him in the centre stalls, which had been purchased from a diner. He was skinny, had one of those long rectangular heads that look okay on camera and inhuman on the street. His hair was done upwards in a small pony-tail, like a medieval Samurai warrior, except he was an end of the millenium she-male stripper married to the woman with the biggest tits on the planet.

"Where's Lola?"

His eyes were dead, but the death was only caused by drugs, not some deeper illness.

If I were undergoing a word-association test and he were mentioned, everything would be coming up: fish, gills, carcass, scales. He smoked a cigarette in the way only a drag queen or an alcoholic actress seems to be able to pull off convincingly, letting it hang in a gravity-defying dangle off the tips of his elongated fingers.

"Lola died in her sleep last Tuesday."

His tone was offhand, bored, but I could see he just couldn't repair himself sufficiently to get his emotions into synch with losing someone he loved.

"How did she die?"

"In her sleep."

"Like that."

"Yeah, just like that."

He talked to me for a while about Lola in a blunted, etherized tone, occasionally laughing callously when he came across an incongruous fact from their past. Apparently her cosmetic surgeon was a former aircraft maintenance engineer, ex-employee of Boeing, where he worked designing control panels. Everything was a convertible skill, he said, quoting Lola. You only had to have the imagination and work on your sales skills. That, and him stubbing out his cigarette, concluded his eulogy. Not a word about her tits. It all came down to sales. It was a short-term market, but the buyers were there.

VIII

I liked Emily, as far as shrinks went. Her whole family had been murdered in the holocaust, and she had watched a trio of thugs pump bullets into her husband's head during a road rage incident on the Santa Monica turnpike. So she knew a thing or two about bad luck. After I brushstroked the general picture, she stated I was dealing with a comparable situation, more I thought by way of gaining the confidence of her new client, but no, she insisted, I had definitely just done a few rounds with a real contender, and fundamentally, I was still ahead of the game, being alive that is, and that it was time to cut losses before something really bad happened.

Her office was in a walk-up brownstone, cubby-holed into a bourgeois neighbourhood on the West side of the city. Plexiglass entrance with the name "NRC Consulting" in copperplate Gothic font, engraved into the glass. Cushioned reception area with a brown-haired receptionist, sexy but toned down with a conservative tweed jacket and her hair tied back into a bun. Just enough to keep the clients inside the office, without knowing why. NRC's fees were guaranteed by the Law Society, and the Law Society only spent that kind of money if they had to. From a business standpoint, it was like insuring thirty year old oil tankers or houses on the San Andreas fault. Just a question of when and where. That explained the glass-encased African fetish art and Brassaï photography gracing the reception area.

Emily waited for our second interview before asking what I thought the main reason was I'd come to see her.

"Not a hundred per cent sure. Maybe the dreams."

Emily smiled. It was a smile I would have labelled saintly, if the saint business hadn't been usurped by the head-shavers, anorexics and self-flagellators. She looked like she had found that smile somewhere else, on a road of her own making.

"Franck."

"Emily."

I liked the sound of her name. Uttering it was like taking a mild analgesic and watching a 60s sitcom.

"You know the personality tests freaks like us like to give? There's always the .05% that fall off the graph. You're in the 0.05%."

"Should I take that as a compliment?"

"You're *sui generis*, Franck. One of a kind. Or almost. You fall between the cracks. I'll have to think up a new name for you."

"Why's that?"

"You're utterly random, without being passive."

"What does that make me? A psychopath?"

"Definitely not. Although I wonder about your recent acquaintance."

"I already feel like we're getting to know each other."

Emily glanced at her bookshelves. They were filled with black binders, marked with file numbers. There were no books on the shelves.

"Depending on how you look at it, my profession, and I use the term loosely, is either a laboratory or a garbage can. And, if the law societies are any indication, Franck, spitting out alcoholics, neurasthenics and shell shocked delayed stress syndromes on a daily basis, it's getting pretty hairy out there."

"And those are the success stories."

Emily smiled. I knew this wouldn't last, that she really couldn't do anything for me, and that she knew it as well but, in the meantime, there were worse ways to spend an hour. It was like wandering into a video arcade and finding a game which suited a hidden addiction.

"How would you define your glitch, Franck?"

"You think I have a glitch, Emily?"

I placed Emily in her late fifties. I wondered what it would be like to fuck her at various stages in her life. As a virgin. During her travels. The day after her husband was murdered. In the sub-basement of a community centre while a B'Nai B'rith meeting was being convened on the main floor. I decided she would be a generous lover, but would only suck cock as a favour for the man she loved, and not out of intrinsic enjoyment. But, a favour she would indulge in once or twice and never again. Something of ritual significance.

"Everyone has a glitch, Franck. We're humans."

"If you had to pin me down, Emily ..."

"I'm not the pinning down type, Franck."

"... I'd say my glitch was sexual."

"So would I, Franck."

"So, where does that leave us? Sex is a big world. It could mean anything."

"It leaves us at square one. Tell me a bit about your past."

"Oh, like the child within. The victim."

"That's right. If we find something, maybe we can sue somebody. Blame them for your glitches."

"What about my dreams? Can't we do some Jungian shit, as long as we're at it?"

"Are you the type that asks dentists to pull all their teeth out before you even get cavities, Franck? Just to get it over with?"

"Why do that when you can go for a cap job?"

"So, Franck."

"Where do I start?"

"Start at the very beginning. As far back as you can remember."

"It might take a while."

"I get paid by the hour, Franck. Take your time."

•••

My first memories are auditory. The tackety-tack of high heels across a linoleum floor. The slap of a face. The deep, steady acceleration of breathing from my mother's bedroom. The click of a powder pack being shut. The ring of a doorbell. The sound of sirens. Coughs in the hallway. Mumbled dialogues uttered in gravelly, sneering masculine voices. And the false soothing drawl of my mother's voice, which could bring everything to a slow governable tempo, all of which she controlled.

My paternal great-grandfather was the largest individual landowner in British Columbia. To this day, there are rivers, islands and highways named after him. His father was killed in a dispute over a five card stud game during the heyday of the Klondike Gold Rush. His only son, my grandfather, inherited enough money at the age

of sixteen to set up a small sawmill on the banks of the
Fraser River. To say my grandfather was a fighting man
would be banal. Every man fought in those days. But,
my grandfather was the dirtiest streetfighter, and in his
own words, meanest *sumbitch* in town. Once he got a
man down, he laid the boots to him, and what was left—
usually not much, as nothing made Grandpa crazier than
watching a man go down under the wrath of his own
blows—would be transported to the local hospital or
even, on one or two occasions, to the morgue.

Grandpa drank Seagram's Canadian whisky or Charlie Rosen's Fraser River Bourbon straight up from noon
to dusk, and he preferred the company of whores to that
of his own wife. My father and his siblings were often
woken up by the raucous cursing of my grandpa stumbling across the threshold of the family home with
whores he'd picked up from the King Eddy hotel, setting
off unholy rows that kept my own Uncle Franck wetting
his bed until age fourteen.

To appease Grandma, Grandpa would buy her perfume and scarves directly from Paris' Hermes and
Lancôme shops, some Cartier jewelry and the odd fur
coat. If his behaviour had been bad enough, and the mill
had just experienced a strong financial quarter, she
might get a Dusenberg, the only one West of Winnipeg,
or a Caribbean cruise, before that became the common-
place. Grandma never referred to herself by name. She
was always Mrs. Franck Robinson. Children shared the
same fate. We didn't have names either, until our mid-
teens. We were the Robinson boys.

Grandpa went insane on his seventy-fifth birthday.
Things started out all right, and finished badly. Grandpa
was always home for dinner, which was held in the
drawing room of our second house, one we referred to

as "the stables," our family home and horse farm located on the southern fringe of the city. At the dinner table, children were to be "seen and not heard." I spent my time counting the number of Charlie Rosen's Fraser River bourbons Grandpa would finish before dinner. One particular Sunday, he had downed seven. Bourbon was Grandpa's way of saying: I can't walk straight and I can't think straight; my prostate is no longer doing its job and I will never have two women at a time again, but I can drink, and christ if I won't drink until my sides split.

It must have been Sunday, because we were eating roast beef, scallions, onions and Yorkshire pudding. Except for Grandpa, who on top of everything else demanded a sixteen ounce rib-eye, cooked *blue*, so he could still see the blood seeping through the meat, topped off with a fried egg, and placed in a pre-heated plate next to his regular meal. I always sat at Grandpa's side. At Sunday dinner, everybody was, children, parents included, *to be seen and not heard* while Grandpa told us what and how to think between shovelling first class food down his throat. Along the length of his Borneo teak table on the starboard side, sat Uncle Franck, my mother and my father. I was still short enough to scope out mother's left hand stroking father's right thigh, and her right doing the same on Uncle Franck's left, while the two of them drank like fish, and generally grinned stupidly at Grandpa's stories.

Grandpa mentioned that Khrushchev, one of his favourite targets, was the son of a Commie whore. What's a Commie whore? I asked. I think I was about seven. Figure it out, he answered. It was his answer for everything. Why is the sky blue? Figure it out. How do you ride a bicycle? Figure it out.

"That *sumbitch*, Sean Kelly, is a son of a Commie whore. I'll break him one day. In two."

Sean Kelly was an ex-IRA thug who was shop steward in Grandpa's mill.

"What's a Commie whore, Grandpa?" I persisted.

Grandpa turned towards me, grabbed my bicep, gripped it while staring fiercely into my eyes.

"Son, all you need to know is that, if the goddam Commies win, the schmucks down at city hall will steal the augur drill at Grandpa's mill and use it to grind up little boys into dog chow!"

The thought of this curled Grandpa's face into a red, choleric mass of suffocating laughter. His breath grew shorter, until his lungs collapsed into a sibilating wheeze, as if somebody had stomped on a bagpipe. We all watched, knowing better than to interfere. Then he began choking. Finally, Grandma walked down the length of the table from the opposite end, and pounded him between the shoulder blades, until he spat out a semi-masticated cube of rib-eye steak onto the table. This was followed by his dentures. For ten endless minutes, we watched Grandpa desperately suck in nano-pockets of oxygen. When he finally recovered from his fit, he fell strangely silent for the remainder of the meal. While the cheesecake and coffee were being served, Grandpa broke his silence, and announced he was disinheriting everyone but Jason, an arthritic, fifteen year old Doberman, whose residual life vocation had become eating Grandpa's leftover baked potato skins. By the time Grandma brought the Porto into the living room, Grandpa was mumbling about hiring a hit man to kill Sean Kelly. That night, Grandpa had his stroke. For the next six months, until his death, nothing further emerged from his mouth except for spittle.

While in primary school, I delivered the *South Fraser Columbian* afternoon newspaper. Part of my route included a diagonal one block street with half a dozen houses. No 17 Park Row was a brothel. In addition to visits from a regular flow of men seeking company, number 17 received the *South Fraser Columbian* from my sack six days per week. One summer afternoon, as I completed my deliveries, I noticed my mother, observing me from the driver's side of a canary-yellow, 1966 Ford Mustang convertible, her right hand resting on the three-speed column gearshift, and her left waving me over to the car. She wore cream-coloured gloves at all hours of the day and a pillbox hat with a front veil, and smoked DuMaurier cigarettes. She was just returning from her extended afternoon absence, which usually took place while my father was off doing advertising work in the United States. When leaving me alone in the house, she would say, Franck, be good, Mommy is going to the moon for the afternoon. Or, Franck, Mommy needs to see the American president, so be good.

I climbed into the off-white, upholstered bucket seats of the Mustang. She scrutinised me for a long moment.

"Is everything all right, Franck?"

"Sure."

"Are you sure, Franck?"

I shrugged my shoulders, unsure what she was driving at.

"Franck?"

"Yes, mom."

"Do you know what a prostitute is?"

"Sure. It's sandwich meat. From Italy."

"That's *prosciutto*. I said *prostitute*, Franck. Now, stop playing games."

She wiped something from her eyebrow, and gazed out the window, drumming her fingers on the top rim of the steering wheel.

"Are you sure, Franck?"

"Sure about what?"

"I'm not going to repeat myself, Franck."

"Sure, I'm sure."

"You are not hiding anything from Mommy, are you Franck?"

This went on for awhile. I tried crying to break the impasse.

"C'mon, Franck, Mommy was just kidding. Let's go home."

She drove for a minute or two without speaking.

"So, what is a prostitute, Mom?"

"A prostitute, Franck, is a woman who sells herself to men."

"Oh, you mean like a *whore*?"

I was born on September 11 at 11:11 a.m. My first core belief as a child was that I was the only human being alive on the whole planet, and that others were phantoms, either working for some god who was testing me for something or they were just generally alien beings. My second unshakeable conviction was that I would die on my eleventh birthday.

I didn't die, but in its own way, my eleventh birthday proved memorable. I mark it as the day I discovered things could change in an instant and nothing would look the same ever again. Early that morning, I heard Richard, my brother, crying from the other room. I guessed he had pissed himself again, but instead of going back to sleep, I decided to check it out.

Mother was in front of a vanity mirror dressing table, wearing a long satin bustier, circa 1950s, the style with bones, and a set of cups on it, with attachable black garters holding up cream-white panty hose. It was the first time I had seen her undressed.

"Now, Richard, you be good today, Mommy is talking with Santa Claus about next Christmas, and you don't want Santa to abandon you, do you Richard?"

She spoke to Richard in the same tone she employed with everyone. A brassy, I'm in a hurry, so don't screw up the program tone. For a moment, I watched her breasts pulsate inside the cups of her bustier. She slipped on an off the shoulder ruffle top and a flare skirt, and puckered her lips in front of the mirror, verifying her lipstick. As she splashed on some Guerlain *eau de toilette*, Richard started jacking off. She turned around, swatted his hand, then returned to her task, which was burnishing her mouth with Coco Chanel mud lipstick. Then, she stopped, laughed, shook her head.

"I hope I'm long gone when you two hit the streets."

Later that day, my father returned from one of his business trips. Surprise, surprise, he announced as he strode into the living room.

"Daddy's home early!! Where's your mother, Francky?"

"Gone to the moon."

"Don't be funny, Francky. Where is she?"

"She went to the moon."

"Where's Richard?"

I pointed towards the basement. His features darkened.

He about-faced, and crashed his way down the stairwell into the basement. I heard an extended moan.

"What the hell!"

Followed by more rapid, heavy breathing, as my father, a four-pack a day Marboro man, chugged his way back up the stairs.

"What the hell did you do to your brother?"

"Nothing."

"What do you mean nothing! You call nothing being strapped into the jolly jumper in the basement!"

I stood on the other side of the table, gripping onto its edges, considering escape routes. He ran around the table. I dove under it, but slipped and he clamped his bear paws onto my leg.

"You little bastard."

After swatting me a few times, father figured out that I was no wiser than he.

"Where's your mother?"

That evening was a noisy one around the house. But, the part I recall best was long past our bedtime, as I lay in bed, staring at the ceiling, unable to sleep. I heard a sort of sick whelp, like a dog, except it was my father.

"You're nothing but a goddam whore. Nothing but a whore. Nothing but a whore."

Then mother's sweet as molasses, mock conciliatory tone.

"Don't worry, Maurice, come to mommy now, everything will be rosy tomorrow, c'mere peachykins, it's been a long day."

My father never forgave Grandpa for not naming him Franck, particularly since it should have been his automatic birthright, being the eldest in the family. But, Grandpa passed him over, preferring to call him Maurice, and conferring the patronym Franck upon the second eldest, in another display of the recurrent Robinson genetic snobbery that causes all of us to overlook moral qualities in favour of good looks.

Franck II returned the favour by forcing Grandpa to hand over the family business for a derisory sum while he lay on his deathbed. And my own father thanked him for that piece of work by robbing the business of half a million while Franck II was stupid, or felt guilty enough to allow him control over the books of the company, despite being nothing more than an ad weasel.

Franck II had a beautiful mistress who stuck to him like a fly on shit once he came into the money. My mother. Mother understood the famous words of Sam Goldwyn. A verbal contract ain't worth the paper it's written on. So, she had everything made out in her name through something even Franck II's legitimate wife could not attack. Insurance policies.

It was a sweltering hot summer day when Franck II was nailed for arson. He violently denied everything, despite a professional arsonist pinning his name on the deed that burned every asset of the Robinson Pulp and Paper Works, covering the full stretch of the Fraser River Delta. Once Uncle Franck was safely lodged courtesy of the Attorney General, mother only had one last reminder of her liaison with Uncle Franck. My brother Richard. Mother used to enjoy visiting Uncle Franck, and would playfully taunt him from the free side of the penitentiary visiting room with references to her "scorched earth policy."

After Grandpa died, people would glorify him at the sporadic family gatherings, when they drank too much, or when they got maudlin and were lamenting the good old days when men beat the shit out of their wives and then bought their way out of it, and generally acted like criminals, which is what the New World is all about, and for that matter, the old world.

I think it was at one of those family gatherings, probably Franck II's funeral after he killed himself in prison, that someone asked me to name Grandpa's greatest achievement. No one really spoke about my uncle, for whatever reason, but Grandpa seemed to inspire a lot of stories, and of course it was *de rigueur* to praise him to the skies. That question stumped me for a long moment and, while I hesitated, several of the attendees now turned their attention towards me. What will the boy genius have to say about this now?

"I think his greatest feat was hanging himself in the garage after he had his stroke."

I looked across the room, taking my focus away from the uproar of protesting voices clamouring and fingers pointing at me, and moved into the abstract zone which preceded the rain of blows which my father was sure to let fall in my direction. Against the dining room wall, between an early Munch sketch of *The Scream* and a reproduction of Picasso's *Guernica*, I could make out my brother Richard, staring at me. He was still pretty young, and so quiet I had always thought him autistic, but, this time, though I couldn't exactly guess what he was thinking, he definitely seemed to be paying attention.

I lived in San Francisco for a while, mostly working assembly line on the Oakland side of the bay, when that type of thing still paid money, and spent most of my leisure time drinking beer and playing pool in a string of dead-end bars located at the core of skid row. I had been drinking since mid-afternoon in a bar called the Cobalt on my twenty-first birthday, when a blonde girl, rasta beads in her hair and a jean jacket, threads hanging in shreds from the cuffs, sat down and drawled, "buy me a drink" in an Aussie accent. Like that. She had something in her eyes, but she was too friendly for her good looks, which to me spelled dependency, as did the needle tracks at the top of her left forearm.

We spent the afternoon drinking beer and shooting 9-ball in the Cobalt, then staggered across the street to the Hotel St-Regis. I think her name was Donna. She made ends meet turning tricks on a low-end stretch of Union Street. Or at least that was her story.

At about 3 p.m., I proposed to her. We weaved down to the courthouse, where we tied the knot in front of a justice of the peace who looked to be in similar shape.

I rented a room at the St-Regis and brought up some cheap and warm bubbly from a Chinatown liquor store. I don't recall much, or even whether we made love. But, when I woke up, she had robbed me of all my money, and all but one of my credit cards. I never saw her again. Our marriage had lasted four hours.

Several days later, it was still raining and I was still inside the St-Regis. The room I rented was on the top floor of the hotel, just under a leaky aluminum roof in sore need of repair. I wasn't thinking a lot about anything. Just listening to the rain ping off the metal, like someone drumming their fingers on the roof. It was a good feeling, going into full drift like that, probably as good as I had ever felt about anything. As if I no longer had any form. On the desk in the room, I had a tumbler filled with crushed ice at all times, which served as a receptacle for the Long Island Ice Teas I was using for fuel as I ploughed my way through a book of crossword puzzles.

On the second or third day, I dropped some blotter acid after ordering another book of crossword puzzles from room service. Then it became hard to tell whether it was day or night. I recall looking in the mirror, and seeing my face stretch out and take on hues of emerald, jade, chlorophyll, as if I were turning the lights on and off. I dropped to all fours, and started crawling around like a baby until I spotted a battalion of scorpions scuttling inside every orifice in my body. My guts were steadily torquing as if I'd swallowed some arsenic. Then, my tongue split into two, and I became convinced that I had transmutated into a human reptile. I only got that under control when I pushed my fist through the mirror.

I left the hotel by a rear stairwell which served as a fire escape, climbed down to the hotel parking lot, and took my Grand Prix for a spin towards the waterfront to cool down. I had cut my hand pretty badly, but it had slowed the brain down to operational. At least thoughts were percolating, and not bubbling right over. It was nothing special, just a mental zone. My brain had more or less liquified, derivative strands of the recent past now streaming down cerebral eavestroughs into a grey, polluted sewer.

I criss-crossed the Golden Gate a few times, staring out the driver-side window at Alcatraz, Monterey, Carmel, thinking shit, Clint Eastwood is mayor and Ronald Reagan is president, what's next? I doubled back East for another cruise through the hookers' quarter. For me, just like a return to the womb. A nocturnal ticker tape parade of bordellos, transexual haunts and strip joints run by the mafia with the tacit blessing of the city's forefathers.

I cruised up Union and down Columbus Avenue, then down around Powell and Union, doing what I like best, which was drifting. Nothing much around the square caught my eye, outside of a longshoreman repeatedly clubbing a drunken Indian prone on the sidewalk. I recall thinking, a drunken Indian is a cliché, then that there were a lot of clichés in that part of town. Then automatic pilot kicked in, the way it always did, and I was drifting, like the other drifters, ten miles an hour, where I spotted her, chewing gum and flashing a stretch of leg from beneath a black leather miniskirt.

I was not much older than her myself, and, like I say, I was making a pretty good salary working in a factory at the time. My '57 Chev Bel-Air was a slick, scarlet machine red/black interior, with a 400 four barrel under the hood, mag wheels and an engine purr so powerful the police pulled me over regularly on sight and sound alone. I had taken it up to 130 mph within city limits and despite its huge size, had lost the cops twice during high speed chases while high on a mix of various high-octane cocktails.

She made a big show of climbing into the car. On her way to the Oscars ceremony. So to speak.

"Wow."

"What's your name?"

"You want a name? No problem. Michelle. That's a name."

She bounced her butt up and down on the front seat a couple of times. I could see she really took to the car. We drove up to a parking lot she pointed out, just behind an old art-deco theatre the city fathers had declared part of the sacred urban heritage.

Later, after she had finished sucking my cock, I lit a Marlboro, and debated whether I would ask her to start all over again. She didn't seem in any hurry to leave, so I offered her one of my Marlboros. As I passed her the cigarette, I noticed her right hand was a little on the knotty side for a girl. Whatever. She gave good head, her scarlet lipstick was liberally smeared on her mouth and the miniskirt looked good on her. That was enough for me.

"Where are you from?"

"Around. Portland. Whatever."

"Like your work?"

"What do you mean like my work? Oh, I get it. You mean, like, do I like my work." She smiled, and something told me that despite her young age, this one had travelled places I would never see, "I just *love* sucking cock."

I let her off at the corner. Her tight butt carved a lazy serpentine curve down the sidewalk like some garden variety of snake. Her black purse hung loosely from a discount ersatz gold chain, and was swung over her shoulders. Her general attitude was far too contrived, far too theatrical, and with far too much of a sense of vocation, to belong to a woman.

For a while, I continued cruising up and down the waterfront, near the Bay, letting my mind drift. The rain had slowed to a drizzle. An undercurrent of percolating, vacuous thoughts streaming through the brain, then halting abruptly for a moment. Like the neap tide. I was thinking, this will not change. I had no intention of really getting formed into anything for society.

Out in the bay, five or six ships waiting to moor in the San Francisco container port facility. Strings of homosexuals, half of them with trimmed moustaches, the other half wearing mascara, hanging around the washroom facility, or sitting on the benches, waiting for someone to come by and suck their cocks, but not willing to pay for it. As I lit another cigarette, my mind shifted to a recollection of the old Marlboro man ads, portraying a rugged cowboy on a horse in Montana or wherever they still rode horses and gazed out on the rugged, limitless prairie. The first five male models to work as Marlboro models died of lung cancer. Like that. They were like Michelle. They believed in what they did. Funny. I remember Michelle's name, but I am not 100% sure about my first wife. I think she said it was Donna.

While flipping through the classifieds of the *San Francisco Chronicle*, I spotted an ad about a university in

Montreal with a law faculty, who accepted just about anyone who could speak basic French and hadn't been convicted of felonies. Law school couldn't be any worse than factory work. I'd at least figured out that, if you didn't have the guts for crime or the inclination to slave your life away for a medal and a pat on the back, it was important to get your paperwork in order, before someone else did it for you. I quit my job the next day, collected two weeks' severance, and returned to the cold country. I found a cheap walk-up on the Main located just beneath Cleopatra's, next door to Fong's Saigon Success.

I hadn't seen Richard in five years. Mother had arranged to have him placed in an asylum in Upstate New York under a nineteenth century "ward of the State" provision no one but her thousand dollar an hour attorney had ever heard of. After his release, he became a drifter, and more or less fell off the map for a while, then recontacted me, saying he'd found employment as a bus driver. I fell into a routine of sending a case a month off to Richard at a post office box address in Albany. They were a coded conversation between Richard and myself. One of our favourite Hall of Fame precedents was <u>Regina vs. Zont</u>, [1977] C.C.C. 2d 351, a murder case involving an 18 year old chess grandmaster with severe eczema who had stabbed his mother to death for trashing his onyx set of chessmen, then sliced off her ears and sold them to a wholesaler named Zont who specialized in Cambodian remedies and placebos. Zont claimed he was nothing more than a middleman, that the appendages were unrecognizable, as they had been brought to him inside two glass milk bottles filled with formaldehyde, labelled "Eustachian tubes." The charge was possession of stolen property, a tough rap to beat, as no *mens rea* had to be proven, but Zont's attorney succeeded in proving that an ear is not a chattel, and therefore "ipso facto outside the perimeter of the incriminating provisions, which, in any event, must be afforded a narrow reading as is customary with penal provisions," another phrase which brought Richard recklessly close to the precipice of a smile. In short, it had all the ingredients to please Richard. It was macabre, sordid, but most importantly involved arcane legal technicalities which were incomprehensible to the public at large.

The other case I had specially filed for sending to Richard was Flint vs. Southall [1973] A.C. 1184, Lord Denning dissenting, a civil matter. The owner of a prize-winning English sheepdog, Treanor, sued Southall, an East London Cockney for having sodomized his dog while under the influence. In his dissenting obiter, Denning J., as he then was, referred to the only bestiality precedent on the rolls of the Old Bailey, an incident which had occurred in Newfoundland, Canada forty-seven years earlier, involving a still operator and a barnacle goose.

I had no idea what was really going on inside his head, but I knew that Regina vs Zont and Flint vs Southall confirmed something for him, as it did for me. Sometimes Richard would send me a one line note, speaking in scraps of Regina vs Zont obiter. "Not within my jurisdiction," or "mens rea not having been demonstrated beyond the shadow of a doubt," and the necessity of having a "narrow reading of the matter."

Strippers performing upstairs at the Cleopatra were regulars at Fong's. They usually dropped in during the late afternoon. A mix of TVs and real girls, but their banter, as they ordered their coffees and lit their cigarettes, was more secretarial pool before the boss arrives. The trannies in particular were big on the things girls must have been big on forty years ago. Powder packs. Pocket mirrors. Furry handbags and petticoats. The atmosphere was kind of Paris Music Hall, backstage. One big family of oddballs, rejects and genetic freaks.

I slid into the booth, ordered Fong's $3.25 pork vermicelli special and a pot of tea. Through the window, I could see a list of cheap Asian destinations at the Kar-Wah Travel Agency across the road. At the bottom of the list, there was a gaudy poster announcing sex tours to Bangkok. The door to Fong's swung open, bringing in a gust of wind and five or six girls for coffee before the early evening revue.

One of the girls stood for a moment, lit a cigarette, then, spotting me alone in my booth, walked over and sat down across from me. She had a peasant ruddiness to her cheeks, looked like she had jumped out of a Millet painting or had her skin scrubbed off in a wooden tub. Her breasts were compressed together and upwards under the combined pressure of different parts of her push-up bra. She ordered tea, and waved Fong away when he pointed a menu at her. She tapped her cigarette twice on the table and pushed it into her mouth.

"Every day, I come in here, and every day you are eating this same soup."

"I live just under the club."

She glanced at my bowl, half full of vermicelli and pork floating in a brackish consommé. Fong flashed her a smile through his stained gold teeth. She looked back at me.

"Quit staring. I know I need a facelift. What's your name?"

"Franck."

"My name's Samantha. Actually, that's my stage name. You work, Franck?"

"Kind of between jobs."

"Sure."

"I just finished law school."

She sized me up, lit a cigarette, decided to smile.

"How old you think I am?"

A tall Haitian girl, standing at the counter, wearing a leopard skin top, like the top of a one-piece bathing suit, jean miniskirt, called over.

"Hey, Sam, he's just a kid. Leave him alone."

"Fuck you, Geena."

She turned back to me.

"Sorry. You want to meet me after the show tonight? I only do the early show. Maybe we could have a drink together. At your place. Just pick up some beers and wait for me. I finish around midnight."

Samantha's real name turned out to be Karin Van Der Velde. She stayed overnight. It was a waystation, and one of the things a girl hung onto was that eventually she'd get out. But, Karin also told me about Hervé Bourque. It was appropriate that a whore would even be responsible for getting me my first job in a law office.

Hervé Bourque's office was on *rue Notre Dame*, between a lawyer's gown shop and the Court Bailiffs, within the shadow of the dismal brown building housing the *Palais de Justice de Montréal*. When I entered his office, it was a Friday afternoon. Six girls were in his waiting room, but the sleaziest looking of them all was a purple-haired harlot sitting at the receptionist's desk fielding phone calls. There was enough fishnet on her to outfit a trawler. If there were a police roundup, they would have gone for her first, although you could smell the street on the half dozen others curled up on the divan in the waiting area.

A man in his early sixties entered the office, sporting a set of eyebrows which hung like tarantula legs from an awning. He extended his hand towards me.

"You must be Robinson."

He waved impatiently.

"C'mon in, I said, make yourself at home. How did you hear of me?"

"One of the Cleopatra girls recommended you. Sir."

"Not exactly a shining recommendation, Robinson."

One of his eyebrows arched into a triangular bivouac.

"Do you know I've been in front of the disciplinary committee more times than I can count, Robinson. How do you feel about that?"

"Ever been disbarred?"

Bourque peered intensely at me, as if my question had answered another question.

"I'm the one interviewing here. What's the most important word in the law, Robinson?"

"I don't know. Guilty?"

Bourque hummed the word "guilty," until it buzzed out of his mouth like a bug on an African verandah.

"Not *guilty*, Robinson. They're all guilty. Retainer is the word. And what is the first rule of the practice of criminal law?"

I shrugged my shoulders.

"Never post bail for a client. They have all, without exception, been in shit up to their ears from the cradle onwards. Which is not a problem, provided you never forget it, and obey one or two ground rules. So, you live below a strip club. You have a taste for seed, Mr. Robinson?"

I shrugged my shoulders. It felt like an interview where it didn't really matter what I said or didn't say.

"What would you say, Mr. Robinson, if one of those girls in the waiting room proposed to pay in kind for professional services rendered?"

"You mean sexual favours."

"For example."

I considered the question. From the point of view of Bourque as a future employer.

"I'd tell her to post her own bail and a small retainer. The balance we could work out in an instalment plan."

Bourque looked at me. He had a way of looking at you sideways or even upside down without even moving his head. I could picture him in front of a witness box, lighting a cigar while cross-examining an international money launderer, or a cop on the take or a sweating politician.

"You're hired, Mr. Robinson. See you in the morning."

Bourque used my services on a regular basis, i.e. from 10 to 12 on Mondays and 3 to 5 on Fridays in remand court, handling guilty pleas, setting down trial dates or posting bail for the Cleopatra girls. It was all about serving time or buying time. After three or four months of this, I answered a call in the office, asking for me. Who is it?

"36th police precinct. Constable Lefebvre. Franck Robinson?"

"Yes."

"I'm calling you on a criminal matter. We require your presence at Royal Victoria hospital morgue. For an identification."

"What's this about?"

"We have someone who says he is your brother in custody. Homicide."

"I'll be right down."

The receptionist in the emergency department of the Royal Victoria hospital wore her hennaed hair in a tight bun. Her name tag said Miss Catherine Jones, R.N. She was attractive enough, but there was something about the thick breasts bulging under her uniform that triggered a whole range of disconnected thoughts. She had somehow managed the female hospital staff trick of being pulpous, feline, servile, friendly and hygienic all at once. But, with a little imagination, and adding ten years to her age, it was easy enough to project her into another time and place. Northwest Wales on a pig farm, surrounded by sows and her own offspring, with a constant drizzle pouring over her head, her absentee husband leaning drunk against a rotting beam of the local village pub. Somewhere near a coal mine. Circa 1965. Miss Catherine Jones directed me to an elevator, where I was instructed in a friendly but firm tone to descend into the sub-basement. A Doctor Giguère would be waiting for me. He would tell me what it was about.

I stepped onto a long, rectangular freight elevator. A reedy man in orderly's uniform stood behind a stretcher. The stretcher had a body on it. The body was covered with a creased, white bedsheet. The orderly's nametag displayed the name Eric Chomsky, L.P.N., but since I didn't feel like looking at Eric Chomsky's face, or the body he was tending, or the cigarette he was making a half-hearted attempt at concealing, I focused on a metal plaque affixed to the wall of the elevator, which identified the manufacturer: Otis Elevators, Chicago, Illinois. The body halted at SSB, two floors underground, and Eric Chomsky wheeled his stretcher out of the Otis lift, just ahead of me.

A tall gangly man stood in the corridor, his hair curly and boyish, as if he were the understudy to the conductor of the city symphony orchestra.

"Doctor Giguère."

He motioned with a palm to the room behind him.

"Come."

The room was bordered by an L-shaped counter containing three sinks, and a set of cupboards. The floors were tiled. In the centre of the room, a bed, fixed to the floor. An overhead neon light, and the low-grade buzz of an air ventilation system. In the rear of the room, an open entrance to an alcove, containing three walk-in doors.

"Wait here, Mr. Robinson."

He walked into the alcove, and pulled open the latch. He opened the door, bent over, and walked inside, disappearing. Several moments later, a stretcher emerged, looking similar to the one which had accompanied Eric Chomsky down to the sub-sub basement. He wheeled the stretcher into the main room and aligned it beside the bed.

"Before I can proceed, I require an identification. You, apparently, are the only person in a position to provide one."

He pulled back the bedsheet.

"Recognize her?"

"It's my mother."

Mother's torso had been stabbed repeatedly, but her face was intact, and even in death, I thought it had a trace of that wry, tight-lipped grimace Richard and I had looked up to for the first twelve years of our lives. Dr. Giguère pointed at one long scar tracing a vertical line up the centre of her abdomen.

"The weapon used was a rapier, similar to the scythes used by Sikhs in ceremonial rituals. There is clear evidence of a sexual assault both prior to and following death."

The Honourable Mr. Justice Aznar of the Superior Court presiding over Courtroom 4.13, formerly Aznar, J. of Remand Court, in Courtroom 4.14 next door, briefly examined Richard, peered over the court record, and ordered an assessment to determine "whether the accused was, at the time of the alleged offense, suffering from a mental disorder so as to be exempt from criminal responsibility." Etc. etc.

The following day, I drove to the Pinel Institute to see Richard. I reviewed the proceeding and decided it had gone well, all things considered. Richard's life as a free man was over, but Richard wouldn't make a scene in the courtroom, and would generally allow the judge to expedite the matter.

When I entered the visitors' room, Richard seemed a little absent. I assumed he was comparing his own experience with <u>Regina vs. Zont</u>, and coldly assessing whether he had done anything unusual, i.e. unusual from a legal point of view, the only one that mattered if your aim in life was to become binding legal precedent, and be immortalized in the legal gazettes.

"How have they been treating you?"

"All right. No complaints."

"I guess there's no point in talking about what happened."

"Not really."

"I have contacted defence counsel."

Richard's eyebrows arched slightly.

"I don't see the point. Strikes me as a waste of money. It's culpable homicide. Way outside the *de minimis* range. <u>Smithers versus The Queen</u>. 1977. Self-defence is a non-starter. Provocation is out. It's life, no parole before 25. Unless section 672 washes."

"I wouldn't bet my last dollar on 672. It's not automatic anymore."

Richard stopped, considering this.

"Who's counsel?"

"I don't think you know this one. I found him through Bourque. He's good, in fact very good, and he's cheap, because he's had some recent troubles with the law society."

"What kind of troubles?"

"He has been under investigation for fronting a sale of six hundred kilos of cocaine through a group of Montreal biker gangs."

"What's his name?"

"Gutman."

"Gut. Man," he mouthed disjunctively.

"No. Gutman."

"That's good. I like that. What do you think he'll plead?"

"I think you can safely rule out reasonable apprehension of bodily harm."

"Don't suppose drunkenness or any specific intent defence is really an option."

At that point, I was still a little naïve. Not about everyone. But, I thought Richard might want to discuss things.

"Richard, why did you do it?"

"I'd rather not discuss it."

"Richard, you can tell me anything. I'm on your side."

"If you're on my side, you know why I did it."

"Honestly, Richard, I have no idea. I'd be the first to admit it."

"I think it's about time you told me why you really came to see me."

It had been a while. Five years. A lot can happen in five years.

"All right, let's say I know why, but, I need to hear you say why you did it."

Richard raised the index finger of each hand, and placed them on his temples. Like two Martian antennae.

"It was the aliens."

"Of course, Richard. But, which aliens?"

"The ones who kidnapped her body. And, who want to poison the water supply of the City. It was purely preemptive. I should get the Order of the British Empire, Franck."

"We're no longer a colony. Okay, fine, Richard, I take it back. 672 might wash. But, forget about the defence for a moment. This is your brother talking. I'm not saying you weren't justified. But, just this once, Richard, I want to know why."

Richard looked around the four corners of the visitors' room. Smiled knowingly. Like, you idiot brother, how can you not see this. Unless you're working for them. He raised his voice.

"I don't care if this is being recorded! Or who you're working for! Hezbollah agent Candice Robinson, my so-called mother. Mossad agent. Funding suicide bombers."

Richard smiled sometimes. But, he never laughed.

•••

"So, that's about it, Emily. The Swiss Family Robinson. A collection of social shipwrecks and mutants."

I sat back, took a deep breath, lit a cigarette.

"Any coffee left?"

"That is one incredible story, Franck."

"Well, you know what they say. You can pick your friends, but not your family."

"So, tell me, Franck, is anything of this, and I mean any small piddling fact true?"

"I don't know, let me think about that one for a second. Hey, by the way, you really do know what you're doing, don't you?"

"If I were a little less experienced, I'd label you a pathological liar."

"Really. So, what am I?"

"I think you're trying to get into my pants."

"I'll be. Bang on, Emily. That very thought had in fact just crossed my mind. Does that raise any ethical issues from your side?"

"Do you know how many of my patients develop this type of fixation?"

"If they don't, there's something really wrong with them. Anyways, why is it a fixation to want to have sex with someone?"

"I'm going to try something a little different next week, Franck."

The following week, as I drove into the West End of the city towards NRC Consulting, I mulled over what it was that attracted me to Emily. On the street, Emily was nothing much to look at. She was almost nondescript. She had white hair, was well into her fifties. I decided the non-descript component had something to do with it. Emily had succeeded where I had failed, and become completely invisible to the outside world. Also, her smile had seeped down to my internal water table. During the week following our meeting, I felt I had come into contact with the forces of good. Whatever. It was better than the options.

I sat down on a mauve divan in the waiting room, picked up a back issue of <u>Psychology Today</u> open on a mahogany coffee table, leafed through it. A man entered the waiting room from the same corridor where Emily had emerged the previous week. The man had the beard and concave forehead of the man on the old John Player's cigarette packages.

"Mr. Robinson?"

During the fleeting seconds he actually met my gaze before spinning into an about-face, his eyes appeared to be jiggling. The man bore a striking resemblance to a former acquaintance. As I followed John Player down the corridor of NRC Consulting, I tried to recall what I could of my friend, the body double of the man I was following. He had telephoned me long distance, reversing the charges, frantically claiming he was being held prisoner in the basement of a Fort Lauderdale scientology centre and had been forced to sign over proceeds from his pension funds. I hung up the phone and never heard from him again.

We entered a room with a capital B glued loosely on the corridor side of the entrance door. The man waved me in ahead of him, closed the door, motioned me to take a seat on an art-deco sofa, about-faced, hunched over and began marching around the room, carrying some *circa* 1973 tape recording equipment as if it were a geiger counter. He plugged it into the wall outlet.

"Okay, Franck," he said by way of preamble, "before I turn this thing on, I want to explore the place in the world where you feel safest."

We briefly made eye contact for the second time. Another memory of his alter ego. That he had been captain of a tugboat. And that he had lost his job, when he was caught masturbating in the toilet by a woman bailiff sent by the courts to seize some stereo equipment he had forgotten to pay for.

"I don't know. I feel safe in an Audi."

"I see. An Audi."

"They handle well. Good for altitude driving. Generally have good sound systems."

"I see. Anywhere else you feel safe, Franck?"

I thought about that for a moment.

"I took an elevator up the Empire State Building once. It was old. But, I felt safe. In good hands. So to speak."

"So to speak. I see."

He noted something down in a coiled notepad on his lap.

"I think I know what you mean."

He peered into my face. For a moment, I wondered whether this wasn't in fact my long lost acquaintance. I decided against confronting him.

"There is one place where I both feel in and out of danger simultaneously."

"I see. Where?"

"Sheba's cunt."

He made another notation in his notepad, which I noticed was quadrilled. It looked like he had sketched Σ, followed by a V, and a word scribbled, which looked like jungen, or jung.

"It's a little unusual, Franck, but I don't see why we can't take a look at this place which you are calling Sheba's cunt. It's a working hypothesis."

He recorded another entry. Then, something seemed to strike him as droll, but he put a cap on that.

"How would you, describe this ... *cunt*, Franck, and by describe, I mean what are its salient features as a physical, organic entity?"

Each pronunciation of the word *cunt* caused him to cringe, which was followed by a nervous titter.

"Well, in some ways, she's like any other woman. She has the usual equipment. You know. Labia. Clitoris."

"No, Franck. I don't know. But you have my full attention."

"Well, for starters, her clitoris seems to have a brain of its own. I'd swear her cunt is equipped with extra-sensory apparati with about a 10,000 kilometre range."

He held up a flat, jaundiced looking palm towards me. Like a traffic cop.

"Stop. Stop right where you are, Franck."

He looked excited about something, wiped his pate.

"What do you mean by *range*?"

"I mean, close up or far away, she has the capacity to suck the brain cells right out of me."

I recalled an image which had been recurring in my dreams since her departure.

"You know the student revolution in May '68?"

He did, or at least his nod indicated that he didn't require a complete re-run of penumbral fifth republic France.

"*Rue Gay Lussac*. The overturned cars running up the street from the Luxembourg Gardens."

"I see."

I took this as a signal to continue.

"If I were to locate her clitoris, the time frame would be May '68, and the location somewhere around *rue St-Jacques*. The CRS are six deep, twenty-five across, wearing plexi-glass face shields and swinging billy clubs. The hairs of her cunt are back at the Medici palace. Just behind the statue of Bacchus."

"I see."

"That is where her cunt starts. It slithers up Claude Bernard. Like a snake. The exact spot where the head of my dick penetrates is around the *Place de l'Italie*. And her fallopian tubes fork off in two directions. One leads to the tapestry factory at *Manufacture des Gobelins*."

"I see. And the other?"

"The other curls into a little pocket at the St-Rosaire cemetery on *boulevard Auguste Blanqui*."

"I see. The anarchist."

"One and the same."

"All right, that's good enough, Franck. I have all I need. Just stay where you are. I will now describe your travels up Sheba's cunt in detail."

He pushed the mike up to his mouth and entered into a first person travelogue narrative of the itinerary I had just mapped out, speaking in an unguent, new-age murmur.

"I am walking up the cunt of *rue Gay Lussac*, feeling the walls of Sheba's cunt ..."

From my point of view, he narrated a more than credible reproduction of Sheba's cunt, at one point likening it to a fifty-two bedroom castle with a cliff view over an islet in the Loire river.

"I'm in the vaginal antechamber. I'm looking through a sunlight into the fallopian tube."

After twenty minutes of this spiel, he pressed down on the Stop button, popped open the cassette and flipped it over to me.

"There. Twice a day, Franck. Or anytime, you're feeling a little stressed."

He entered a final notation on his notepad, ending with a checkmark and an exclamation point.

"Here is what I think, Franck. You have been confusing this Sheba with the city of Paris. I think that, under the circumstances, you have only one choice. You have to go back and fuck the city of Paris."

"How do you fuck a city?"

"I don't know. But, your answer lies in there somewhere."

I looked at him more closely. He began fiddling with his pencil.

"It's you, isn't it, Paul?"

Still staring at his back.

"Who are you talking to, Mr Robinson? My name is Hen ... Hender, Hederickson. Henderson."

"Paul."

"I'll be with you in a second, Mr Robinson. Just have to unplug this infernal cassette."

He stood up, turned around. His features sagged momentarily, then tightened into a grim mask.

"I'd rather not talk about it."

"It's you, isn't it?"

"I've put all of that behind me. I've got a good job. Nobody asks me anything, and then you turn up. This is problematic. I've got a good life."

His voice had slightly picked up in rhythm, taking on a chirpy lilt.

"Take it easy. Your secret is safe. Last I heard, you'd been abducted."

"Not exactly. It was a Dianetics thing. All right, I was kidnapped. Look, it could happen to anyone. Don't get me wrong. There are some good sides to Scientology. Look at all the celebrities involved: Travolta, Tom Cruise."

"But, you bailed out."

He was holding a framed photo in his hand. The photo was of Ron Hubbard, ex-marine, founding charlatan supremo of the Scientologists. There was a signature on it.

"It was a cultural thing. I never got used to Baton Rouge. At least what I saw of it. The centre had rented the local where Lee Harvey Oswald stayed just before the assassination. I had to distribute flyers to people. They'd just disappear, get sent off to other centres. Eventually, my family sent in a deprogrammer. Patrick, I think the guy's name was. I guess you could say I was only reborn once I left the movement. Reborn as a psychologist. But, let's get back to you."

I recalled a moment back in the city, sitting in a café on the *rue Montorgueil*, on a stool beside a young, bespectacled Englishman, alone, drunk despite the early morning hour, spilling his guts out to a waitress who ignored him while he flipped her twenty franc tips. He had been babbling, "Just let me take you out for a drink. I cannot bear to live without you." The heavily caked makeup of the tart freezing into a sneer as she poured out another *démi-pression*, slid it contemptuously across the counter at double the regular tarif, then retreated to the opposite end of the bar to dream, not about beauty, or the ephemeral nature of life, or the Louvre or the sun king, but how she could skin another mark to pay for her daily coiffure.

Like Bosch`s miser. At the brink of death and still reaching for the dish of gold pieces held out by the devil. Or like me, reaching out for a cunt. Throwing away a lifetime's effort for an afternoon *pipe* at discount. Or generally doing what men are good at, which is passively buying into a confidence game, no matter how cheap. My thought was interrupted by John Player, as he pushed his recording equipment into a grey, metal filing cabinet pull-out drawer.

"Would you consider taking me back with you? I don't need to do this anymore."

"I'll send you a postcard."

It was bad enough being inside my own brain without dragging another piece of spiritual flotsam across the ocean to where I was going.

IX

Practicing law is like flying an airplane, or fighting a war. Not to be done by half. Whether you have one file or six hundred, contingent liability and professional negligence is always lurking round the next corner. You should never, ever dabble. Dabbling brings you within the microscopic focus of the Law Societies. Creaky-wheeled bodies. Right up there with the revenue authorities under the "to be avoided at all costs" rubric. If they get spokes into your wheels, you can sink into a permanent mire. It's one of the reasons I stuck to personal injury — no one likes plaintiff counsel, but the equation is simple enough to work out. Cover the costs up front, hit the client with a 30% contingency. If you take on twenty claims in a year, eight were bogus, eight could be settled out of court, if you played the jury card properly, and knew how to get them crying *at the injustice of it all*, while convincing the client it was a crapshoot, you had a couple of big winners per annum, and year in year out, once you got rolling, three to four million easy. To sum up, the principles of the stock market applied to human suffering.

Then, there's the dog files, and the worst of the dog files involved clients who were suing on principle. Holly Reichman had accidentally had both ovaries removed when she was slated for a caesarian, by a hatchet man, an Armenian named Masbourian, another Bourque referral. She was a tricky case, not dog file *a priori*. Even had PR value, page two item in the daily press. *Doctor X stole my vagina! A horribly true tale of menopause at age twenty-nine*! On the downside, Holly was married to Isaac Reichman, Hassidic Jew, which is neither here nor there, except she'd already had ten kids. So, I won the case, which made Isaac happy, and more importantly satisfied Holly's jap vanity. But bringing in a medical expert from the Mayo to prove a woman's uterus was cut out by a surgeon as opposed to atrophying all on its own due to Isaac's wish to break post-modern records for procreation is a costly proposition. In short, damages were nominal, which made it any self-respecting lawyer's nightmare—a win on principle. All the case law supported us on the merits, but I couldn't dig up anything decent on quantum. And for any of you unfamiliar with the dour propensities of Scottish-Canadian judges, let it be known that some part of their brain just doesn't compute the notion of punitive damages.

On the winning side of the balance sheet, Kimberly Sutherland was a quad in a halo brace who had been training for a try-out with the Olympic figure skating team. Two million settlement, and probably worth double that. Plus, Paris was calling again, and the New World looked like a black and white universe compared to the city of light. It was time for some creative accounting. In my books, it was a case for natural justice *à la Franck Robinson*, which involved a classic squeeze of two ends against the middle, and me having to use large chunks of Kimberly Sutherland's award to pay off disbursements in the Holly Reichman case. It looked bullet-proof at the time, but I hadn't factored Spike Nussbaum into the equation.

When someone goes to see a lawyer, it's usually the worst day of their life. So, on the odds alone, there were bound to be dog files and clients like Spike Nussbaum. Fifteen per cent of clients were write offs. Loss column. The Spikes were another category, as hard to factor as the odds of running into a psychopath in a bowling alley, or being born with six toes. Couldn't be quantified. But shit attracts flies, so sooner or later you have to deal with them.

Four times that particular morning, I'd watched Spike Nussbaum's number flash up on call display. By this time, I only called in temps for any secretarial work, so I was stuck with answering the phone myself. Which put me in the direct line of fire.

"Robinson."

"Mr Robinson, sir? Spike Nussbaum."

Nussbaum was a Vietnam veteran, the type who would even call you sir just prior to strangling you.

"Mr Robinson, sir, I really need to talk to you. Sir."

"By all means, talk, Mr Nussbaum. You have two minutes. What can I do for you?"

"What I have to say needs to be said in person. Sir."

"I'm afraid that just wouldn't be possible. I'm on a four week trial right now."

"Sir, during my spare time, when I'm not taking care of Kimberly, I've been doing some research. Since you never actually sent us a copy of the judgment, I went down to the courthouse and picked up a copy."

"Very enterprising of you, Spike. If I were a betting man, I'd say you have a future."

"Sir, it says here that we were awarded two million dollars. Sir. Plus compound interest since the date of service of the writ."

"I don't mind saying the jury appreciated my arguments, Spike."

"How come then, Sir, we only got 350 clicks at the end of the day."

"Because, Spike, at the end of the day, that's all there was left."

"But, it says two million dollars!"

"After six months of applications, discoveries, and, don't quote me on this, but there were dilatory tactics on the part of defence counsel which bordered on the unethical. And, as you well know, we had expert witnesses brought in from the outside. It's the unfortunate, dreadful procedural side of *the system*, Spike, but it's not my job to remedy that."

All that to say, the city was drawing me back again, its gravitational pull increasing in direct proportion to my boredom. I picked up the phone and dialled international. The voice that responded was Joel, Wee Willie's Lyonnais chef, whose reputation was enhanced by rumours that he had tortured men during the Algerian mess.

"*Wee Willies, bonjour.*"

"Joel? Franck Robinson here."

"Franck, you old devil! When do we see you again?!"

"What's on special today, Joel?"

"*Cèpes à la Bordelaise. Croûtes Comtoises aux Morilles.* Come back and join us. We'll party again, Franck!"

"I'll be there tomorrow. Make sure the place is crawling with slatterns, Joel."

PART II

Chambre 52, Hotel du Quai Voltaire

Changed locales, Hervé. One step ahead of the law, as they say. Further to my last missive, check Account 332-555 672. And, Hervé, give me a break, and drop the talk on trust accounts and fiduciary duty, otherwise no more phone calls. I don't depend on you for cash, you depend on me for entertainment. Besides, this is *force majeure*. Remember Nuremberg, Hervé. I was just following orders. Your orders are: Transfer the funds. Call up Sam Harder, you remember that wine-soaked lunch we had a few years back at Club St-Denis. If he gets antsy, cook up a power of attorney. Do whatever it takes. I'm counting on you.

Haven't quite decided what to do next, but somebody should end up dead to punctuate this little tale in an appropriate manner. Or who knows, maybe everything will turn out, ha ha. Just kidding, only a bullet in the head is going to loop this baby out. In the meantime, thought I might continue my little journal of the john, fully annotated version, concerning my life, such as it is. A Darwinian log-book of sorts. For your personal enjoyment. Top ten popular myths about the john. The food we eat. How to become a john. Favourite john fashions. Why our mothers still love us.

I am writing this missive from a haunt known as the *Café Byzantin* which is frequented by the scum of the universe — johns, pedophiles, rapists, abortionists and pimps — the other human debris slouched in various positions at the bar and in the stalls of *Café Byzantin*. Each of them pouring Leffes and Pastis down their gullets, and each one of them probably with a variation to tell on my own theme.

None of us actually chose this life. We drifted into it, because we didn't feel enough drive on our way to the initial destination. It was a question of vitality. A choice between decadence and ethics. Those from the world referred to as normal, or day-to-day or moral fail to fathom why certain women are willing to step out on St-Denis and suck strange men's cocks, day in and out, and why certain strange men are willing to pay to have their cocks (the instrument of life!!) sucked, or have their life-giving jism dribble out uselessly down the diseased, gelatinous thighs or scarred faces of women who have performed the same task dozens of times the same day with men of *unspeakably foul habit.*

So fitting, that last phrase, Hervé. Don't you see what's happened here, Hervé? I have committed the ultimate sin. Not whoring, not stealing from the trust funds of quadriplegics, not avoiding child support payments. That's nickel and dime shit. No, my true sin is identifying myself as *part of an oppressed class.* But, let me continue my guided tour of the gutters of *rue St-Denis,* the septic tank of the Western world.

I

The bed was in the "green room," on the first floor, overlooking *rue des Martyrs*. I looked out the window at a *boucherie chevaline* on the opposite side of the street. Workers standing outside of a delivery truck, in blood-soaked aprons, hauling down horse carcasses. I looked back inside the room. Alena squatting over the bidet, douching her cunt with a lime-green rectangular terry-towel, watching me. Flashing what she called her smile *troublant*. Then turning it off.

"That's good. Where'd you learn that?"

"What?" she said, her lips pouting.

"The smile."

"I imagine a schoolgirl caught masturbating. It is part of my repertoire. To slow the men down. Looking is free. But then, nothing more until *cash*."

She took a couple more dabs at her cunt with the towel.

"I have a gift, mister Franck. I can make any man stop. I am like a disease."

"You should have gone into sales."

"To sell what. Fish?"

She folded the towel and placed it back on a rack at the edge of a small sink. Turned around, a cigarette now in her mouth.

"Light my cigarette. If you are a gentleman."

That word again. *Gentleman.*

"I have to make my monthly visit to the Commissariat today. To regularise my taxes."

"You pay taxes?"

"*Pauvre con,*" she pronounced, "of course. I am *profession liberale.* Look."

She reached into her purse, pulled out a sheet of paper, neatly folded into four. An excerpt from the *Registre de Commerce de Paris*, identifying her as a *péripaticienne.*

"Social benefits, tenants tax, property tax, the crèche, the audiovisual tax, the value-added tax. I'm telling you, Franck, nine thousand tonnes of paper. Nine thousand. And what ever is left goes to Yannick. But, inspecteur Chanvre, the assistant prefect, is a customer. He shows me how to organize my paper work. *Donnant, donnant. C'est cool.*"

Everything about Alena suggested sloth. She moved at crawl-speed. Her voice dripped out in languid streams. As if she had been waiting for a decade or so for the right person to come or the right thing to happen, then figured out that stagnation was her natural state. I liked her style, and her way of reducing fucking to routine, marinated in indifference. With Alena, you weren't really there. She had to show up for work; otherwise she wouldn't eat. She had to wiggle her ass, because that got your dick hard, and if your dick was hard, she might squeeze an extra couple hundred francs for the promise

of something never really delivered upon. And she needed that cash, for cigarettes, to feed her kid, for whatever.
But the client, although essential, was interchangeable,
fungible. Like a Ken doll coming off the assembly line.
But with venereal disease, or a grudge against his mother, or nothing to do before attending a Church meeting.
Or the occasional brutes. Savage, thick-skinned and
thick-headed. The type that see women as slabs of meat
or punching bags. The kind that made it nice to have a
pimp close by.

"Franck, would you accompany me?"

"Sure, no problem."

Maybe I'm not normal, but to me, being invited by a
whore to walk down the street during daylight hours
meant something. Kind of an acknowledgement that I
was now part of Alena's world. More than that. It was
an honour. Which shows that I was either very stupid,
or I adapted well to different environments.

We walked together through the *Faubourg Montmartre* towards the St-Denis post office. Just after turning off *Réaumur*, we stopped for a moment to watch
Pascal, an oversized brute with a squashed nose and
quick hands, who was running a dice game. His straight-
man, Abdul, stood at the other side of the collapsible
card table used for their operations. Another crony wearing an amused smirk, watching the mark being played
out, who that afternoon was a small Portuguese man
wearing an oversized bowler hat which left only a brushy
moustache and a stubbly chin visible.

Abdul was in phase two of the sting operation, staring into Pascal's eyes, as if he were his father, or as if he
were being handed inside information by the vice-chair-
man of the stock exchange just prior to a public offering
of telecom shares. Abdul stared and then stared some

more, clutching a handful of hundred franc notes in his left hand, struggling to keep them from jumping onto the table.

"What do you mean, it's easy?" he asked, his eyes bulging, incredulous. "I will kill you if you lie." This followed by a long theatrical pause.

"But is it possible, are you really the one I have been waiting for, the man in the dream?"

Abdul inched back towards the table as if he were being pulled back by an invisible leash.

"Please, kind man, you suck the marrow from my bones and the will from my spirit, but speak the truth, please, just this once, oh kind man, let destiny turn my way."

"*C'est très simple,*" Pascal responded, summarizing all of life in his bland, authoritative response. "All you have to do is guess where the die is."

"Sure, it's simple, why am I trusting you?" Abdul shouted protestingly, performing a splenetic jig, a grimace twisting his features. "Just this once, Allah, guide me through the desert to the promised land!"

A little girl stood skipping rope in the middle of the street. A Sunday afternoon theatre troupe trudged through. A jumble of harlequins, worn bass drums completed by a trio of clowns hauling a makeshift box constructed to simulate a royal coach. Abdul was blind to it all, and frantically threw three hundred franc notes on the table and smacked his palm flat onto the middle cup.

"There! I'm sure of it!"

Pascal lifted the cup, his granite features immovable.

"Three hundred francs for the *beur.*"

"*Allahu akbar, allahu akbar!*"

He stuffed the hundred franc notes recklessly into a snotty *mouchoir*. Despite the whole thing being an utter sham, the same suckers still showed up, with a few new customers lagging around, who had seen the trick performed a thousand times, yet walked up, and after the ritual hesitations, analyses, back and forths, squinting of the eyes and smacking of palms, placed their money.

I accompanied her as far as the St-Denis post office, let her continue. There was a letter waiting for me in the *Poste Restante*. No return address, something from Montreal.

> Dear Franck,
>
> I am writing you from my hospital bed, where I have been prostrate for ten days. I know that means nothing to you, that you have forgotten my very existence. Your daughter asks every day when daddy is coming home. I have told her you are looking for diamonds in South America, and that you will return as a millionaire. You are a real son of a bitch, Franck. I know that nobody has ever meant anything to you, but, if you have any decency, you might send us a cheque once in a while. I don't have enough money, but when I do, I'm going to hire a contract killer, and do the world a favour.

I momentarily attempted to conjure up an image of the sender, and failed, despite having lived with her for years, and fathered three of her children. The effect of the letter was similar to what I might have felt upon discovering that I had left a phone bill unpaid at a former address.

As I completed my reading of the unsigned missive, I found myself in front of a *tabac*, stepped inside and picked up a box of Danneman cigars and the Friday night race card for the Vincennes track. Alena's pimp Yannick had given me some inside information on a trotter named *Hollywood or Bust*, carded on the fourth race, which according to Yannick was going to be thrown. *Hollywood or Bust* was pegged at 48-1 on the preliminary card. Those types of odds on a quinte win meant enough for six months of whoring and plenty of pocket change for rounds of Ricard. For my new *friends*.

Outside of Tranh, a casual relationship at best, with no risk of going anywhere, there was no one in my life. Unless you counted whores. My whole existence was being played out in the mind. There was death to consider, which meant being buried or cremated somewhere, but even that could be outsourced. Or, you could just opt for the default button, and die in the street, and be tossed in a garbage truck with the rest of the waste of St-Denis. Maybe they'd send the invoice to my ex-wife under the Decree of Thermidor Year II, concerning the duty to dispose of the remains of family members.

The key to the city was picking your *arrondissement* and sticking with it. Each one of them had a personality and, if you made the wrong pick, sooner or later you would be forced to leave out of apathy, disgust or fear. The second and ninth provided everything you needed if your predilection was vice: bordellos, sex shops, *clubs échangistes*, S & M, wine caves, and meat shops threaded in and out of the quarter, underlining that we were all just meat at various stages of the coil from breeding ground to slaughterhouse. Which brought me back to a core realisation. If my life had any limited meaning, it was only that I belonged in Paris. It provided me with the one thing I had truly sought out of life. Anonymity. Sheba had been a brief interlude, during which I suffered from the hallucination that she could answer a question which even I didn't know how to formulate. Or so I thought at the time.

I spent most of the following morning hanging a set of erotic sketches drawn by Eisenstein which I had recently purchased. The walls of number 2, *rue de Mulhouse*, were now covered with paintings, drawings, lithographs, etchings, sketches of women. Kama sutra postures, Munch adolescents, Picabia pastiches of meat grinders titled *Voici la femme*. Garish harlets, schoolgirls in pleated skirts, nubians covering their cunts with flat palms, as if their uncle had just walked into the boudoir and was preparing to rape them.

As I stepped into the corridor, I caught sight of the old woman, down on her knees in the communal toilet, vigorously scrubbing the inside of the cracked porcelain bowl with a brush. Skinny as a pole, rigidly balanced on a set of scrawny, doorknob knees. She wore a pink set of thirty year old babydolls. Her stubby backside visible through the meshed layers of her negligée. Inside the W.C., three clothes lines criss-crossing, wall to wall. Panties, hosiery, bras, bustiers, corsets hanging from the lines. A curl of cigarette smoke wafted upwards from the crack between her skeletal buttocks, sending out unspeakable invitations. A cemetery of her past and whatever it contained.

Her door was a little further down the hall. On the outside, a label, reproducing the name I had seen on her postal box downstairs: C. Ducastin-Chanel. Ducastin-Chanel had taken up the habit of saluting me whenever I passed by her door in the early evening on my way out.

"*Vous descendez en ville, monsieur Franck?*" she squawked.

Her head swivelled, revealing a gnarled, crooked mouth and beady eyes.

"*Vous descendez en ville, monsieur Franck?*"

"What's it to you?"

"Sin wasn't invented yesterday, my friend."

"Get back to your scrubbing, old woman."

"You know the last time I cried? Forty-seven years ago. It was a Thurday evening. Standing outside the Bobigny. You know. Just by the Bastille?"

"Can't say that I have."

As I descended the stairwell, her squawking voice resonating from the top floor.

"You ever ask an old lady her first name, *monsieur Franck*?"

The city had been dark and grey for weeks. Two months into spring, and nothing but rain. The Seine had overflowed, and there were no signs of water levels abating. Tainted water seeping out of the sewers, onto the street in a slow, relentless progression. The trains had been on strike for seven days running, emptying Paris of the movers and shakers and the suburban workers. The local *riverains* were back in control, and the tone had changed back to traditional Parisian rude self-contentment.

Over time, my appetite had been gradually, but progressively increasing, taking up larger and larger parts of the daylight hours. Part of this may have been brought on by my nascent friendship with Tranh, but there were other reasons, ones I explained by the fact that I was getting over Sheba. There was no getting around it. The stronger the addiction, the worst the cold turkey. It was better to return to soft drugs, like wine and food, and the result was more than salutory. By the time evening arrived, I was now at the point where, if on a binge, I could devour a ten course meal.

I dropped into a butcher shop on the St-Denis exchange operating under the name *Charcuterie de l'Orient*. The meat on display, particularly the lamb, had a distended appearance, as if the animal had crawled a few last steps across the slaughterhouse floor after the first swing of the axe on its head misfired. I ordered a Merguez sausage sandwich from a grinning, buttery faced ogre sliding a chain of sausages through his thick palms. Two young men, clad in butchers' aprons, were engaged in casual discussion beside me. They were drinking acrid coffee, smoking Marlboros as they discussed the legs of a young short-skirted client, or more precisely, the cunt perched bare centimetres above its hem, and just exactly how they wouldn't mind sticking a few *merguez* into the vaginal crevice within.

One of the two mentioned that earlier that afternoon he had masturbated in the breaded mix for the *escalope milanaise*. His colleague nodded blandly, adding that he never completed a shift without shooting off at least one wad of jism into one of the mixes for *pâté* or *mousse au canard*. I considered for a moment whether this was braggadocio or a case of something else. It was not pleasant to contemplate, but neither was eating eggs, if you thought about it too much. That was the key. Not to think too much about things.

On the bigger playing field, hoof and mouth disease had swept the continent, but within Paris, a stubborn, well-anchored form of madness had possessed the locals. The restaurants, shunned by fearful tourists, were selling meat at cost, bringing in the lower end of the social spectrum. Everywhere, but nowhere more than in *les Halles,* the ragged dregs of the city had temporarily repossessed their chairs and tables from the Japanese and the Americans, and seized the occasion. A large blackboard sign in the terrace area of *Aux Tonneaux des Halles* advertised Ricard at one franc, over a sign:

Have you caught Hoof and Mouth Fever?

The inside of the bistro was packed to overflowing. A twenty-something, female accordionist, rust-coloured hair in ropy braids to her waist, a pleated skirt over striped leotards and high-heeled saddle shoes, rouge forming two blazing suns on her cheeks. I spotted Rhanya. She was weaving across the floor just behind the accordionist, waltzing very unsteadily with a *beur* half her age. The *beur*'s eyes were half-closed, his head pushed against Rhanya's large head nurse breasts. The regular clientele had been replaced by kitchen staff and dishwashers, six garbage men in Ville de Paris lime-green coveralls, drinking pastis. The employees wolfing down Chinon wines and the cheapest tripe, *rognon*, giblets, *ris de veau* and other unidentifiable offal being sold at discount.

I moved down *Montorgueil* towards St-Eustache church. The Indian beggar standing at his post at the side entry into the nave. He spotted me, broke into a smile.

"Once a gentleman, no?"

I nodded, flipped him a franc.

"Ever been to Gujarat, my friend? You can have a woman for eight rupees."

I moved onwards towards the old commodities exchange, and a few more tripe and pigs foot joints. At the *Pied de Cochon*, a heavy set, tall, stooped, silver-haired man was gathering himself from the ground. He had a fresh cut on his forehead and a streak of mud on his cheek. Two men, shaved heads, both wearing black pants, white shirt, black tie. Their arms folded.

"I am chair of philosophy at the University of Chicago. Alistair Needham. You fools, how could you not have heard of me. Alistair Needham!"

The taller of the two men shook his head.

"*Ça ne me dit rien. Et, toi?*"

His accomplice shook his head.

"*Que dalle.*"

Alistair Needham tried to push past him.

"*Désolé.* No tourists. For the poor today."

"But, I can pay!"

"Come back tomorrow. Tomorrow."

Inside the *Pied de Cochon*, two men in waiters' uniforms were sleeping on the floor, partially blocking the entrance. In the centre of the restaurant a table of twenty men, in from the slaughterhouses, still wearing their bloodied aprons, were throwing knives into the walls in a makeshift competition which the owner watched with grim resignation. The rest of the *Pied de Cochon* filled with derelicts who had briefly abandoned their begging at nearby St-Eustache church to join in the orgy. For the lower urban classes, hoof and mouth was manna from heaven. It meant they could eat properly, if only for a few days.

I took a window table, looking out onto Place St-Eustache and the Commodities Exchange. The taller man who had just refused entry to the American dropped a menu on the table.

"What's on special today?"

"The temptation of St Anthony."

"That'll be fine. With a bottle of Moselle."

Two minutes later, the waiter returned with an over-sized, shallow soup bowl, filled with a steaming heap of pigs tail, knuckles, *museau*, dismembered corpses floating in a thick brown gruel. He dropped a large, wooden salad-mixing spoon onto the table.

"*Voilà,*" he said. There. You're served.

I dug into the food. Food was a solution for everything. If people were worried about getting afts in their mouths, or developing a mutant strain of sclerosis because the cows were mad, that was their problem. This was Europe, and the general genetic balance periodically called for a plague, or a war or a genocide from time to time to bleed the collectivity and keep everyone on their toes. If you didn't like it, you could move to America where filth was a strict liability offence, and you could keep a weapons arsenal in your kitchen, provided it was cleaned once a week.

I decided to stop in and see Millie, who operated solo out of a *chambre* on the sixth floor of the Hotel Clauzel on *rue des Martyrs*. She had set up a makeshift waiting room out in the hallway, consisting of two chairs and a coffee table near the elevator. She had left a book open on the coffee table, at a page with the following quote underlined in red pencil:

> My soul is a black maelstrom,
> Immense vertigo surrounding emptiness.

Millie emerged in the corridor, cheerfully, but briskly escorting her previous john, a skinny, bald-headed coot, to the elevator. She had coarse salt and pepper hair braided rasta style, which hung like a bead curtain to her shoulders. She wore a white miniskirt and a long garland which slithered its way down her ankles, drunken Judy Garland style. She walked right past me, escorted the bald eagle to the elevator, watched the doors shut, then turned towards me.

"So, when's the last time you had your cock sucked, Franck?"

Usually, the non-French product I sampled was shipped in from Guadeloupe, Dominican Republic and former French African colonies in the Indian ocean.

Millie, however, was from Chicago, and the only on-duty American whore I ever met in the city of Paris. She had taken up whoring after being fired as a heavy-duty machine shop operator and had to dig up some cash quickly to have her uterus removed. At least that was the way she stated the case to me, the words blasting out of her Cherokee-Irish mouth like heat from a kiln.

We returned to her room, She had made little effort to remake the bed, and the sheets were rumpled still from her previous client.

"So, what is it today, Franck?"

About two or three minutes into humping, I suddenly felt Millie's vulva grip the base of my cock like a Venus fly-trap. The stem and head of the penis, however, seemed to be stretching out, as if it had embarked on an independent speleological expedition into a cavernous grotto of the Pyrenees. I could only guess what tracts and canals my dick was peering at through sensory devices whose existence I had never suspected prior to now. For a moment, I imagined the giant worms of Frank Herbert's *Dune* trilogy, burrowing through extra-terrestrial sand to locate life-sustaining water. In retrospect, the loss of her lower body had caused me to lose control of my mind. The undertone of rumbling utterances gained slightly in cadence as the rhythm of my own humping increased, which led me to believe it was just one of those parallel mental tam-tam reverberations which knocked the walls out of my brain anytime I found myself in a bordello. Nothing special was registering on the mental Richter scale. Millie, right in the middle of fucking, started repeating a phrase:

> *"... je suis une femme pour qui le monde extérieur est une réalité intérieure."*

The simple resonance of the phrase seemed to coagulate with the acrid stench of the room.

Millie bent over and touched her toes, demonstrating an age-defying, aboriginal suppleness worthy of a contortionist. I stared for a moment at a scar, dead centre of her back, which resembled a paddlesteamer, while I attempted to light a cigarette. A poster on the scarlet wall behind her scrolled upwards and downwards as I moved into a steady hump. Up, down, up, down.

> Conferencia Futurista
> José de Almada-Negreiros
> Teatro Republica
> Sabado, 14 de abril 1917
> 52 cts

While examining the toreador posture and inflated pleat trousers of the futurist poet of the previous century, I heard another snorting noise, and perceived for the first time that it was coming from Millie herself, who was now rigid. She looked to be in a trance. Although her body was stiff and immobile, her Cherokee straw hair bobbed up and down over a string of black moles strung out in a semi-circle between her shoulder blades. She pointed her ferret-like snout forward, sniffed, wheeled around and stared up at me. Her eyes rolled upwards, briefly exposing a long, pointed, ghoulish set of eye-teeth. Then she regained her focus and smiled, her eye-teeth still visible. I examined my prick, which now hung limp and lifeless, its vitality depleted by the clinical squeeze of Millie's vulva. Fucking Millie was like masturbation. Desecrating a grave.

"Stick around, Franck. I'll pour you a drink. Fuck it, I miss talking to Americans."

"I'm Canadian."

"You'll just have to do."

She poured me a Kronenbourg.

"What do you feel when you fuck me?"

I shrugged my shoulders.

"Nothing. Nothing personal. My mind's elsewhere."

"Didn't you even notice? I mean my machinery. It's gone. I've been gutted. Disembowelled."

I watched her examine herself in front of a vanity mirror, brushing and rebrushing a straw mane of hair nonchalantly, swinging it over her shoulder as if she were Lady Gueneviere and not a chronically unemployed Illinois heavy-duty machine shop girl who had to become a trans-Atlantic tool operator to earn enough back pay to cover costs to remove her own body parts.

"You still hung up on *la gamine*?"

"Have you heard something?"

"Forget her, Franck. Do you know how many men she's done her number on?"

"What number would that be?"

"Don't think you're so goddam special, Franck."

"You have no fucking idea what she did or didn't do."

"Oh yes I do. I know exactly what she did. That's the problem with you men. Even you goddam johns think you're special cases. But you're replaceable. Jesus, she's probably out doing some john who's got ten times your cash flow."

"So, you've seen her."

"Getting a little paranoid, are we Franck? She's already done her number all right."

"I'll take care of her."

"No you won't. No one ever takes care of *la gamine*. She's in a league of her own. Listen to me, Franck. I'm from Chicago. A West side slum, Franck. My brother is doing five to ten for armed robbery. Take it from me. You're an amateur."

"Who are you, Mary Magdalen?"

"Who the fuck is Mary Magdalen?"

"A whore."

"Fuck you, Franck. You think I read Pessoa, and I don't know who Mary Magdalen is? No wonder you're always in shit. Why do I try to help people? Fucking waste of time."

"Don't worry about it."

I looked past her, out the window of the sixth floor of the *Hotel Clauzel*. A slight mist clung to the building across the street, enshrouding a billboard advertising French *haute cuisine* fast food version. Behind it, the silhouette of the night sky transmutating into early morning cobalt.

Three bangs on the door signalled that my time was up and that another john had arrived in the Hotel Clauzel.

"I'm part Cherokee. If you really want, I can put her in a grave. From a distance. Better than fucking arsenic, Franck. And no bad aftertaste or evidence."

"I'll think about it."

I was still sticking with my own system. I had discovered the *Café Byzantin* by way of an Atget photograph in a press agency near the old Figaro offices on Montmartre. The photo showed a whore plying her trade in the '20s in front of 143 rue St-Denis. Behind the photo, but still in the file Brothels in Paris, a 1944 transcript of a radio report claiming Glenn Miller had been found dead in the arms of a whore in a brothel at 143 St-Denis. The whore in the photo was square-shouldered, very buxom, dressed in black. She looked happy enough, and eager to do business. Then, under an 1863 charcoal sketch of Victorine Meurent, modelling nude as the whore for Manet's *Olympia*. But, 143 was now the *Café Byzantin* at the corner of *Réaumur*, and like anything else on *rue St-Denis*, had fallen into disrepair and become another anonymous haunt of the strip, which exerted an organic gravity on all higher forms of life, pulling them down towards the gutter.

Pierre, the stocky, curly haired Breton bartender, slid a foamy Meteor down the brass counter towards me. Only one other patron, excluding an off shift waiter, six feet away, pouring tap water out of a flagon into a cylindrical glass with yellowish green Pastis in it. Behind the man, in the recesses of the café, three hookers drinking coffee. I turned around 180 degrees, propped my right elbow on the counter and gazed out the window. A perfect North view of St-Denis. I spotted her again. The same one. Every night without fail. Black hair waxed together, Mali-style, then coiled into an arced labyrinth of flat metallic sheets.

Another glass of Meteor appeared in front of me. The off-duty waiter nodded in my direction.

"On me. I'm getting married in the morning, can you believe it? Fourth time. Every time a disaster. This'll be no better."

He was older than thirty and younger than forty-eight. His shiny bald scalp, aquiline features and rangy build made anything more precise impossible to estimate. Beside him, a shorter acquaintance, sheepdog hair hanging over a set of thick glasses, pasty complexion, making an attempt to intervene in the conversation.

"I know exactly, *précisément*, what I mean to say is ..."

"Sure, go ahead, buy me a drink," said the off-duty waiter. "But I wasn't talking to you. I was talking to *ce-monsieur-là*," his finger hanging like a crooked branch in my general direction.

"*Ce que je veux dire par la ...* "

"Shut up! I told you, I'm talking to *ce-monsieur-là!*" backhanding roughly in the direction of the short man. I downed my beer and stepped out the door. Direction Magnetic North.

She wore a set of hotpants and suspenders, which stretched tautly over her breasts like airplane struts. Her lips smeared red, protruding vaginally. I thought I saw a cane leaning against the door, and wondered whether she wasn't blind. But, when she turned, her glazed eyes locked onto mine.

"*Je vous emmène?*"

I followed her down a corridor into a courtyard, watching the sands of her gravelly ass shift back and forth inside her turquoise, terrytowel hotpants. Forty per cent of the Zaire army has AIDS, and I want to get on line. I recalled Lola sitting inside that cheapo Montreal diner the week before her death, describing the design and engineering of her own set of silicon pontoons. As if genetics were trying to equip humans with survival equipment for the next great flood.

I noticed she was limping up the steps, and that her right leg was skinnier than the left, possibly a residual effect of polio, which her rigid Buckingham Palace Guard posture had successfully camouflaged on the street. Halfway up the steps, she grabbed onto the rail to steady herself, gasped for breath.

"*Merde. T'as pas une clope?*"

I passed her a cigarette. She took a few drags, butted it out beneath her pump. She pulled some tin foil from the pocket of her hot pants, rolled the stub inside, shoved it back down her pants.

I followed her past a black pimp sitting in a chair at the first level stairhead. Further down the hall, I could hear a female voice snarling *"allez, salaud, tu viens ou quoi, merrrde?"*, rolling the rrrs out sharply in a rough Basque *patois*. The slovenly middle-aged bald pimp could have been the upstairs tenant, except he was someone who didn't mind sitting around while women sucked other men's cocks for him. If you didn't get too hung up on product, he was basically running a franchise operation with all the usual headaches. Copyright, industrial property, confidentiality clauses, customer loyalty, quality control. Whether it was hamburgers, whores or muffler shops, the principles remained the same. Success depended on predictability. Remaining open twenty-four hours a day, and having a generic storefront at every street corner.

We hiked up to the next landing. The room itself was only accessible by an outside *passerelle* clinging precariously to the building, and which resembled a suspension bridge.

"*Ici*," she said.

"After you."

She had a lumbering, worklike manner of removing her clothes, reminding me of a drydock crew I had witnessed pulling down rig and tackle from a trawler that had run aground in Oostende. Once she stripped down to her lingerie, I could see she was gelatinous. There were no definable contours, once freed of the moulds formed by bra cups, corsets and garter belts. Judging from the positioning of the scars on her body, someone had propped her onto an operating table and had inserted implants. Someone who either no longer or never had been engaged in what is loosely called a *medical practice*.

Prostrate now, her knees up as if ready to give birth.

"*Tu viens, chérie?*"

I reached into my pocket and pulled out the Marlboros. Lit a smoke, and threw down an extra note.

"I have to make a phone call. When I signal, I want you to take the phone."

I dialled the cell phone number. That voice at the other end, transforming two syllables into an aria.

"*Allo?*"

"Listen to this Sheba. My new girlfriend. From Mali."

I waved the whore closer to the phone. Passed her two hundred more francs.

"Uhh, uhh, c'mon baby."

I pushed the phone up to my own ear.

"You should see her tits, Sheba. No traces of silicone. The creator's work left intact."

The voice, was pleasant, measured, oozing over the phone.

"Franck. *Ça me dit que dalle.* You must have the wrong number."

"You fucking cunt. You can't hide behind a cell phone forever, Sheba. C'mon, baby, tell me where you're hiding."

Then a taunting laugh. Machiavelli and Marilyn Monroe.

"*Pitoyable. Pauvre mec.*"

I hung up the phone. Looked at the undulating mass gawking at me from the bed.

"*Alors, tu viens ou tu viens pas?*"

"Ever heard of Dr Cooper?"

"*Docteur qui?*"

"Best liposuction specialist in Vegas. You better have a little talk with your pimp, honey."

"*Ça, alors.*"

While descending *rue Montorgueil.* I spotted Tranh inside *Aux tonneaux des Halles*, seated alone in front of a bottle of Médoc, three-quarters gone. He caught sight of me, waved me impatiently inside.

"What a coincidence, Robinson! Come and join me, sir, I've not yet ordered!"

During the first ten minutes following my arrival, he continued drinking while haranguing the waiter about the cooking of his *rognons* during his previous visit.

"*Entrecôte* it is then, *monsieur Tranh. A point*?"

"*Absolument pas. Saignant.*"

"*Saignant, alors. D'accord.*"

"But, first bring us some *Pâte de sanglier.* And the *céléri remoulade.* Not too acidic."

I'd seen foreigners do this. Inanely specify things to show they hadn't just arrived in the city. In Tranh's case, it seemed to be his way of saying he also was stuck in the city and doomed to act out a secondary role for the remainder of his *ritualised existence*, but that, as the son of Nguyen Vo Giap, conqueror of the French at Dien Bien Phu, he deserved a minimum of respect. It was all about respect.

"I once fell in love with a whore, Egmond. She was from India. I still remember the day when she entered my studio. At the time I lived in the 16th. Things actually were going well for me then. I was having an exhibition. She walked in off the street. Wearing one of those hounds tooth outfits. You know, one of those suits the royals like to wear. I can assure you, she had a real effect upon me. I had planned on proposing to her. It was a foolish idea, one which I luckily did not have the opportunity to execute. Her brother was sent from Bombay to retrieve her. On the very day I intended on springing my request, she was kidnapped. I never saw her again."

He ran the tip of his finger around the inner rim of his wine glass.

"What do you think lies behind your attraction to whores, Robinson?"

"They don't require user manuals."

Tranh's laugh like mice scuttling through an attic.

"I don't believe you. When a man does this, an older man, he is wrestling with the idea of his own death."

"I don't see the connection."

"Of course you don't. You Westerners never speak of death. It is a taboo. That is why it is present everywhere around you. Its certainty and finality paralyses you, because you do not believe in reincarnation. But, things preceded us and things will follow us. The total energy will remain identical. This is a law. It is inescapable."

The *entrecôte* had arrived. Blood seeping to the top of the cut. He examined it with satisfaction.

"Do you know why I do not fear death, Robinson? Because I have had so many good meals since I was released from prison."

"That's why you asked me if I'd done time."

Tranh tested the Asian inscrutable smile on me, reached for the wine list, ordered another bottle of red.

"Have I told you my wife has multiple sclerosis?"

"It's possible."

"There are those who think that a spouse with multiple sclerosis is a prison. They could not be more mistaken. I have no problem controlling my wife, Robinson. We discuss her death every night. Her greater fear is that I will not kill her once she is helpless. She refers to it as a sadistic torture borne of compassion."

He emptied his glass. Poured out more for both of us.

"I have been observing you in my own way, Robinson. You are a man on the run. You spend your life leaving jobs, friends, women. You never know where you are going. Then, you discover a woman. She epitomizes everything you have wasted—lost dreams, lack of direction, sloth—but in your initial illusion, you believe she is the remedy for everything that has ever ailed you. You are disappointed. You leave her. You drink. You whore. Still, nothing satisfies this insatiable thirst. So, you envisage suicide. But, you do not want to die. So, your emptiness becomes wider, more vacuous, like a Russian steppe. Nothing is left. Nothing. But you are still breathing, still alive. What can you do? Nothing. I can't go on, you say in your rare moments of lucidity, I can't go on. But you go on. Not even religion can save you. You believe in nothing. You have created your own hell, and nothing will satisfy you until you have deteriorated from disillusion into sheer misery. Then your thoughts turn back to this woman, even though you are insane now, and you know she is insane, you feel she has given you something. Something which you cannot obtain elsewhere."

"So. What's your point?"

"You are missing an essential part, Robinson. But, your problem has no resolution. Whatever you must do, do it. Spend no time considering the consequences. That is weakness. An unforgivable trait in an amoral man. Your life is not so important. Enjoy what is left of it."

I imagined Tranh, or one of his uncles, torturing French paratroopers held captive in underwater bamboo cages.

"Tell me, Robinson. This woman has caused you immeasurable grief. Yet you insist on returning to her. Why?"

"What are you talking about? She's a piece of tail, Tranh. End of story."

"You are lying. You have already thrown away everything for her. You have lost your taste for everything else but her. And, forgive me, Robinson, but all she can do is fuck. It is pathetic."

"If it's so pathetic, why the grin?"

"You misunderstand me, Robinson. Please do not take this personally, but your own fate is a matter of complete indifference to me. On the other hand, your decline interests me tremendously on scientific grounds, as do the reasons behind your conduct. Please, I invite you to dine with me, as I must hear more."

We wandered up St-Denis after the meal, and landed in *Le Byzantin*, where we lodged ourselves between a table of whores and three young *beurs* planning a Brink's robbery. The table littered with Choucroute Garnie, bottles of Gewurtztraminer and Oude Kampen Sumatra Cum Laude cigars. Hoof and mouth hysteria had moved into a new phase. Government ministers now devising disinformation campaigns, spreading rumours that farmers were deliberately contaminating livestock in the hope of gaining government subsidies. Which suited me perfectly, for the price of meat was descending into dot.com territory. The Africans were a two hour plane trip away, no doubt wondering why a continent with food to spare was butchering everything alive to wipe out a disease that couldn't be transmitted to humans. But, things had never been better for Tranh and myself. For several weeks running, we had been engaged in a two-man carnivorous orgy. Tranh grinning at me, threads of *blanquette de veau* hanging from his teeth like the closing curtain at a bankrupt theatre production. He clutched at the neck of the *Côte de Bourg*, swallowed a long draught directly from the bottle, and wiped his mouth with his sleeve.

"Have you ever wrung the neck of a Cambodian chicken, Robinson?"

The question was purely rhetorical. Whenever Tranh was feeling joyous, he'd refer to Spengler or Darwin and the imminent downfall of the West. He saw the whole world as a perennial plant, reproducing itself endlessly, occasionally lying fallow, undergoing droughts, followed by temporary periods of plenty.

"Take the Vandals for example, Robinson. A Germanic tribe who ravaged Gaul, Spain, North Africa and Rome in the fourth and fifth centuries, destroying books and works of Art. We live in such times. But they pass. Paris has rules of its own, and the Parisian is lazy, stubborn, dissolute, and yet conservative. Napoleon wanted to raze the city to the ground. Give me twenty years and old Paris will disappear into a chasm, he bragged. Of course, he failed. Then it was he who was erased from the planet. Largely because he had no understanding of the Parisians. No one can ever understand Paris. It is beyond comprehension.

"Look at the Pompidou museum. A perfect example of the avant-garde movement. Deconstructivism, Robinson. In only two decades this monstrosity has taken on the appearance of a dilapidated Meccano set. The infrastructure is rusting and rotting. It will be torn down in its turn. But you should have seen the quarter before ... jugglers, flame swallowers, anarchists ... I once saw a whore pulling up her skirt and flash her *con* at a police officer. Two old biddies witnessing the spectacle reached down and hiked up their own skirts in a show of solidarity. Quite fascinating, Robinson. Every day produced something tiny, unrecorded, but memorable. There were moments, *inoubliable*, Robinson, *inoubliable*. And then, a presidential decree and it is destroyed. No matter. It is the city of the guillotine. The most pervasive legend of Paris is that of St Denis, who carried his own decapitated head through the city. A perfect symbol of modern man. His head removed, and yet somehow still alive."

Tranh returned to the topic of his wife, and their agreed-upon plans for the inevitable phase when the muscular sclerosis paralyzed her to the point of irreversible decline.

"Euthanasia is performed routinely in the Netherlands. I have contacted an agency which specializes in death tourism. It is a routine matter. The authorities in the low countries turn a blind eye to this sort of thing. Passing strange, Robinson. When the Americans controlled the South, we dug thirty thousand miles of subterranean passageways to subvert their overwhelming power. And now, decades later, I am stalked by my own invisible enemy, digging thirty thousand miles of cellular trenches in my wife's brain."

We left the café, walked South through the Marais until we arrived on *Ile Saint Louis*. A cold wind sweeping across *pont de la Tournelle*. We stopped and gazed into the flushing currents of the Seine. The high waters of spring floods washing a sluice of brown liquid against the underside of the bridge. A *peniche* and a *bâteau mouche*, both unmanned, knocking against the limestone banks of the river, stagnant. The *square de l'Ile Saint Louis* vacant, but for a bald homosexual masturbating into the river, his trenchcoat flapping in the breeze as he balanced precariously from the peninsular tip of the island. Behind the man, the wrought iron railings protecting the gardens behind the grey silhouette of Notre Dame Cathedral. Tranh pointed out the pervert gratifying himself, laughed briefly.

"Let me summarize once again. You step beyond the usual moral constraints, indeed, beyond the point of return, if you are to be believed. But, this is Paris, Robinson. Nothing in your experience convinces me that it lies outside the realm of human experience. Look, Robinson, *rue St Honoré* is just across from us. That is the street where the ox-cart would carry victims up to the Concorde for the guillotine. Imagine, six thousand heads cut off in a year. So, a man runs into a French woman with a death wish, well, there's really nothing exceptional about it, is there?"

He looked over the bridge into the Seine.

"For something to be outside the norms, it must only be comprehensible in relation to itself, and not in relation to anything else."

"You see that bench over there, Tranh? One day, Sheba and I were having a little sit down. It was a beautiful day, and for me, I thought there was only Paris, me and her. Nobody else existed. There was an old man sitting at the neighbouring bench, minding his own business, feeding the doves. Sheba was wearing a long skirt, with a slit up to the thighs. She allowed her leg to slip out and began tracing out circles into the ground. She caught his attention, and then just flashed him one of her looks. But, he turned out to be paresthetic. What followed, Tranh, was not a pretty sight."

"If I understand correctly, you struck some sort of faustian bargain with her?"

"That's right."

"There is something you haven't told me. Fine, you are not ready. But, you seem driven by some need to penetrate to the inner enclaves of the world of vice, as if it will provide you with some answers. You are not just transgressing a code of ethics, or the ten commandments. You see the cunt as some form of oracle."

"That's right! I've always thought that Cunt, per se, is something that has nothing to do with the woman. It's an independent parasite that lives off the the host body. And, Paris, Tranh, it's like a big Cunt. It's why I never feel like I'm walking down St-Denis. I'm slithering down the fallopian tubes of Paris. From one Venus fly trap to another. A honey-dripping lure, drawing me towards her again, to the lair, to her nest, the Queen Bee. She used it like a supra-spiritual vacuum cleaner to suck out any rational thought I had ever had. As if her labia talked to me, whispered to me the same secret over and over again. You know what, Tranh? This may sound insane, but I'm convinced that cunts communicate with each other. They may even come from another planet!"

"But, Robinson, you have understood absolutely nothing! This woman, can't you see, she doesn't even exist! She is a reflection of your own mind. That is what is driving you crazy. There is nothing wrong with what you did. You fell in love with this woman. That is all."

"You know what, Tranh? You're the one who doesn't get it. Sheba is part of the background. My relationship is with her cunt. If I could sever her cunt from the rest of her body, it'd be a perfect relationship."

He drank down the remainder of his wine. Poured out two more glasses.

"*Alors, ça, c'est fort.*"

"I haven't finished yet."

"What is different about this Sheba?"

I sucked on my cigarette.

"I've played out marks, and I've been played as a mark. But, this was like a progression. Planned in advance. First, I fucked her. Then, for a while, we were fucking each other. Then, it moved onto her turf. She fucked my mind. Like she moved right inside my brain."

"She wouldn't have moved in without an invitation."

"Probably not," I conceded, "but, that's beside the point. I have a feeling I'm going to run into her again. This story isn't over."

"It's her Frenchness."

"True. French girls still give head."

"If you are to engage with the French, you must understand the French. The key to them is to realize that their esthetic of beauty and their revolutionary nature is directly linked to their taste for cruelty."

· Tranh was drunk, but had honed the talent of remaining articulate long after the Médoc had dismantelled his cerebellum into its constituent parts, which gave his speech a tangential flavour of automatism.

"Tell me, Robinson. When you last visited Père Lachaise cemetery, did you notice the engraved message at the entrance? It says: *La mort est un sommeil éternel.* The man who ordered the engraving was named Fouché. The most dangerous man who ever lived. A vicious, cold-blooded atheist. The man who orchestrated Robespierre's downfall. I have examined paintings of this man in the Louvre. His most pronounced features are his hooded eyelids. This man moved with consummate ease from the secretive cells of the extremist left to the far right, where he eventually became the chief of police in post-revolutionary France. The new millenium, Robinson, will be the era when the Fouchés of the world regain their place in the corridors of power."

"What's your point?"

"My point? My point is we are lucky men to idly speak of these things in the early morning."

Dawn was breaking. The rear façade of Notre Dame etched a silhouette against a charcoal sky. We stood mute, watching a streak of blue on the horizon disappear into a mass of cloud. Then, back to the rain. The night shift girls would be checking into the *Byzantin* for coffee before returning home to sleep through the daylight hours. Tranh pointed back towards the *Brasserie de l'île.*

A woman stepping onto the bridge, her head down, enveloped in a scarf, and a transparent plastic cape over a blouse, mini-skirt, four-inch pumps.

"Look, it is Alena," he said, as if he'd conjured her up himself.

Tranh waved in her direction. Her head was tilted downwards unnaturally. She drifted momentarily towards a passing car, staggering uncertainly. She about-faced, her heels bent inwards as she regained her equilibrium. She continued in our direction, then stopped again, kicked her heels off, placed them side by side on the *trottoir*. She looked up, caught sight of us. She stared blankly, then lost her footing, propped herself against the balustrade.

"Something is wrong."

Tranh moved towards her, quickening his stride, then breaking into a run.

"Alena!"

Alena had climbed onto the balustrade, and was now balancing precariously, her eyes riveted on the river. Tranh advanced until within two metres of her, slowing to a walk. She took one step towards Tranh, her arms extended outwards. Like a child, performing a hop-scotch. Tranh opened his arms.

"Just keep your eyes on me, Alena ... easy ..."

She was close, an arm's length away.

"*Non. C'est trop dur.*"

She about-faced, exposing a Christian Dior backpack.

"You're having a bad day. Come down, we can talk about it."

We were interrupted by a shout, and the appearance of a man coming from the direction of the Left Bank, running onto the bridge.

"*Stop! Espèce de salope!*"

It was Yannick, the doorman. He was choking from the effort of running. The rain pouring down in a steady torrent. I looked back at Alena. Mascara running in rivulets down her cheeks. She leaned forward. Shivering, her bare feet sliding along the chalky surface of the balustrade. Her gaze locked onto mine. She smiled. Recognizing me for the first time.

"*Quel con*. Goodbye, Franck."

She looked down for a moment, then jumped. The current immediately caught her, flushing her towards the tip of the square St-Louis. For a moment she looked skyward in surprise, floundered, disappeared, then reappeared, her arms slapping absurdly against the current. I gripped Tranh's right arm.

"Forget it, Tranh. It's too late."

Alena caught by the undercurrent, was engulfed by a thick, swirling brown eddy. When she reappeared this time, she was face down, and the brown rush of flood waters smashed her roughly against the rock edges of square St-Louis. Yannick standing at the edge.

"*Putain, putain*, why did you go and do that? Oh, *putain de merde, je vais me flinguer*. Fucking hell, it's all over."

He fell to the ground, pounded his fist onto the roadside, weeping uncontrollably.

"Come, Robinson. Let's go. There's nothing we can do here. The police will be asking questions, and those questions will lead to more questions."

We walked towards the *Place du Châtelet*. The first buses of the morning arrived. Tranh climbed onto the 27, heading towards St-Lazare station.

"Just go home, Robinson. Just one of those things."

I bid him goodbye, then moved back towards the river again. Two white Renaults had arrived on the bridge. A plainclothes frisking Yannick. His accomplice looking in my direction. I turned left, paid no attention. Walked along the *quai des Célestins*, then stopped. I lit a cigarette, stared at the river for a while, not thinking much, other than the usual default reflection: what's the difference Franck, they're all phantoms, you're the only real one, they can't help what they do, and whatever mutant deity created them is far sicker than anybody walking the planet. So, forget about it. There didn't seem any way out of things, other than dying.

It was one of those pit and pendulum thoughts which made me nauseous. Wasn't really my style, but I vomited on the ground. Then, I started crying. It was early morning, and I was drunk, and alone. And, in a way, I was enjoying myself. It felt good to be maudlin, shedding tears a woman who sucked cock for a living. Or at least did until then. I knew that, if I saw my ex-wife jump out of a thirty storey building, it wouldn't make page 17 in my brain. And somehow that struck me as more evidence that I was where I wanted to be. It made sense to cry over a whore smashing her head on the banks of the Seine. I spotted a cab coming down the quai, and flagged it down.

"Take me to Pigalle. *Boulevard Clichy.*"

After drifting up and down *boulevard Clichy* for a while, I noticed the cab driver examining me through his rear view mirror. His nose had been broken a few times. A thick, waxen sheet of black hair draped to a set of shoulders tailor-made for a yoke. His hands oversized, bloated paws which gripped the steering wheel with a contained ferocity.

"Where to now?" he asked.

"Turn North."

"We just came from the North."

I pulled a few notes from my billfold. He lifted up two fingers of his right hand, retrieved the notes, then glanced back again.

"You know this area?"

"Yes. I know it."

"You looking for someone?"

"I haven't decided yet."

The *Moulin Rouge*, a slew of strip clubs and porn palaces, fronted by impresario types trying to lure wandering johns into their haunts, all reassured me that nothing fundamental had changed. We crawled up and down the boulevard a couple more times. I directed him through some of the smaller streets. *Rue des Martyrs, rue Houdon, rue des Abbesses.* Then a sweep wide towards *Père Lachaise* cemetery.

"Turn down Sebastopol towards *St-Denis*."

"People know me up here in Pigalle. I am an ex-wrestler. *Champion de catch.* Could have been champion of France, if it hadn't been for a fight one night. Cost me four years in *la bagne*."

St-Denis had its familiar ramshackle look. A pestilent oasis, ridden with human maggots, but an oasis all the same for those of us who seek such places to relieve us of other malaises ill understood by the healthy of spirit. The driver interrupted my thoughts again.

"My wrestling days are finished. I was bouncer for a while at the *Folies Pigalle*. It was all right. But, there's nothing a group of transexuals like better than a fist-fight, and whenever the fights broke out, one of them always wanted to take a poke at the biggest man. My last night there, a coked-up tranny in a spandex dress shot me from behind. In the *nuque*."

He pushed his right forefinger inside the track of the scar along his nape.

"Nobody could get me down on the mat, then some fifty kilo drug addict takes me out. *Tant pis.* Then I ran into money problems with the *milieu*. Had to stage my own death. Simplify. Now, I drive, and when I don't drive, I play my cello at home."

He glanced into his rear-view mirror, exposing an ugly grimace.

"You think it's funny, a big ox like me playing the cello?"

"What's funny about it?"

"You on the run?"

"Stick to your driving."

He shrugged his shoulders, shook his head.

"You're the client."

The real-life outline of the buildings enveloped with an undulant silhouette. Excessive fatigue, or the lousy weather. Or time to see an optometrist.

"Listen, you wouldn't be interested in some cunt, would you? I can bring you to a place with some first class girls. It will cost you a bit, but they're *clean*, you know."

"Is Club *le paradis* still open?"

He shook his head, but seemed to cheer up after I passed him one of the notes from my wallet.

"This is Paris, my friend. We don't find your *paradis*, we'll find you something else."

Then, as if the thought had just occurred to him.

"You ever want some protection, my friend, you call Victor on this cell phone. You might need it. Things happen to people in this city. Things they never dreamed possible. Some of them are good things. Some of them are not so good."

"Fuck it, let me off here."

I had spotted a café at *rue des petits carreaux*, opening up for textile workers arriving for the day shift. I entered, ordered a coffee, smoked a half dozen cigarettes. Then, decided to call up Ducastin-Chanel. Take her out to lunch. It made sense. A lot of insane propositions make sense at the tail-end of an all-nighter.

I sat in the stairwell for two hours waiting for Ducastin-Chanel to prepare herself for our little date. The taxi took another long hour, while she shivered at curbside *rue de Mulhouse* and I finished another half pack of cigarettes. It was the first time I had seen her with teeth in her mouth. On her chamois skin, she had stroked a long ivory shadow with her rheumatic claw from lids to brow bone, applied dark brown shadow in creases, then lined her upper eyelids from inner to outer corners with black kohl pencil, curving the line upward at the outer corners. This was capped off with two coats of black mascara on the outer periphery of the upper lashes.

Didier, our flat-nosed Aveyron waiter, dropped a couple of *kirs*. Paid her a compliment on her crinolined evening dress and white opera gloves. Ducastin-Chanel responded that they were a replica of Gina Lollobrigida's costume in 'La Morte Ha Fatto L'uovo.' "Or was it: 'Death laid an egg'?"

She berated Didier upon learning he had used Muscadet instead of Bourgogne Aligoté in the Kir.

"Give a lady a cigarette, Franck."

I passed her a Marlboro. She cradled the cylindrical shape in her fingers like a trophy.

"You don't believe it, do you, Franck?"

"Believe what?"

"That these chapped old lips ... you know, Franck."

"No. You've got something. I could see you giving a man pleasure."

"Not just pleasure, Franck. I could deliver pain. And pain could be lucrative."

Didier dropped a bottle of *Grand Vin Château Tayac*, a Cru Bourgeois 1993. Ducastin-Chanel stared at the glass. She pushed her knuckly hands around the stem of the glass, lifted it to her lips, which hung like rotted bark. For a moment, she was impervious to me, staring through the glass with that glaucoma glare favoured by the geriatric. She was like anyone old. When they get you at close quarters, they won't give you what you need unless you listen to the rest. And the rest never matters.

"What about the *gamine*? You said you'd tell me where I could find her."

"When you get older, people no longer respect you. I don't blame them. I was a *balance* for a while. Passed on information to the *Brigade Judiciaire* on Pierre Lescot. But the younger ones didn't respect me. I don't blame them."

She smiled coquettishly, looked at her empty glass.

"Can't a girl have some fun, Franck?"

I waved Didier over. She had something, although it had become a little bit *sthpeshial* with the passing years.

"They were good days. You see, Franck ... *it's Franck, isn't it?*"

"Yeah ... what about *la gamine*?"

Her teeth clamped shut at fair velocity. That skinny claw of hers suddenly gripped onto my left wrist, and her look became ferocious, confessional, as if she'd waited since that night at the Bobigny forty-seven years ago to release the secret within her.

"Listen to me, Franck, we gave people a destiny. The bordellos in those days were beautiful places. The johns circulated freely through the rooms. There was entertainment. Dancing, *bal-musette*, smoking rooms. Of course, we had to deal with the police, but this is France, Franck. Things can be discussed. I need some money, Franck ..."

She glanced down at her crotch.

"It's all over now. I don't blame them. Why should I blame them? Franck, you know something ... you look terrible."

The boudin and mashed potatoes arrived ...

II

One of the reasons you keep running into the same actors in the global café scene is that these places are basically high-end franchise operations for the lost souls of the world. Whether it's Harry's Bar, the Café Carlyle in New York or *Le Fouquet's* on the Champs Elysées, which I was about to enter, you can program these people as easily as the consumers at McDonalds or your local Burger King. Just substitute Chablis Laroche for the root beer and *souris d'agneau confite au romarin* for the big whoppers and you have the ticket.

I always walk into a café periscope up, do a quick survey to see if there is any loose *poontang*, as the hillbillies call it, and park myself within a table or maximum two of the prey for the evening. As the thermal sensors moved to the right side, who do I see, but Sheba herself sitting at a table with a Paki wearing too many rings, looking bored, dabbling idly at the remains of a *Baba au*

Rhum, while sipping a vodka martini. She wore a fur coat that looked pretty fresh off the rack. Her eyes bugged out when she saw me, no doubt at the promise of an escape route from her current beau but, credit where it's due, the enthusiasm was there.

"Franck!"

Waving me to a table on the other side of *Le Fouquet's*, at a safe distance from her escort.

"Franck, it is really so good to see you. Where *on earth* have you been? Come, let's sit down, Franck. You have to tell me everything."

She pulled a cell phone out of her purse. I glanced over at her Paki pal, picking up his own unit five tables away.

"Ranjit, something has come up, and it's rather serious. I had better meet you back at the hotel. *Non, non,* I beg your pardon! You want to tie me up with what! Ridicule, listen, later, I can't get into it, just go back. *Chérie.*"

Ranjit understood and Ranjit laughed and Ranjit stood up, good-naturedly waving the waiter to his table.

"So, Sheba, tell me all about Ranjit."

"Him?" she inquired, as if conducting an archeological dig. "Nobody, really. I'm helping him, in my own way. You seem awfully curious, Franck. Who are you working for these days? The CIA?"

"Not at all. I'm strictly private sector."

"I once worked for the DST. The French secret service." She stopped short, recalling something. "Franck, have you figured out the answer to my question?"

"Ask a question, you get the answer. Anything, Sheba."

"About your fantasy."

"I actually did give this a little thought recently. Let me tell you a little anecdote, Sheba. When I worked criminal assizes, occasionally, it was pretty rare, but occasionally they'd catch a big fish, someone who actually ran things, as opposed to being a runner, or an enforcer. One day, a kingpin, the genuine article, was escorted into the courtroom for a preliminary hearing. His name was McNeill. My partner, Hervé Bourque, represented him. McNeill always had a few big-hair, big titted broads hanging from his elbow, and had a phalanx of thugs, ex-boxers and hit-men at his beck and call, laughing at his jokes, pushing reporters away, generally scaring the shit out of people. That particular day, I think I was entering a few guilty pleas, and wondered whether McNeill didn't have a lot more figured out than me. Shortest distance between two points type of thing. McNeill's dead now. But still, he had it figured out in a way."

She laughed. And the laugh was genuine. Even now, particularly now, I can see there were times she found things genuinely amusing.

"You want to be a gangster, Franck! Oh, that's so funny. Franck Robinson, gangster. What next!"

"Don't worry about it, I can switch fantasies, no problem. You remember what we talked about in Montreal? Olive tree, overlooking the ocean, all of that. I'm thinking that nothing could make me happier."

She frowned, as if I had resurrected a bad memory.

"All right, all kidding aside. I actually saw a shrink back in Montreal. You had some kind of effect on me, baby. I asked her what my problem was. Assuming I had a problem. She said my fantasy was to fuck the city of Paris."

She stared at me. Come to think of it, it wasn't just her cunt. It was the cumulative effect of the saliva oozing up like a long dead geyser between her lips, her Grecian ass, her siren voice, and how they hypnotized me into believing that satanic cunt and its insatiable desires were actually good for me.

"Fuck Paris?"

"That's right."

"*Baiser toute une ville. C'est quand même curieux.*" She smiled. "Who are you running away from, Franck?"

I reached into my own grab bag of enemies and pulled out a recent candidate.

"A man named Spike."

"Spike, horrible name. What does it mean, *clou*? So *américain*. I am so glad to see you again, Franck. Should we get married?"

She pulled out a powder pack, flipped it open, looked into the mirror.

"Don't worry about it, Ranjit's gone back to the hotel."

She laughed.

"*Tu es vraiment marrant, Franck.* Now, I recall why I liked you. You are funny. What do you need?"

"I think I might need a little haven for a while. And I'm flush, provided Spike doesn't show up."

"My car's outside, Franck."

"What about Ranjit?"

She laughed, and I like to think that, in her own way, she was enjoying the moment.

"I missed you, Franck. I had totally forgotten you, but I missed you all the same."

We drove all night, and arrived in La Rochelle right on the Atlantic coast in the Southwest in the late morning. She parked her Audi at beachside, and we walked along the ramparts of the port area, passing under a medieval clock marking the entrance into the walled old city. Her flat was on *rue Gambetta*, accessible through an inner courtyard. We walked up to another door, marked Escalier B. She punched in a four digit code, and the door clicked open. She walked down the corridor ahead of me and turned around.

"*Chez moi.* For now."

Once inside, she showed me into her living room, and disappeared into another room. I dropped onto a California divan, scoped out the place. On the wall opposite, a star of David hung, dead centre. Beneath it, a jangle of pictures in a calculated disorder, each portraying Sheba in different poses. A vampire. An interior shot, her back to the camera, staring through a window onto the desolate Atlantic shore. An Audrey Hepburn *Breakfast at Tiffany's* pose. In the next, an artful twist of a beret and a set of shades gave her the look of a terrorist. The last, a black and white shot from the back of a vintage Citroën. She wore a black pillbox with Egyptian motifs, a checkered dress with a v-neck and held a Colt 45 flat against her loins. Her left leg was propped up on the bumper.

I recalled a conversation with Hervé over Scotch one evening back in Montreal. Hervé was a rare enough bird, had been through wars, both domestic and military, and understood most of the base rules of engaging in human conflict. I inquired whether it was true that French broads liked to throw knives and dishes around as a form of foreplay.

"It's been known to happen."

"I've heard those Mediterranean sluts are breathy little whores, but a little on the petulant side."

He'd shrugged, smiled knowingly. Poured me another Scotch.

"*Mon cher ami*, I'm from the Midi. If a woman throws a plate at you, you fire two back."

"And if that doesn't stop her?"

"Then it's a good *aller-retour.*"

An *aller-retour*, he explained, was an open-ended cuff across one cheek, quickly followed by a backhand on the other as the recipient regained her balance. A *return ticket*.

Sheba re-appeared with a bottle of *Moet & Chandon* on a silver plateau, two champagne flutes, six lines of coke and an assortment of pharmaceuticals."

"For you, Franck. *A ton service.*"

She poured out a glass of the bubbly.

"Try some of this. Christophe bought it for me. He's a rep for the Rothschilds. Christophe has done a lot of things for me."

"I'll bet he has."

"How long are you staying here, Franck?"

"I haven't decided yet."

"What do you think? That you can just stroll into my house, and fuck me, like a *pute*?"

I pretended to mull that one over for a moment.

"That's right. I'm going to fuck you. But, not like a whore. I'm going to fuck you my way. Now, give me some more of Christophe's champagne."

I felt better immediately. Whatever we were preparing to do would take a while to play out.

She walked across the room to a window overlooking her terrace, which in turn overlooked the old harbour, and a skew of yachts and catamarans moored for the evening. Behind that, a stretch of the Atlantic ocean. She had lit a Dunhill cigarette. She liked Dunhills, because the packs contained miniature retro lithographs of Dusenbergs, Bentleys, Rolls-Royces. The cigarette pack disappeared and, in its place, she held a sheaf of papers. In her left hand, a gold butane lighter, a yellow-blue flame shooting out of it towards the bottom corner of the paper. For a moment, she allowed the flames to lick up the A4 sheet, then tossed the whole scroll of paper carelessly out the window. We watched the flaming bundle fall downwards, its smoked edges rising upwards.

"That was my last will and testament, Franck. I think I need to revise it."

"Very wise to review these things periodically. Guess what; you're looking at the meister of the two page will. Bullet-proof, honey."

"Are you in receiver mode, Franck? *Tu me reçois cinq sur cinq?*"

She glanced out the window.

"I once defenestrated a man at this very spot."

I sat back on the couch, taking it in, sucking on a slim Danneman cigar, listening to every word she *evoked*, for the words that came out of her mouth were entirely disconnected with the message she was conveying.

I drank another glass of Christophe's champagne and smoked a cigarette. This was relatively new turf, so it was fairly important to lay down some ground rules. Generally, the trick was to never give a woman what she asked for right away. Once you made them beg, they were yours. Which led to another set of problems.

At some point in the conversation, the coke kick-started me, and for a second, or an hour, who can tell, my mind drifted. When I came out of it, I was staring at the photos of her. Sheba had disappeared again. Her voice from a room down the corridor.

"Franck."

I waited a few minutes, took my time, then strolled up to her bedroom. What was the rush? I was already inside enemy territory. But, she didn't call again. I give her credit for that. She had rigged up a semi-transparent veil, which hung from the ceiling—like one of those mosquito nets in the African Queen. She was nude, and lay in the bed, beneath that veil, not moving, not saying a word.

I had a strange feeling at the time, as if I were trapped inside one of those old 16 mm movie cameras, and had somehow become part of the celluloid.

I took off my clothes, lifted the veil, climbed onto the bed. I looked into her eyes. The right eye seemed to scrutinize me. There was something lifeless in it, like a fish eye. The left eye was a conductor, a lightning rod, seemed to suck everything into a maelstrom behind the iris.

"So, Franck. Fuck me your way."

I thought her eyes were agate blue that first evening, but I never really learned the real colour. She had as many sets of lenses as she did shoes. Generally, fucking a woman is a time of day when you can finally look at her objectively, beneath all the dissimulation, and the makeup and the fine sentiments, and you can see her in her bare moment of need, when she comes clean and tries to own you. I could already see that Sheba worked differently. She was a consumer, and I was perishable goods.

We lay there for a while. Then I turned her flat onto her stomach. Pulled her up by the haunches, and stuck my prick into her.

"Franck, hit me Franck, please."

I was pumping into her, really enjoying it, but the parallel thoughts were there. I was wondering at the time, even as I pumped into her, what do normal human beings do? What the fuck do they do with their time? Her voice intervened.

"Non, Franck, *je veux que tu m'encules*. C'mon, Franck, stick it right up my ass, just pretend I am really your little Afghan fuck boy. You can do it, Franck."

I pulled my prick out of her. She was on all fours. A female mammal in the receptive period of the sexual cycle. My prick was chafed. Her head turned around to face me.

"Please, Franck. I am begging you. Have mercy, Franck. *Encule-moi.*"

Later, sometime in the middle of the night, I woke up, like I always did. I pulled back the veil hanging over the bed, walked into the other room, lit a cigarette, sat down at a laptop I'd brought with me, started writing a letter. Occasionally, I looked out the window, onto the beach. The Atlantic ocean. Not that long ago, I had been on the other side. Montreal.

I heard a voice, whispering behind me, which I initially mistook for the Atlantic waves lapping onto the shore. Then, it came again.

"*Salaud.*"

I turned around. She looked really pissed about something. Her eyes flashing. Brief hallucination that she was twisting in the middle of a windstorm.

"Don't you ever do that to me again."

"What's the problem?"

"Nobody leaves me in the middle of the night. Nobody."

I stubbed out my cigarette.

"Too bad. I'm not nobody."

I returned to my typing. Lit another cigarette. Men have pricks, and they're like heat-seeking missiles, and the detectors pick up the cunt, and the cunt is at the service of a woman, and god knows what they want, but the cunt is the best thing going for them, and masks whatever lies beneath. I might even have been writing some such thing to Hervé, because I was distracted for a moment, or an hour, who knows, and during that time gap, she went into full flight, and caught me real good on the side of the face. Clawing out miniature trenches. I took her roughly by the shoulders and shook her until her head bobbed like a puppet's. Then a voice coming out of me I didn't recognize.

"YOU STOP IT OR YOU'RE GOING RIGHT THROUGH THE FUCKING WALL, HEAR ME!!"

She flopped like a rag doll. Her eyes closed.

"Christ, baby, are you okay?"

Her eyes opened. She nodded and I helped her to her feet. THWACK. She delivered a savage direct straight to the nose, breaking it. Then, just like automatic pilot, KERSMACK. I backhanded her hard enough to knock her right in the air, then down to the floor. Everything went quiet for a moment. Just her laying there, and me standing there. A trickle of blood came out of her mouth.

Then, she did something which made me so damned hot, I think I must have gone a little bit crazy, maybe even permanently. She crawled onto the floor. Propped herself up again, like a dog. She was petite, and she just waited there, passive, expectant. Her ass at that point was still unscarred, but I was staring at that CUNT of hers. Like, we're having a low-grade bacterial, syphilitic conversation, just me and that CUNT. And the cunt is saying: "You better just fuck me, Franck. You just BETTER FUCK ME!!!"

III

Say what you like about women's liberation, in my experience the legal profession is still pretty well divided along sex lines. Basically, men only went into practice for the money. Women had other reasons, some of which eventually led them to bail out, or seek the protective awning of a bureaucratic office so they could still feel they were doing something useful. But, once they found their niche with the government, they could make your life miserable enough. So, my first call from Margaret Tillman of the Law Society was not necessarily a sign I was up to be appointed Queen's counsel.

"Mr Robinson."

"This is Robinson."

"Margaret Tillman. Law Society Investigations Branch."

"Good morning, Canada! What is it, about forty below in the Great White North? How are the Maple Leafs doing?"

"I'm not calling to discuss the weather, Mr Robinson. Or ice hockey."

"Get to the point, Margaret. Haven't I sent my annual dues?"

"We've received a complaint filed by a certain Mr. Spike Nussbaum. You were counsel for the plaintiff in Sutherland vs Lloyds, Mr Robinson?"

"Not on behalf of Mr Nussbaum."

"So, you do know him."

"The worst kind, Margaret. The unhappy spouse of a client."

"What does the name Finister Ebrams mean to you?"

"Name rings a bell."

"He was a witness for the defence in the Holly Reichman trial. Mr Ebrams has indicated that you threatened him with criminal proceedings."

"I strictly deny. Look, Margaret, it is Margaret, isn't it? I don't even practice law anymore."

"That's not what our investigators have reported."

"I think you have the wrong Franck Robinson."

"Thirty-five writs have been issued in your name in collections matters over the last six months. Defendant counsel was surprised to discover that you were unreachable when they tried to contact you."

"Well, who the hell is doing that? Get off your butt and do your job, Margaret. Throw the book at him. What year call to the bar are you, anyways, Margaret?"

"Do you have any children, Mr Robinson?"

"What's that got to do with it?"

"Are you familiar with the recent deadbeat dad legislation? Let me fill you in, as I understand you've been out of the country. As a defaulting debtor under Montreal Family Court Order dated 14 December 2001, your driver's licence has been revoked and your banking assets frozen. You have also been set down for a disciplinary hearing before the Benchers Committee to be held in two weeks."

"Sorry, booked solid."

"For the moment, I only require an address for service of process, Mr Robinson. You have a fixed address, Mr Robinson?"

"*Rue Scribe,* number 9, ninth arrondissement. Paris."

"Isn't that the American Express office, Mr Robinson?"

"A home away from home. What of it?"

"Good day, Mr Robinson. You'll be hearing from us."

I returned to the beach, spotted her sunning under a parasol. She wore only the bottom of a bathing suit, her back arched, as she gazed out into the half moon bay where we now spent our afternoons.

"You see those three islands, Franck? *Ile de Ré* was for the celebrities. *Ile d'Oléron* for the regular tourists. And Fort Bayard the Southwest's version of Alcatraz. But, you and me, if we stick together, we can have that and a lot more."

I realized it wasn't enough for me to have her or possess her. I wanted something more and, though I couldn't pin it down, I knew she still had plenty she hadn't given away, and that somehow, I would never get. We listened to the waves lap onto the shore in silence, me behind her, my arms wrapped around her waist. She reached for a hexagonal container of coconut cream and handed it to me.

"*Tu veux bien, chéri?* If you oil me down, I will tell you a story. I am sure you will like it."

She lay back, and exposed her tits to the world. Every time I was privy to a close up of a woman's breasts, I did a mental gauge of how long it would be before things deteriorated. Physically, so to speak. In Sheba's case, you knew it couldn't last forever. On the other hand, it didn't seem she could ever be anything but beautiful or dead. Nothing in between.

"There was a girl in my class at the *lycée*. She was demure and modest. A real egghead. But, she had obviously never had a boyfriend. I had been observing her for some time. Initially, I ignored her completely, or I would mock her. Oh, here's *crâne d'oeuf,* how is *crâne d'oeuf* doing today? Just that simple comment, I could see it crushed her. Because I was convinced that she found me very attractive and was thoroughly intimidated by me. Then, from one day to the next, I seduced her. We became best of friends. When she told me her sixteenth birthday was upcoming, I immediately insisted that she must come for dinner, my parents will be absent, I said, it'll only be the two of us. During the week preceding her birthday, I would bump into her physically, as if by accident, and I could see it was having an effect on her that she didn't even dare confess to herself. So, on her birthday, when we arrived *chez Maman et Papa,* oh-la-la, if you could have seen the suppressed fear and embarassed desire in her face as we climbed the hill ... like Jesus during the passion or St-Sebastien as the arrows pierced into his torso. I was explaining to her that I wanted to "do her up" like a real lady, that I could see the *unbelievably* sexy woman hiding beneath, well, Franck, I have always been amazed at the hidden vanity of even the homeliest people, it is amazing how easy it is to bring it out. Upon entering, I brought her directly upstairs to the *boudoir. Tu t'imagines, Franck?* Can you imagine? I was terribly aroused."

"By her?"

Sheba brushed her hair, surveying the waves rather than me as she considered the question.

"Don't be a fool. No. I saw the possibilities of trans-forming human beings. Moulding them. But, there was something else."

A young girl walking along the shoreline before us. The tide turning to low, and the waves lapping lazily onto the shore before receding. Sheba frowned.

"It was an energy entirely contained with me. I had wound myself into a real state. But it wasn't desire. No. Something else ..."

She paused. A jagged, crepuscular streak of crimson now traced a path across her cheekbones.

"No. I felt angry somehow. I wanted to hit her, slap her hard across the face. As punishment. She was a superficial fool to renounce her intelligence for the cheap parlour game I was playing. I detested her for it."

"But not enough to stop."

"Of course not. I commanded her to disrobe immedi-ately."

"In those words."

"As a matter of fact, yes. I was very ... imperious," she responded, her eyes now limpid, vacuous. She smiled at her tendentious, arcane language. "Besides, Franck, I had no choice. Makeup demands control if it is to be a weapon."

She fell silent again for several minutes. Then she wound her torso, until her eyes met mine. I looked past her. Three more windsurfers ogling her, commenting. They appeared to recognize her. They had definitely no-ticed her.

"Have you ever seen photos of Dachau or Auschwitz, Franck? You would never guess these people had once been lawyers, doctors or bankers. *Pillars of society.*"

The phrase pushed her lip into a curl, as if her taste buds had unexpectedly come across a sliver of lemon rind.

"Once the person has surrendered her right to her appearance, you are more than halfway there. Not that the issue was ever in doubt. Once I knew I had her, I became increasingly stern with her. It was so interesting, Franck. As if she were inside one of those medieval torture devices, and I was turning the wheel crank methodically, according to my own rhythms, until I had her whimpering. It was *extraordinaire*. I think it was the first time that I had watched a human being completely surrender her will."

She fell silent.

"That's it?"

"That's it."

"Sorry, that doesn't cut it as an end of story."

"*Non*? Well, too bad, Franck. The rest isn't worth telling. Besides," she added coquettishly, "it's privileged information. But trust me. The rest was easy, Franck."

A strange image appeared in the mind's eye. Her skin a tropical aquarium, and lurking inside, a lime-green reptilian shape, eyes bulging from the head, unblinking, prehistoric, the real driving force of her being, and the rest just a shell. The grains of sand had heated up the beach, making it increasingly difficult to remain seated.

"The next day, once we were together in class again, I chose a reverse role. I treated her abominably. As if I had caught her defiling herself in a sacred place. I whispered things to her, told her she was *dégueulasse*, that she had defiled me. I had orchestrated the whole exercise from A to Z, but I insisted to her it was a sign of dementia. Then I flew into a rage, and started shrieking at her that she was a slut, depraved, a whore."

"How did she take that?"

"First, you must tell me what you think."

"I don't think anything. She entered into the bargain freely. It was her problem."

"The following day, while walking home from school, we spotted the S.A.M.U. ambulances outside the house and a long trickle of blood on the sidewalk outside. She had hurled herself right through the window of her fourth floor study, committed suicide."

She had been in front of me throughout this conversation, and I could not see her eyes. Now, she pivoted to the side and faced me, examining me in the process of examining her.

"What do you make of it all, Franck?"

"Well, speaking as plaintiff counsel, a dead person isn't worth much, quantum-wise. Now, if she'd broken her neck, or suffered brain damage, but survived, different ball game altogether."

She frowned.

"Franck, I want to know your personal opinion. What you really think."

"Let me put it this way. You never actually shoved her out the window, right?"

"Of course not."

"In fact, you weren't even there at the time she jumped."

"No."

"Case closed. Motion for dismissal. No triable issue."

"Franck. You don't believe me, do you? That it really happened."

"Why wouldn't I? This stuff happens all the time. Survival of the species and all that. Not everybody makes it. Sounds to me like her time was up. Maybe she thought she could fly."

She mulled that one over for a moment or two, then reached for a hairbrush and began pulling at a tangle in her hair.

"So, what's with all the questions? Police look into the matter?"

"Oh, there was an investigation, but nothing much. No, it's just sometimes I think about the expression on her face the last time I saw her. It intrigued me. Like something had crumbled inside her. It really left an impression on me, Franck. Later, I went home, and tried to imitate the expression she had in my mirror. But I couldn't do it. Somehow, it escaped me."

She shrugged.

"She was naïve. Nothing more. *Une pauvre fille.*"

A few days later, we took a day trip on the Poitiers line in Vienne. She had brought a small picnic basket and was wearing a red and white checkered summer dress to the knees. Outside the train, the land a long, uninterrupted stretch of reclaimed swamp. She had just informed me for the first time that, unlike an earlier version she had served up, her father was still alive.

She wore a slight trace of makeup, and her hair was tied back in a bun, Simone de Beauvoir style. Demure, placid, timid, dutiful.

She reached inside her purse; and pulled out three black and white photos. The first showed a soldier, his face agape, the jaw hanging and his body slack, as he was carried down a stretch of road in front of a military barracks. He was in a state of drunken hilarity.

"He looks a fool. But it is the only picture where I have ever seen him happy."

The second photo showed three men standing in the midst of a stretch of the Algerian desert. Each of the three were dressed in standard issue khaki-coloured uniforms of the paras. The man in the middle had his left foot propped on a box. He stared into the camera. The nose aquiline, and the features dark, Mediterranean, saturnine.

"My father ... no one has met him before you. He lives as a recluse. He was an Indochina veteran. They took him prisoner after the Dien Bien Phu debacle. Later, he was a *para* in Algeria. He is *lunatique*, my father. Very moody."

The third photo showed the same man, this time standing in the doorway of a villa, overlooking a rocky, chalk-white promontory on the shore of the Mediterranean somewhere. The man wore broad cotton pants, and what appeared to be a denim shirt. His face young, but now his hair grey and cut crew. Like a crag of an eroding limestone quarry. The shirt was pinned up on the left hand side at the elbow.

"He lost his arm in the war?"

"No. That happened later. In Algeria. He was trying to defuse a bomb."

The train slowed to a halt in front of a small, yellow building. SNCF Lusignan. We descended, and stood for a moment on the quay. An outdated schedule half torn from the outside wall of the building. A uniformed man, wearing thickly rimmed glasses walked past, ignoring us.

"We have to walk from here. There is no other way."

The house was perched on the upper rise of a road leading towards the village centre. The rear garden was a graded, mezzanine of tiered plots overlooking a deep ravine. The old man sat in a chair under the shade of a pear tree. He was holding a chamois, which he used to strain blackberries into a large metal vat. The nose thick and the face hidden by a thick *bacchantes* moustache, twisted upwards at the extremities. When he caught sight of us, he stared for a moment without making any move to rise or extend a greeting.

A pre-school infant held his forearm, watched us without moving forward. Her shoulder-length, stone-grey hair was tied back in a ponytail. She wore a white blouse over a navy-blue pleated skirt. She lifted her arm, pointed at me.

"Papy, c'est lui mon nouveau papa?"

"Tschh. Embrasse ta mère."

She skipped towards Sheba. Stopped short in front of her and curtseyed. Dutifully kissed her on each cheek, then reached for her hand, a little on the coy side, I thought, for a kid.

"Bonjour, maman. Je suis contente de te voir."

The two of them turned together, descended a set of curving steps, and entered a wine cellar. He pointed at the flat surface he was working on, the stump of a fallen oak.

"Rabelais lived in this house. He is thought to have planted this tree, while it was still a tree. Until the storm, at the beginning of the year. I had to take it all down."

Sheba and the girl reappeared, Sheba carrying a bottle of champagne and three glass flutes. She placed the champagne on the table. The old man motioned towards her.

"Open it."

Sheba popped the cork. We watched the bubbly flow over the neck of the bottle onto the ground. She poured the champagne. The girl watched me, saying nothing. The old man pulled her closer to him, turned towards Sheba.

"Have you paid your respects to your mother?"

"We will visit the cemetery this afternoon."

"Bien," he responded. The tone was flat, pro-forma. He shifted his unsmiling gaze back to the girl.

"Now you will have a new home. But not before the marriage."

Sheba interjected.

"We haven't yet set a date, papa."

She turned around and walked towards the house. She now wore a white apron over the dress, which was tied in a bow behind her back at the waist. He tracked her with his eyes until she disappeared.

"How long have you known my daughter?"

I shrugged my shoulders.

"A year," I hazarded.

"Not long. She has been *odieuse* with you?"

I said nothing.

"If she hasn't yet, don't worry. *Ne vous inquiétez pas.* You will know her before long."

He glanced at the girl.

"*I raised that child.*"

Sheba re-emerged from the rear of the house. She approached us, keeping her eyes on her father.

"We cannot remain any longer, papa. Monsieur Robinson has an appointment."

"*Bien.*"

He turned towards the young girl.

"*Viens, chérie. On accompagne ta mère à la gare.*"

The girl ran towards her mother, stopped, curtseyed once. Kissed her mother on the cheek.

"*Merci pour la visite, maman.*"

For an impromptu performance, it looked pretty rehearsed. I wondered what the old man's wife might have to say if she were still around. The girl and her grandfather escorted us out the gate and down the road towards the train station, Sheba and I behind, the girl hopping and skipping alongside her grandfather, filling in the space of the missing limb.

We arrived at the Lusignan quay three minutes prior to departure. The tracks were lined with uprooted trees and the rain was starting to fall. Work crews were surveying the damage from the storm, pulling fallen trees further away from the tracks and cutting them into portable pieces with electric handsaws. We walked past the unmanned ticket office and onto the quay, the young girl singing:

> *... lundi matin, l'empereur sa femme et le petit prince*
> *sont venu chez moi, pour me serrer le pince*
> *comme j'étais parti, le petit prince a dit*
> *puisque c'est ainsi, nous reviendrons mardi ...*

Then stopped suddenly and covered her ears as the screech of the train halting drowned out all else. The old man whispered something into his daughter's ear. The young girl kissed her mother. Now, the old man turned towards me, shook my hand, then turned away. Just a series of freeze-frames and sketches for a future composition. Title: *Départ sur le quai*. Watercolour. Artist unknown. Title: *Le Manchot*. Oil on canvas. Discovered in the attic of a local prefect murdered five years previous. He trudged down the length of the quay, his shoulders slumped, the girl skipping alongside to keep up. He never said much during the visit, other than that laconic *"we raised that child."* He had obviously not regained whatever he had lost on the bigger battle field a long time ago. He had the girl. That seemed to be enough for him.

As for his daughter, maybe he even loved her, if love is a taciturn stare into the bottom of a glass, or a rueful shake of the head. Or maybe, if he didn't love her anymore, he once did. Or maybe, before civilian life did a job on him, he enjoyed his life in the military, if a photo of an infantry gunner being dragged dead drunk across a stretch of Saigon road is enjoying life. But, by the time I got to him, he was a one-armed silhouette you would scarcely notice walking down the main street of Lusignan, a village of seventy-five people. He even walked down that railway platform like it was a gang-plank, after planting a kiss on Sheba's cheek that looked more like a warning than anything else I could make out.

The train rolled out of the Lusignan *gare*. We watched the old man and the girl climbing the road outside the train slowly exiting the Lusignan station. Then the train rounded a corner and they were gone.

"*Un vrai salaud*," she pronounced delicately, still gazing out the window.

She remained silent for a long moment. When she looked back at me, she faintly smiled, as if recalling my existence upon emerging from a coma.

"Do you know, Franck, I wanted to kill my parents when I was young?"

"How did your mother die?"

"It doesn't matter how. It is why."

"All right. So, why did she die?"

"She died because her time was up, Franck."

I followed her gaze. The train was passing through an open field towards a small forest in the shape of a figure eight. It didn't really matter where we were going. Somehow the visit confirmed for me that Sheba could take care of things, that it wasn't my turf, and that I should stop worrying about it. I relaxed slightly. Things would happen. I would deal with them then.

"Have I ever told you the legend of the Mélusine fairy?"

"No."

"Every day, she could be seen drawing water from a well in the village of Lusignan. Her presence drove many men mad, unable to stand the sheer force of her beauty. One day, a brave man, very handsome, courted her. You may love me, she responded to his courting, but during the night, from Saturday to Sunday, I cannot see you. Ever."

I half listened to her, while performing my own usual mind split. She was a pure lunatic, but from my standpoint, what woman wasn't, or for that matter, what man wasn't? Nobody looked very good close up.

"The man loved her, became possessed by her within hours, until finally it was not enough to have her six days out of the seven. All of this happened within a short time. When Saturday fell, he followed her back to the well. And took her against her will."

As far as I could make out, it was either a warning, or some way of punctuating recent events. According to her psychic talmudic tablets and ethical scrolls, and her need to be *clean*, papa had been dealt with and would never enter our lives again. As for the little girl, only time would tell. Maybe she would become a whore like her mother. Or reverse the trend and become a chartered accountant. These things are impossible to predict in advance. When you come right down to it, it's a question of personal taste more than anything.

Several hours later, we arrived at *gare Montparnasse*. As we emerged above ground, I caught a view of *boulevard Montparnasse* where it crosses *Vaugirard*. I could see the signs for *La Rotonde* and *Le Select*. The last time I had been in *Le Select*, it was for a champagne breakfast before catching a plane for the Dry Tortugas and a photo shoot of barracudas. And now, centuries later, I was touring the city with a whore, my life mate. Til death do us part.

"Wait," she ordered, disappearing into a Guerlain shop. As I lit a Marboro, a young woman approached, but instead of entering the boutique, she lingered, peering into the display window of the shop. She was a sassy looking henna-streaked thing, wearing a pastel, cut-away dress. Her whole appearance had something accidental about it, in appearance unplanned, but in fact a collage of items and impressions which had been carefully prepared to deliberately produce the effect referred to by the French as *insouciant*. A partially executed brush stroke on the canvas. Spoiled and self-indulgent, right down to the crocodile stickpin on her skirt and the pillbox hat with the veil. On the other hand, she looked sane. I lit another Marlboro and considered for a moment what it might be like to live with someone who both gave good head and paid taxes. The thought didn't seem sustainable as a world-view, but it stayed there long enough for the girl to evaporate. I stared through the spot where she had been standing, down the gullet of the 14th *arrondissement* of this whore of a city, reviewing my remaining options.

I briefly considered leaving her. Letting her work the thing out herself. Whatever the thing was. Paris was good for that. You could walk around the corner, lose someone and move on. People did it every day. I had employed the strategy myself, but doing it now would call for a different approach. I had improvised before.

But I was lethargic. My will was fading. Something vital was being steadily sucked out of me.

IV

I was driving a steel-gray Renault Talisman down a Vaucluse road in the direction of the Luberon mountain range. The Talisman was designed and drove like a smart bomb, as if the Pentagon were tele-guiding you towards an as yet undetermined target. The road divided the *Côte du Rhone* vineyards from those of *Châteauneuf-du-pape*. On the left side, the caked clay soil of the *Côte*. On the right, a chalky soil covered by small stones which surrounded the vines planted in the bitumic soil, reflecting the sun onto the base of the stock of the vine.

She slipped a CD onto the player, a Rojas tune called 'En la Orilla del Mundo'. She closed her eyes, her features relaxing into a posture of pleasure, or at least as close to pleasure as she could come. It didn't matter what went on in her head. It was a core realization — my own form of satori — that you never really knew what was going on in anyone's head, not even your own. Just because people cried didn't mean they were sad. It just meant tears were rolling down their faces.

We were on another *route nationale*, well into the Luberon range now, approaching a village named La Coste, perched on a hilltop, and principally known as the childhood abode of Donatien, Marquis de Sade. The sun hard and glaring, the high whistle of the Mistral wind causing the car windows to rattle.

"Sade was right, Franck. Not everyone deserves freedom. Some people defile the gifts they have been granted."

I pulled onto roadside, stopped, turned off the ignition.

"I'm beginning to think you were right. It was in the cards, you and me. We had to finish things off together. It was meant to be."

I shoved the car seat back and she crawled on top of me. She looked at me, another question in her eyes, riding up and down. She could do things that would look ridiculous on anyone else, like the bandana she had wrapped around her temple. I'm fucking her, looking past her out the window at cars passing by, she is talking to me in a rhythmic monotone, trying to explain something through her desire, the only thing that could hold her captive.

"Franck," she's saying, "it's a two-way street. When I fuck, I want to extinguish life, and when I extinguish life, I want to fuck. Can you understand, Franck?"

The chateau was a few hundred metres away, jutting out of a steep, rising promontory overlooking the departmental road where we had parked. I started up the car, then turned onto the access road, which wound upwards in an S curve, over a river, then through a tree orchard, and lands cultivated with corn, soya, sunflowers. The remainder of the property was forest and heath, with a spring running through it. Closer to the chateau itself, a large round swimming pool, several older dwellings, a large hangar. Outbuildings, the signs of a farm manor or former estate. Then a series of tiered gardens, leading up to an asphalt driveway to a four-car garage at a lower level on the East side of the manor.

"They call this a *Maison de Maitre.* The Manor of the Master. Positively feudal. Wait until you see the inside, Franck. And the owner. Some people, they occupy positions in society, Franck, and they are nothing better than *merde*."

She slammed the door, and walked up a path rising towards the main entrance, with two Corinthian pillars marking the perimeter of a hemicycled porch. After a few minutes, she still hadn't returned. I walked up towards the entrance, lit another cigarette. As I approached, I noticed the door was partially ajar. I could hear her voice. An elderly male voice, responding in a rapid, tremolo register.

"This is just not appropriate. You must leave."

And her mild, but firm rejoinder.

"It's time for your check-up, *monsieur le baron*."

"Really, I just cannot see you now. Please, go."

I entered a large lobby, decorated with Louis XV furniture. At the entrance, an Egyptian mosque lamp and a Bohemian enamelled humpen, for welcoming guests. 17th century Venetian glass. Clear, colourless cristallo, decorated with enamelled and gilt decoration. The wall was covered with paintings. Still, nobody visible. On the west side of the room, another door ajar, leading into an oval drawing room. I followed the sound of Sheba's voice and the high strung elderly voice. The man looked like he might be the president of a yacht club, or a freemason. An ascot tightened around his neck. Blue blazer, My eye caught a glass-enclosed wall case with a collection of Montoyo cigars.

"I have something for you."

She opened her purse and removed an ivory, pearl-handled hairbrush.

Monsieur le baron stared at the hairbrush, as if it were a handgun. The hairbrush reminded him of something.

"*Madame la baronne* has gone shopping for the afternoon and *monsieur le baron* looks elsewhere for affection. *Mais le chat ne nous caresse pas. Il se caresse à nous ...*"

She continued to tap the underside of the brush onto the palm of her hand. *Monsieur le baron* stared at the brush, and the longer he stared, the more he seemed to become something, or somebody else. He seemed to be struggling with something, then his head bowed slightly. He retreated a step. She advanced one step towards him, cradling the brush in her hand. Something about their movements struck me as rehearsed. Then, he noticed me for the first time.

"Who is that?"

"Ah, Doctor Thompson, you have arrived. Excellent. Before the examination begins, I invite you to survey the premises. We have quite a collection here, Doctor Thompson. Seven Watteaus, nine Bouchers, eight Fragonards. A nice series of Dutch 'little masters' of small-scale landscapes and genre scenes. If you toured the galleries, Doctor Thompson, you would see Rembrandts, not to mention some masterpieces by the Flemings Rubens and Van Dyck. I seem to recall a Velazquez. And, interestingly, absolutely nothing after the 18th century. A veritable Luddite, Doctor Thompson."

She crossed the floor to a glass-enclosed display case.

"Tin-glazed earthenware in the form of Hispano-Moresque and Italian maiolica and French lead glaze. That piece looks like Palissy ware. I could be wrong. But, over here, we most definitely have prime examples of

English slipware and some more exotic samples of Iznik and Persian ware. Some: 18ᵗʰ-century celadon vases and a pair of Meissen ewers and two cups. Arms & Armour, ceramics, enamels, gold boxes, metalwork. The ancestors of our subject were decidedly more of the buccaneering variety than our domesticated subject. But, the blood grows thin, Doctor Thompson, the blood grows thin ... Doctor Thompson, the patient was most uncooperative during our last visit ..."

She paused. Frowned. Tapped the floor with the tip of her pumps. Acupuncture. She had pushed a button to the Baron's personal time tunnel, as his facial expression grew younger and younger. Seventy, sixty-fifty-forty-thirty-twenty-ten. A ten year old, naughty child with a lot of time on his hands.

"Such a good family, and such a naughty, naughty little boy. The unworthy heir to all this unearned wealth. So, we have had to train him, as best we can, in domestic duties and punish him when he is disobedient. Come here."

Speaking in a stern voice, cradling the pearl-coloured hairbrush in the palm of her hand. Ready and available for use.

"*Madame la baronne* has been overwrought. She doesn't have the energy to discipline this naughty little boy. Come here."

She sat down, turned her back on him. The baron seemed to have forgotten me. He crossed the floor, his head downcast. She passed him the brush. He began to brush her hair. The baron began. Began to brush. To brush her hair. The baron brushing her hair. Her profile visible to me. She snapped her fingers. And then, said this:

"Colonel Mustard. With the hairbrush. In the oval drawing room."

Upon hearing this phrase, the Baron flushed. He continued mechanically brushing her hair. A sixty-something child with a lot of time on his hands, brushing Sheba's hair.

"Doctor Thompson, as we discussed at our last conference, it is universally accepted that a significant number of men abuse their wives. What is not generally recognised is that women can, and do, abuse their houseboys. Now, there is a distinction here. Abused females can appeal to friends, relatives and even the police. They have access to shelters and help-lines. Estimating the number of battered wives is relatively easy. On the other hand, men who suffer pain and humiliation at the hands of wives, sisters, mothers, and female employers must hide their pain and shame. Up until very recently, studies reflect the belief that only a tiny minority of men are victims. Today there is a considerable weight of clinical evidence to the contrary. Men are victims, but they cannot appeal for help. Ergo, their interest to our laboratory as potential subjects."

She prodded the baron in his backside.

"And, why is this so, Doctor Thompson? One word. Fear. Fear is the essential ingredient in training any naughty boy. It may be fear of humiliation, fear of pain, or simply an ingrained terror of a strong dominant woman. But, once they are trained, Doctor Thompson, oh-la-la, you can do anything with them. We hope to present our findings in this regard at our next worldwide conference. How is our patient doing, Doctor Thompson?"

"He's behaving."

"Continue to observe, Doctor Thompson. To cement the obedience procedure indelibly in his mind, a mistress must arrange at least one witnessed event. It doesn't matter who sees him thrashed in his pink panties. It could be a relative. It could be a complete stranger. But until you can truthfully demonstrate your authority in front of a third party he will always believe he can revert."

She stood up, angry.

"And this is why the baron has been trying to avoid me. After two years of perfect obedience, still the old way of thinking persists! But, now I've got you back, don't I? Answer me!"

"Yes."

"Now, you little selfish *bitch*, who committed the murder?"

The baron emitted a diarrhetic giggle. Like shitting his pants. She cupped a hand around her ear like a sea urchin, as if she hadn't heard properly.

"*Pardon?*"

"Mrs. Peacock," he babbled, saliva dripping down his chin, "with the dildo in the pantry."

She smiled.

"That's better. Mrs. Peacock. With the dildo in the pantry."

The baron was sweating, glancing at the door of his own house. But, he seemed paralysed. She stared at him, in mock surprise.

"Is that something I see beneath your *blouse*? Are you secretly wearing your frilly petticoat ... *Maryse* ... ?"

The uttering of the name gelatinised the old man's insides. Six centuries of haughty nobility destroyed by the mention of a set of knickers. Then, as suddenly as she had assumed the persona of clinical dominatrix, she let it drop, a sneer of disgust crossing her face. And, I'm thinking of a sixteen-year-old girl who jumped out of a window a long time ago.

"*Il me dégoute.* Look at him, Doctor Thompson. The same person who was calling me a *salope*, only fifteen days ago. And, now, just a little boy, shitting himself. *Dégueulasse.*"

She walked across the room to a glass-enclosed, dark mahogany bookshelf. Tapped on the glass.

"You remember our last visit, my little *salope*, when we discovered your little *jardin secret*? Fifty years you've been keeping these papers secret, and now, finally, finally, the little dirty secret of secrets has been revealed."

"*Non.* That is not part of our agreement."

"That is not part of our agreement," she mimicked. "*J'en ai rien à branler de tes agreements.*"

She opened the cabinet, pulled out a sheaf of documents. Passed them to me.

"Read the first one, Doctor Thompson."

DOCUMENT NI-9912
Richtlinen fuer die Anwendung von Blausauere (Zyklon) zur Ungeziefervertilgung (Entwesung)

"These, Doctor Thompson, are guidelines for the use of Prussic acid, also known as Zyklon, for the extermination of vermin. Human disinfection. Thinning out the weaker elements."

"So, he's a Nazi. Big deal."

"Doctor Thompson, this document is one of the core pieces of revisionist historians, and various other old men — Freemasons, royalists, members of their little *boys' clubs,* groups trying to prove that the Jews were not killed during the Second World War. No Drancy, no Vel d'hiv, no Auschwitz, no Buchenwald. Here is another one, a volume authored by a certain J.C. Burg, titled *Maidanek in alle Ewigkeit?* And another: 'On the circumstances underlying the alleged "gas chamber" homicide of Struthof, the three successive and contra-

dictory confessions of Joseph Kramer.' Proof that the
Nazi gas chambers never existed. And, that's not all.
Here, we have a little departmental memo, dated 7 July,
1942:

> 'Attention: René Bousquet
> From: Vice-Prefect Dalmas
> Date: 7 July, 1942
>
> It is far preferable that the *Préfecture* organize
> this operation, rather than allow interference with
> a strictly French administrative jurisdiction. It can
> be justified on the same grounds as the August '41
> operation: Communist agitation after the Wehr-
> macht invasion of the Soviet Union.
>
> In the event the operation is approved, teams
> have been organised for July 16. 4 500 gendarmes,
> gardes mobiles, officers of the *police judiciaire* or
> from *renseignements généraux* shall make up the 900
> teams. Each team will be made up of three to four
> men. The operation will cover both Paris and the
> suburbs. I have requisitioned fifty buses. I would
> suggest that, if the public is concerned, we respond
> with a further instruction that, as a humanitarian
> gesture, *children should be permitted to accompany
> the parents of arrested Israelites.'*

"Truly, a piece of genius. But, during one infamous night
in '42, Doctor Thompson, over 22,000 Jews between the
ages of 16 and 55 were arrested by the French police in
the Paris region. Often blamed on the German occupier.
But, they never could have done it without the assistance of Bousquet, *Secrétaire Général* of the Police. The
Baron's immediate supervisor. You probably wouldn't
have noticed a piece of Juden vermin named Rebecca

Goldenstein, *n'est-ce pas?* But, our memory is long, so long, *monsieur le vice-prefet*. And, there are some things which are never forgiven. Not even on Yom Kippur."

She reached inside her slouch bag. Pulled out a pistol. A nine millimetre. Browning. High power. She pointed the trigger to his temple, cocked it. Kept her eyes on the baron, who was mute.

"They are all the same. All of them. First that grin while they look me over. Then, when they see 'such a pretty little girl' holding a pistol. Can you imagine? A 17 round detachable box, four inch barrel on it, a terrorist's dream, and all they can see is a pretty little girl. Do you see what television does? But after, they all look the same. *Pourquoi je ne te buterai pas sur le champ, monsieur le baron?* Give me a good reason not to put you out of your misery."

She cocked the trigger, pressing the barrel of the Browning harder against the temple of the old man.

"What is it you want?"

"Do, you know, Franck, that Goering was a transvestite? Just like the baron here. These were the superior *aryans* who planned our extermination. In private, cross-dressing sodomites. Now, tell us where you were transferred in 1942."

"Bordeaux."

"He worked for the Prefect of Bordeaux. Maurice Papon. And, what did *monsieur le baron* do for Monsieur Papon?"

"He made lists."

"Lists, and lists, with names and names. Notice how easily these people speak of themselves in the third person. *He* made lists. But, that's not all *he* did. *He* also organised train schedules, didn't he? To what destination? Answer!"

"Drancy. Please, if you want money, take it, I beg you, anything, but just leave me alone!"

"*Putain de merde, ça me donne envie de niquer.* You know, Franck, acting as judge, jury, executioner, that makes me so bloody hot. *J'ai besoin d'une sensation forte.* Franck, just wait for me outside, it will be just a moment, no *problème.*"

I turned and exited the house. It's hard to recall exactly what was running through my mind, except that it had nothing to do with me. It was a private matter. Old country feud. As I crossed the threshold, two muffled shots punctuated the afternoon. Sheba emerged at the front entrance, spotted me, and held up two fingers, turned around, closed the door, pulled a handkerchief from her purse, wiped the door handle. Then, she stood for a moment, examining me, neither of us moving. She looked calm, but for a thin bead of sweat beneath her eyes, which she wiped away delicately with her index.

"Everything's fine, Franck. We can go now."

I drove for a while, neither of us speaking. Carcassonne, Bordeaux, then up the West coast, through towns littered with human refuse baking under the hard sun of the Southwest. As we turned into the *périphérique* road ringing Biarritz, she spoke for the first time.

"Give me a cigarette. From the compartment, Franck. You look funny, what's the problem? *A quoi tu penses,* Franck?"

We were passing by a petrochemical plant located on a deserted industrial zone inland from the coast. I pulled onto the shoulder of the road. Turned off the ignition. I wasn't sure about anything yet. Just waiting for my mind to catch up with things.

"That old man would have been dead in a year or two. So, what the hell was the point?"

"How convenient. If it's any solace, a lot of people think like you, Franck."

"It's not convenient. It's survival. It's the way it is. Why can't you just bury the past?"

"That's how we bury the past, Franck. By revenge."

"Why the fuck is it you people can't just move on?"

"The point, Franck *chérie*, is that someone has to feel the suffering we did. Nothing else suffices. It doesn't really matter who. But they have to feel senseless, random pain."

"I don't get it."

"Look, Franck, you're free with me. If you don't like it with me, *prends la caisse, et tu te tires.* I'm not stopping you. I have the feeling you haven't made up your mind about something. You're free to go. I never said I had any hold on you. But, I have to know."

She was wearing a fur coat, and a miniskirt. Beneath the skirt, that cunt, percolating, effervescent. I could always leave her. She wouldn't stop me. She wouldn't have to. If I left, I could go to Beijing or the Galápagos or Baffin Island, and that cunt would draw me right back to its owner, and I'd be back to square one. So, what was the point? There would be consequences, but what was the point?

"There's only one problem with that. I'm in love with you."

"*Putain*, I never thought I'd hear those words from you."

"Why else would I stay with you?"

"It's all a film, Franck. The whole world has been in a film for so long that we can't escape. We are holding up a mirror to ourselves, and we cannot bear the image, so we are killing each other and ourselves, just to purge the world of the ugliness of our image."

She smiled. The smile reminded me of Père Lachaise cemetery. *I hope it's not all talk, Franck.* We returned to the car.

"There's something I want to tell you. The day after my mother died, I went to a porn shop on *rue Saint-Denis.* I purchased twelve porn films. Not erotica. Everything *hard.* I spent the whole day watching these films, studying them. Then the day after that. And over and over again, for a week. Finally, I stopped. I had succeeded in burning the bizarre and the source of men's desire right into my subconscious. I had discovered my calling."

We drove for a time without saying anything. She was staring straight ahead when she spoke again.

"My first client was Malagasy. They are experts in death. I told him what I had done. He explained everything to me. He said, for the dead person to meet with the ancestors, they must disappear from the memory of those who are still alive. Can you imagine, Franck? I can't remember what she looks like, Franck. I can't remember what my own mother looks like. When I try to picture her, sometimes she is four years old, and I am her mother, sometimes she is a hundred years old, like a tree suffering from Dutch elms disease, rotting into mulch. Does this mean she is with the ancestors?"

"You never told me how she died."

"Franck, there are others, like the baron. Once I have finished with them, all this will stop, and we can be *tranquillos.* I prefer you know right from the outset. If you don't like it, *mais tu prends ta caisse, et tu te barres. Oh merde, j'ai envie.* Pull over the car. Pull over, Franck. Stop the car. *Putain, Franck, j'ai envie. Faut que je baise. Tout de suite.*"

We moved into another apartment, just outside of town at beachside. The flat was on the second floor, just above the *Vendée Globe* café, overlooking the ocean. It had been built as part of a development which included a Monte Carlo Casino next door. We were awoken in the mornings by the sound of the Atlantic waves crashing onto the shore and sand spraying onto our front balcony, where it accumulated, etching and grinding marks into the sliding glass doors.

The steamrollers and backhoes criss-crossed the beach through thick gusts of Rochelais wind, blowing sand across the levelled beach. A huddle of windsurfers in wetsuits, drinking coffee under the awning of the *Vendée Globe* beneath our apartment. *Ile de Ré* and Fort Bayard, an island prison, visible in the distance of the half-moon bay. The industrial machinery retreated, as the waves gained in vehemence, and the high tide brought the sea closer to our apartment.

She entered the room, carrying a flat tray. Coffee and *tartine*. She placed the tray on a coffee table, rejoined me in bed, propping herself onto the pillow, her legs crossed in a loose, lotus position. She wore a multi-coloured African scarf, wrapped around her head like a turban. She reached for a cigarette and curled up beside me.

"Tell me about Spike, Franck."

"Disgruntled client."

"But you told me you never lost a case, Franck."

"I didn't. Never took anything to court I couldn't win hands down. I won this one, two million dollars on the nose. Spike, unfortunately, wants all of the two million. And, it doesn't work that way."

"How does it work, then? I mean, if Spike only gets, say some of it, who gets the rest?"

"There's a lot of mouths to feed in the court system."

"And you're one of them, aren't you, Franck?"

"Sure, I'm one of them. You should consider practicing law, Sheba. Personal injury."

"No, Franck, I think you should consider returning to the practice."

"Out of the question. It's a full time job."

"But Franck, as a team, there are a lot of things we could do."

"Actually, Sheba, money is not really a problem for me these days."

"But Spike is."

"Forget Spike, he's not an issue," I said, holding out a *brioche*. She pushed it away, reached for another cigarette.

The wind blowing ripples of sand insistently across the water outside the flat. Three young boys in wetsuits shrieking as they windsurfed up to the shore. She walked the one step separating us, pointing her finger at my heart, pulled her imaginary trigger and blew on her fingertip as if it were the smoking barrel of a Glock 17.

> You've read the story of Jesse James
> Of how he lived and died
> If you're still in the need of something to read
> Here's the story of Bonnie and Clyde.

She laughed, innocent as a pristine virgin.

"I don't need to kill people, Franck. Not any more. Do you love me, Franck? Would you do anything for me? *Aller jusqu'au bout*? Are you starting to see what I am about? I hope so, because you are an accessory after the fact."

"Funny, I was thinking the same thing."

"Franck, it's just too easy for you. You have never even asked why I do anything, or why I became what I am. It's all so easy for you, Franck. You see a seductive woman, she is there to solve all your temporary problems, and you won't do anything to show that you're willing to take a real risk for her. That's why you're always stuck in your little world, Franck. *Ton petit jardin, quoi.*"

"Give me an example."

"You're in trouble, aren't you, Franck? I mean, that's why you're doing what you do. It's why you're with me."

"You have to handle that if you're a lawyer. Usually the storm passes."

"Unless someone is deliberately trying to get to you."

"True enough."

"And you've got a number of people after you. Your ex-wife, this Spike person. Among others."

"Not to worry. People have to go through the motions sometimes."

"No, there's more to this. This is about revenge, Franck. They think you've taken part of their lives from them."

"Well, I don't know where these types find the time to blame all their problems on me. If anything, I improved their lives."

"Something in you offends them, Franck."

"I mean, I have a specific pattern figured out, a sort of modus operandi, and no matter where I find myself, I can figure things out. If that offends people, fuck 'em. End of story."

"A stable full of horses, right Franck?"

"Yea, a stable of horses. I've said that before?"

"Doesn't matter which one comes in."

"That's right. I'm more of a quinella bettor than an exactor man. If you know what I mean."

"This is different, Franck. Only one horse wins the race we're talking about. You better make the right pick."

She smiled. Cross-examination adjourned.

"Does the rest matter, as long as we're together, Franck?"

"For now, it doesn't matter, Sheba."

She turned away.

"The dream returned last night."

"Refresh my memory."

"I am organic, *végétal*, a plant. I am trying to push through the surface soil and attract the sun's rays. But, one of those steamrollers comes by and ... it crushes me. *Ca m'écrase.*"

She fell silent. The early morning sky darkened, blurring her features. She turned and faced me. The iris of her left eye had retreated into full eclipse, dilating, enveloping her pupil. The uttering of her dream seemed to have pulled her back to a place she visited in spite of herself. As if she were out on a day pass from the prison of her own mind. She tore her gaze away from me once more.

"It is as if there are threads and tendrils pulling on my brain, Franck. First, there is a clarity, almost approaching ecstacy, of such an exquisite purity. Then, a rough diabolic voice, taunting me with unspeakable fantasies, taking possession, repeating over and over: 'You're mine now, come back to me.' It is so horrible, yet pleasurable. Like being raped."

She briefly consulted her fingernails, as if they contained the oracle of Delphi.

"How does it feel when you fuck me, Franck?"

"Like a hole being bored through my brain. Like I'm nuking a third world village, or piloting a 737 into a skyscraper."

If you really think about it, sex is a strange concept. For starters, no one thinks about sex per se while they are having sex. It's all a projection of where the mind happens to be at that particular point in time. And the way my mind works is that, whatever those things happen to be, they should be brought to their logical conclusion. Since the *concept* of sex was strange *in the extreme*, yet didn't offend any of my *core beliefs*, it was logical that its essence could be best discovered by trying it out with someone who was a graduate of the school of the bizarre.

She was now undoing my pants, removing my belt, rebuckling it and placing it around her throat. She retreated several steps to a door, wrapped the loop around the doorknob, then hung herself, and began rubbing her clitoris beneath the V of her mauve merrywidow.

"You see, Franck, what I bring people is not satisfaction, but more desire. What eventually kills them comes from inside, not from me. I only awaken it. Do you know, Franck, there is a certain class of men and women whose deepest dream is to be extinguished? Do you want to be extinguished, Franck? Is that what you're looking for?"

V

Our morning walk took us along a path through a gently intoxicating blend of lavender, eucalyptus, palm trees that removed you from the usual time cycles and left you with only one desire — that nothing should change. We were engaged in a half-serious discussion on the art of the deal, and how it varied on each side of the Atlantic.

"Whether you want to make cash in a domestic or foreign jurisdiction, basically the same rules apply. The keys are cash up front, measure the risks, bring in a fall guy, adopt a brand name for mystique, hire a prick, whatever."

"You have genius, Franck. But you have squandered your talents."

"The world is filled with geniuses, Sheba. The unemployed, the corner drunk, the ad weasels. All neglected geniuses. All squandered talents."

I recalled the last time I had lapsed into philosophy. It was a thousand dollar pool game in Macau, and a Chinese hustler was softening me up with compliments.

"Nothing original about it, Sheba. I borrowed the idea from the ad world. They borrowed it from somebody else. Nothing's new anyways. The trick is not inventing ideas, it's reducing them to their essence. Run it through the meat grinder. Turn out packageable spam for the masses."

"Even if the idea is already good?"

"Especially if it's good. The first aim of the marketers is to kill ideas. It's kind of like making dog food. It's not what's in it, it's what you add that counts. That's why they call it the *add* industry. It's not the contents. It's the repackaging."

"So, you can repackage anything."

"Oh yeah. Not nearly as hard as it sounds."

"Tell me, Franck, tell me how it works."

"Simple. Once everything is product, you're three quarters of the way there. Once it's product, it has to be sold, and for product to sell, everything has to work in triangles. Whether it's three punks playing in a garage band or thirty thousand yes men slaving for a multinational, or three hundred members of an extreme left ecology party, it all breaks down into threes. Who's got the idea, who can put a face on it, and who's the prick who handles money matters."

"We can do something with this, Franck. You told me you sold citizenships before. In Hong Kong."

"Over. Part of China now."

"No, but we just repackage it, Franck."

Her eyes were glistening. Nothing made her happier than the prospect of future victims.

"Franck, I have the target group. Arabs. Terrorist groups, Franck. They'll pay all kinds of money. Dmitri told me the Canadian passport is the best in the world. Even the Mossad uses them."

"Who's Dmitri?"

"He works with the Kosovans and Macedonians. Moving people across borders."

"Non-starter. It's an endgame."

She frowned, fell silent. Our walk took us along the ramparts, past the Chateau Grimaldi, then through Juan les Pins. There's something about the Mediterranean that seems to make you disregard the risk factor. In retrospect, the only explanation was cunt. There was a direct ratio between the enticement factor, and the amount of high-end property you had to be acquiring if you wanted to stay in the game. Or it was the sun, or the way those Mediterranean waves lapped up against the ramparts.

In the old village centre, we stopped at a café, sat down at a table outside just in front of a Morris pillar, advertising local bull fights, boxing matches, a *guignol* Punch and Judy puppet production.

"Franck, are you looking at that column?"

"I'm looking at the column."

"The picture on it, Franck. The one beneath the ad for the boxing."

"I'm looking at it."

The poster displayed a front shot photo of a man staring into a camera. A second photo of the same man in profile.

WANTED
Franck Robinson, aka Jake McMurphy, aka Jack Shrivner
White Male
DOB: 09/11/58
Brown Hair
Brown Eyes

6 foot 5 inches tall
210 pounds
Fair Skin Tone
1" scar on right buttock
tattoos: miniature whore on right bicep
Warrant Number: 01CR1878
40 Counts Rape of a Child
40 Counts Aggravated Sexual Battery

Additional Information: Franck Robinson is wanted for 40 counts of child rape, 40 counts of aggravated sexual battery, impersonating a lawyer without proper qualifications, fraud, larceny, impersonation, international terrorism assisting and harbouring illegal aliens, failure of Registration of Offender Violation under District of Montreal Criminal Court Case 500-02-0001431 and Parole Violation 01-5493 for Aggravated Indecent Solicitation of a Child.

Franck was last known to hang around carnivals and whorehouses in the Paris Pigalle district in France.

This individual is considered armed and dangerous. Do not attempt to apprehend him yourself. Report any information to the nearest *Brigade Judiciaire*. Or Sergeant Spike Nussbaum at 06.49499999

Information may also be reported anonymously to the RCMP Crime Stoppers of Canada by calling **(416) 267-9111**. You may be eligible for a cash reward of up to $10,000 if the information you provide leads to the location and arrest of a profiled fugitive.

"Franck! That's you in the photo!"

"It definitely could be me."

"It *is* you, Franck. Look, there's even a description of your tattoo."

"So there is."

"Franck, you have to come to a decision. I told you, this Spike will not just go away. I know how to deal with this. We're seeing Dmitri right away. Put on your sunglasses, Franck. This man is trying to destroy you, Franck. He has to be exterminated. We have to wipe this *pourri* off the planet."

"Let me give Hervé a call. He'll have some useful advice for us."

I flipped open the cellphone, dialled Hervé's office number.

"Hervé, you old buzzard!"

"Franck. I've been trying to reach you for two weeks."

"Sorry, Hervé, just keep forgetting to turn on the cell phone."

"Franck, I've just received a call from the Law Society. Something about the Sutherland case I referred to you. The ATV accident, you recall."

"What's with the formal voice, my man? This is Franck! Franck Robinson the Third!"

"This one won't go away, Franck."

"Greed rearing its ugly head, Hervé. Greed and resentment. Amateurs trying to get in on the big game. Nothing to fret over."

"They've threatened joint and several liability on this, Franck. I've forwarded your bill of costs on the file. And your time sheets."

"Time sheets! What the fuck are you talking about? I work on contingency!"

"They're questioning the propriety of several items."

"Sue them, Hervé. Sue their asses off. It's defamation *a posteriori*. If I had the time to get back, they wouldn't try this bullshit."

"For starters, your retainer of a hundred grand has raised a few eyebrows. On Bar and Bench."

"The resentment of the public service, Hervé. Nothing illegal about getting money up front. We're all whores in the end. Question of price."

"I don't think I'm getting through to you. It's never the direct things that bring us down, Franck. Always an event which initially appears trivial, that just won't go away. Ever see *Lawrence of Arabia*, Franck?"

"That the story about those sand niggers who bombed the Turkish railroad?"

"You get the picture, Franck. And, you're whooping it up in Medina, my friend."

"That doesn't make me a bad person."

"Franck, have you ever met Margaret Tillman?"

"She gave me a call the other day. Dry as a prune. Over the phone anyways."

"In her leisure hours, Franck, she works at a battered women's shelter. Not likely to be sympathetic to your cause. She's also a dyke. A dyke with a good reason for being a dyke, if you catch my drift."

"What has she got on me?"

"What's that got to do with it, Franck? You personify everything she is fighting."

"Unfair editorial comment, Hervé. You're the woman beater. Remember, the *aller-retour*? I recall you were the one who defined it for me. You sound short of breath, Hervé. You inhaling or exhaling?"

"Franck, you're more than out of the loop in the City. You're right up there with urea formaldehyde, my friend.

Christ, even conversing with you might make me some kind of accessory after the fact. Listen, Franck, I'm a few deviations from the norm. We all are. We're judged behind our backs, in our sleep, or before the courts. But you're getting involved in something different. Criminals — and here, I refer to the *criminal classes*, and not some poor bugger who sods off his wife because he lost his job — operate differently. Type that kills you because of the way you look at him. Or because he hasn't been laid in a week. You've cross-examined these sub-humans, Franck! Come on! You can still come back."

"No, this is home now, Hervé. Where the heart lies."

"I always thought of you as a convenience man, Franck. But you are something else. For what it's worth, you're signing your death warrant."

"You're a good man, Hervé, but you're wrong. Everybody is toast sooner or later. Or, in my case, everybody is *croque monsieur.*"

"Go ahead, Franck. But, I can't communicate with you anymore. Nothing personal, but I've never been a fall guy."

"I know the rules of engagement, Hervé. Quit worrying so much. How are things back home?"

"I'm selling the property. Too much to tend in old age. Not that this would concern you, but the taxes are too high."

"True enough, definitely not on my radar screen."

"In the long run, you can live with taxes, Franck."

I hung up the phone.

"What did he say?"

"He said we'd better talk to Dmitri."

Dmitri's twin diesel yacht, the *First In, First Out*, was moored on the *Jetée Nord* at the *Club Nautique d'Antibes*. The upper saloon of *First In, First Out* was lizard lounge all the way, minus the strippers, but overloaded with plasma screens, DVD home cinema, cellphones, TV sat systems, and antique sextants, compasses and maps of the world, circa 16th century, with the entry *Terra Incognita* over large parts of the New World. In the far end of the Upper Saloon, a wall covered with pictures of young models, posing.

Dmitri's look was 1950s film noir star, which suited his broken nose, hooded eyelids and mallet head. The way he held his whisky looked precious for a man with his face, until you noticed that he was missing three fingers on his right hand.

"I wondered where you'd gone, Sheba," he said as he lined up three whisky tumblers, a bucket of ice and a bottle of J&B on the oval teak table of the stateroom. "You disappeared for a while."

He poured out the whisky, still wasn't looking at me. He poured out doubles, on ice. I went into drift, started running a mental list of 1950s film noir stars. Definitely not Delon. Remnants of Belmondo. Jean Gabin? Close, but no. Lino Ventura. That was it. The Slavonic Lino Ventura.

"I don't like something about it. But I said I would help you," says Dmitri. "So, I'll help you What's this *somebody*'s name bothering your friend here?"

Dmitri pulled a thread from between his teeth as if it were the remains of the last *somebody* who had bothered one of his friends.

"Spike," I intervened, "Spike Nussbaum."

He poured himself another J&B. Nodded towards my glass.

"Another finger?"

"No, I've got enough on my hands."

Dmitri frowned, like he was noticing me for the first time, or was taking a stab at calculating two to the third power, or found himself in front of a traffic light which stayed red for three minutes running. Then, he grinned and shook his head.

"I am from Russia. Siberia."

"Nice. What's a one-way on the Trans-Siberian set you back in rubles these days?"

"Even today, there are cannibals in Siberia."

For a moment, I even forgot Spike. The Riviera. Hideout for Arctic cannibals.

"On second thought, give me a finger. Of J&B."

"Tell me, Robinson. How come everybody got short names in America?"

"What's short about Robinson?"

"No, like Bill, Bob, Gus, Sam."

"We have bad memories."

"We have no memories in Russia. Vodka."

"But you have long names."

"Not everybody. Joe Stalin is short."

"Funny. He looks tall in the pictures."

"So, what is the problem with this Spike *somebody*?"

"Money."

"And you got no money."

"I have money. But none for Spike."

"Just tell this Spike somebody, no worries, Spike, you want the money, you come by and pick up the money. Then you tell him you're waiting for him here."

Dmitri passed me a business card pressed between his thumb and forefinger. Hotel del Monte. Villecroze. Diner-Spectacle. PMU. *Cuisine Provençale.*

"Just like that."

"Just like that."

"Then what?"

"That's simple. Then, I take care of things."

"What's your end?"

Dmitri looked at Sheba.

"You said he wanted my help, Sheba, know what I mean? So, he wants my help, or he don't want my help?"

Right at that moment, I was thinking, you can write your own rule book and escape unscathed for a long time. Until society's various bounty hunters, the Spikes and the Margaret Tillmans, put the squeeze on you, money, the great lubricator, dulls the critical mind. Everything is equal and everybody's your friend. That was my little ozone layer until now. Lovemaking in the morning, *pétanque* in the afternoon, drinks and the casinos in the evening. It seemed like it could go on forever. Sooner or later, I had to pick my friends. Even if I had to pay for them.

"All right, Dmitri, fair enough, I'll invite Spike over. You do your thing, and then we'll discuss terms after the event. Sort of a commission deal."

"Sure. A commission deal. Don't worry about it. Know what I mean?"

VI

We were listening to an old Argentinian soul music number from Astor Piazzolla titled *Oblivion*. She wore ruffled, white satin panties, white bra, white pumps. She was combing her hair, looking in the mirror, talking casually. She reminded me of a dragonfly when she performed her monologues while beautifying herself. She dabbed some foundation around her right eye to mask a bruise which had appeared there. I had just finished whipping her backside with my belt, opening up the now thick scars criss-crossing her buttocks and calves, which were partially covered with gauze to stop up the thick suppurating flow of ooze coming from her wounds, giving an effect of venetian blinds.

"Franck, I don't want you to be afraid. No matter how much I kick up a fuss, I invite you to be brutal. If you do it carefully, increase it by degrees, then I can take it. But the worst thing you could do is stop, Franck. I would never forgive you for that. Beauty doesn't last forever, Franck. I would prefer to kill it off myself than have time do it for me."

She stopped applying some mascara, looked into the mirror at me, verifying something.

"Can't you see, Franck? *I am no better than an animal.* But, while we are acting this thing out, I prefer not to have to stop and give you instructions. You can understand that it defeats the whole purpose. Oh, I almost forgot, there is something I want to show you."

She walked out of the room, and returned with several bound packages, of varying thickness, each tied around with lace, and a label with the first name of a man. Henri. Cédric. Jack. She pulled out the first stack, unlaced it and began reading.

"Even now, from Ward K ..."

She glanced at me.

"*Non, mais tu te rends compte*, Franck? Ward K. I cannot believe they still use letters. It makes it sound just like a prison."

She continued reading aloud. The first letter ended with a promise of suicide.

"You see what these buildings can inspire? *Scandaleux*, Franck."

She continued reading, then moved onto the next sequence of letters, addressed by a certain Cédric.

"A pilot. For *les grandes lignes.*"

Cédric's letters alternated between effusive confessions of love, pleading for her return, and threats of police action.

"Cédric was less than a man. And he betrayed me. So, I seduced his brother. He was no better. A defective genetic code. I believe the scientists study these things in Iceland. And Tonga ... yes, Tonga."

She read from another letter. It was a long, rambling diatribe, at times pathetic, at other times coldly analytical. Someone who clearly hated himself for having become involved with her. The letter concluded with a servile, obsequious request to have a large sum of money returned.

"Vincent was Dutch. When I met him, I owed a rather large sum of money to someone, in the Var, and the person needed the sum immediately. You know what the Var people are like, Franck. Codes of honour. Vincent turned it into a moral issue. Insisted he pay the debt. But, later, I received a letter from a woman, in a truly execrable French, insisting that as his *vrouw*, she was entitled to ask that the sum be returned *illico presto*, or else the police would become involved."

She held her finger out, as if drawing a picture, and traced a rectangle in the air, then smiled.

"Could she have meant the Dutch police? I have never understood how the Dutch have survived. They are not like us."

The next letter was from Vincent's grandmother. She asked for clemency as Vincent had been a good boy, and needed the money for his next campaign to become a school board trustee. His one chance to make good.

"Clemency! *Nul*. Then she had the nerve to ask for the money in guilders. How could I possibly calculate that? You know how much I detest *les maths*. I told her I might arrange for payment in Euros."

That might have ended the exercise, had it not provoked a recollection.

"Tell me about your past, Franck."

"Nothing to tell."

"There were other women ... you are brutal with me. Brutality comes from experience. Were you married?"

"Sure. I was married."

"Tell me about *your* ex, Franck."

"Which one?"

"The one you loved."

"What about her?"

"Why did you leave *her*?"

"Problems."

"Were the problems *vertical ou horizontal*?"

She held her index stiffly upwards, then laid her hand flat, as if lowering a corpse into a tomb.

"There was no problem *horizontal*, there was no nothing *horizontal*."

"How big were her breasts?"

"What difference?"

"I saw a picture of her in your wallet, Franck. It was disgusting, *dégueulasse*. I don't understand. Were you looking for a cow to milk, Frank? Haven't you heard of the risks of mad cow's disease? How old was she? Oh, god, Franck, sometimes you really lean towards the low-grade. Promise me, Franck, that you will never leave me for another woman unless she is younger and more beautiful. *Promis, juré*, Franck?"

I lit a cigarette. We watched each other in silence for a moment. We were seeing each other in a new way. Sizing each other up, maybe for the first time. Like a couple of sparring partners about to go at it for the nth time, then suddenly realizing that only one would survive. Although, that wasn't quite so clear at the time.

She had wound a transparent Indian sari around her torso like a funereal shroud. She appeared ephemeral in it, as if she could fade away and become part of the firmament at any given second. A faint smile appeared on her face. She had a way of making the smile appear, as if emerging from the depths of a translucent forest mist.

"Call your wife, Franck. I want you to kill her. I must have this proof of your undying love for me. Kill this cud-chewing ruminant. A mercy killing."

Her stare was limpid, her skin transparent. Her mind nuclear.

"You, I might consider killing." I mused aloud.

"Why were you drawn to me, Franck? What was it? No man has ever answered this question properly. Do you remember Père Lachaise, Franck?"

"Yeah, I remember."

"When you took me, in the mausoleum, what did I look like?"

"Like a silhouette. A corpse."

"That's it, Franck. It is our wish to destroy ourselves that brings us together."

"Self-destruction is a solo flight, Sheba. It's not a dance."

She wasn't listening. Or she was desperate. I tried to recall what was novel about her.

"The difference between us and the others, Franck, is we know we won't get another chance."

"Actually, that's not it at all, Sheba."

"What is it, then?"

"We're just not concerned with what is going on around us."

"I see it another way, Franck. I think we are precursors of something yet to come. I have these visions. Everything fire and ashes. Everything destroyed. Not just you and me."

She was marking me. I was marking her. She had used the lines a hundred times before. I didn't buy into the lines; the content was superfluous. It was the delivery and the sonority that made considerations like truth secondary. The delivery and that ass of hers. And something else, but at the time I didn't admit it to myself.

"We are anti-celebrities, Franck. No one will ever know who we are. But at least we are voluntarily choosing our fate. Franck, let's kill someone. Why don't we make a sacrifice to the gods, Franck? Let's sacrifice your ex-wife."

Sheba was now leaning back against the tiled wall of the square shower-bath stall, had removed her lingerie, but not her pumps, and was spraying her cunt with the coiled metal shower head she held in her left hand as if it were a flowerbox of pansies. She had smeared her body in coconut oil, which enveloped her in a larval cocoon. She ran her finger up and down her thigh, prying open her cunt, spraying her clitoris with the nozzle end, scrutinizing me, then retreated into her silence, but the silences were losing their mystery. Like the intimidating glare of a boxer with a losing record. Statistics stronger than anything the soul can muster.

"We were supposed to be like *this*, Franck."

This was illustrated by her holding up her index and forefinger, side by side like two sentries standing face to face during the changing of the guard on the Pall Mall.

"Who could possibly be more like *this*?" I inquired, holding up two of my own fingers, and jamming a Marboro between the two of them. Then lighting it.

"No, no we are not like this. We can never be like this, as long as you insist on not being transparent, Franck. You can't keep hanging on to your *jardin secret*, Franck. Why are you looking at me like that, Franck? What's the matter, Franck? You don't love me anymore?"

I walked across to the kitchenette bar counter. Reached for some whisky. Poured several ounces into a glass. Drank it down. Looked through the two portals and, at the end of the tunnel of vision, her, washing that cunt. As if it could never be too clean. She looked calm, which was a bad sign. I was getting used to it. You can get used to anything. I reached for a steak knife, slid the saw-toothed blade between my thumb and forefinger. Laid it down again. Premature.

"Franck, I was just thinking that today might be a good day for you to call that *salope*, and tell her exactly what you really think of her. And prove, once and for all, that you love me, Franck. Or at least, that you have *cojones*. But that is a question you've never really answered, isn't it, Franck?"

Her tone was still even, controlled, but the cadence had slowed to an inquisitorial crawl. Her right eye darkening into ebony translucence. Maybe it was her lenses.

"Sometimes, I wonder whether it isn't you that caused *everything*."

Her hand dangling the shower head against her cunt, the eyes retreating, the rising crest of a wave ready to lash onto shore.

"*Everything* Franck, is *everything* that has created this storm in my head that is lashing against the wave breakers and dykes of my very mind, Franck, and *everything* that has given me bad dreams and causes me to do these things I do to other people.

"I am starting to wonder whether I wasn't mistaken in letting you fuck me, and sodomize me and stick that cock of yours into my mouth. Why am I wondering this, right now, Franck? Why?"

During one of those *whys*, her left hand had inched its way downwards and shut off the cold water. She swung the nozzle towards me, spraying the scalding hot water into my face, then lunged at me. I side-stepped her, and she slipped, falling to the floor. I wrenched her wrist hard, pushed my shoe into her neck, pressing her face harder into the tile floor. I held it there until I was pretty sure she had calmed down a bit.

"You going to behave?"

"*Bien sûr.*"

I removed my foot, allowed her to rise. She walked out of the bathroom at an easy pace, into the living room, up to the wall telephone.

She wrenched the jacks out of the wall.

"Late twentieth century telephone. *Ringard*," she decreed. She crossed towards the coffee table, picked up a multi-coloured lamp, rotated it in front of her for me to see.

"Rococo. Very kitsch. Personally, I am a minimalist."

She allowed the lamp to slide through her fingers. The porcelain shattered into pieces across the tiles of the bar area.

"Franck, you know, one of the arts never mastered by Americans is letter-writing. Here, if something is even typed, it is considered to be an insult. So, you can only imagine what I think of you ruining the harmony of my life with *this*."

I think *this* was a Ricoh, or at least was a Ricoh until the machine smashed onto the ground. She held two crystal champagne flutes in her hand.

"Something to drink, Franck?"

The first glass flew towards me, smashing the wall behind me.

"What are you looking at?" she inquired, as if I'd walked in on her toilette, or was caught gawking at her through a one way mirror, or was masturbating in a shopping mall.

She fell into her now methodical default routine, tearing pictures out of the wall, smashing glasses one by one, then plates, then overturning the furniture. She stopped and briefly surveyed the day's wreckage. Stared at me. Sneered, allowed me to catch a glimpse of the venom and hatred in its essence, then shut that off.

"I almost forgot, Franck. It's almost time for dinner. Would you like dinner, Franck? Or would you like to fuck me? Or do you want your wife? What is it, Franck? What do you want?"

It was unsustainable, but it was a style. At some point, it would be time to vacate, but I could see why Cedric, and Vincent, and Christophe, and Dmitri, and all the others stuck around longer than was good for them. Compared to Sheba, everything else was black and white, and each of us needed a little bit of colour on the canvas.

As suddenly as it rose, the tempest abated. Nothing had occurred. Just a minor epileptic seizure. She was sitting on a stool in the midst of debris skewed throughout the living room. Little Miss Muffet, except, instead of eating curds and whey, she is shaving her cunt with a razor.

"Franck, I know I can be a little psychotic sometimes. When I feel my impulses, I am just like an animal. What is it, Franck? What is it I'm missing? I am missing something that other people have, am I not, Franck?"

"Everybody's missing something, Sheba."

"But I find even the passing of time difficult, Franck. People say time flies. Not for me. Every minute is long, oppressive. And the people around me. Other human beings. Their very existence is offensive to me. If I had access to a nuclear bomb, I would pulverize everything in existence."

"You probably just have too much time on your hands. Why don't you take up rollerblading or something?"

"I took up painting for a while, Franck. But, I could only paint myself, Franck. For me, Franck, the world has no meaning outside myself. No one exists. Not even you. Some people call this narcissism or obsession. What do you call it, Franck?"

"Being a woman, Sheba, it's like being in a prison, isn't it?"

"Oh la-la. Why would you, of all people, make such a statement?"

"I've been having these weird dreams lately. I'd never really considered it, but your whole existence, it's to seduce. To attract."

She was covering that peach of hers with foam, processing my latest theory.

"So, basically, outside of the fact that you *attract*, the way honey attracts bears, or shit attracts flies, I mean what else is there?"

She slid the razor alongside the edge of her labia, starboard side. I wondered momentarily whether she might not self-mutilate. Just to gauge how I would react.

"*C'est ça, le mystère.*"

"No, no mystery at all. None. A pretty little package. Another illusion down the drain. Nothing more. Even this death trip of yours is all part of the game."

"Do you really believe that, Franck?"

"Sure, there's no evidence to the contrary. Why wouldn't I believe it?"

"There's a line you shouldn't cross with me, Franck."

An early morning light deflecting off her angular cheekbones. She looked clean, pristine. The twenty-third virgin bride for the caliph.

"Do you think I do what I do out of amusement, Franck?"

"In the end we're all stuck with ourselves. That's just the way it is."

"There are only two reasons men are attracted to me. The first is animal attraction. The second never has anything to do with me. So, what is your second reason, Franck?"

"With you, I don't have to think about other things. In the short run, that has its advantages."

"You know, Franck, there's always one thing that eats away at a man over time. Something he hasn't solved. If you don't face up to it, it eventually devours you. Like a tumour. So, don't worry, Franck, I won't force you at gunpoint to do anything. I don't have to."

"That girl at your father's place. She's your daughter?"

"*Et alors?*"

I was debating about whether or when I would cross her imaginary line. Then thought better of it. Everything in good time.

"You know what we have in common, Sheba? We don't think we're anything special. So, we take whatever we can get. But it doesn't make us very popular with the working classes."

Even when she was considering homicide, she could find space for a smile. It was a form of intelligence.

"People who think they are special make the best clients."

"That's another thing we have in common. We make cash out of others' disappointments. The bigger the disappointment, the larger the retainer."

"You have a talent, Franck, for talking and talking without saying anything real about yourself. Tell me something about you. Something that matters."

"What matters?"

"Only two things. Where you come from, and where you're going to. Tell me about your family."

I shrugged my shoulders.

"Not much to tell. In the current jargon, I'm what you call a deadbeat dad."

She frowned.

"Not that family. I mean where you come from. Where's your father?"

"Dead. A tumour. Something devoured him."

"What about your mother?"

"Dead too."

My mind was on a basic rule of trial strategy. Never introduce evidence of good character, if you have something to hide. Opens you up to cross-examination. Sheba smiled expansively. All the earlier troubles of the day had vaporised. Something on her face, something like, this oyster took a good week to shuck, but lookee here, what a pearl inside.

"Take off your sunglasses, Franck."

"What for?"

"I want to see your eyes."

I removed my shades, lit a cigarette.

"How did she die, Franck?"

"Let's just say it's my *jardin secret.*"

"You feel responsible. But, you aren't."

"Sometimes, I wonder. Let's just say I unwittingly may have provided the *modus operandi.*"

"I'm listening, Franck."

"Let me put it this way. Society might not call my mother a whore, but she was a whore. Which never really bothered me. But I had a brother, Richard, who was strict on standards. He had a code. In his books, she had broken the code. Betrayed him."

We were outside in the yard at this point. It seemed like the day had been going on forever. She was wearing an apron over a blue flowered peasant dress, a scarf, wooden clogs, and was hanging the wash on one of those ancient clotheslines in the shape of a sawhorse. It was one of her strengths — providing appropriate settings and props.

"Have you ever thought of your mother in other terms?"

"What do you mean, other terms?"

"As a woman. With her own needs and desires."

"It was pretty hard to think of her as anything but a woman. So, anyways, Richard, for his own reasons, fucked mother. And, while fucking her, he stabbed her. So, why do you think he would do something like that, Sheba?"

"Because words failed him, Franck."

"What about your daughter?"

"What about her?"

"I've never quite figured out what the story is there."

"There's no story, Franck."

"Don't you want to take her back?"

"Franck, you really are naïve."

"Why wouldn't you?"

"If I could, of course I would."

"What's preventing you?"

"She serves as currency. A sort of *monnaie d'échange.*"

"I don't get it. What's being purchased?"

"Silence. *La paix.* Why the sudden curiosity, Franck?"

"Well, daughters usually live with their mothers."

"Children usually live with their fathers."

"That's different."

"*Vraiment.*"

She was wearing a spaghetti-strapped top and a white miniskirt, so short that her lower buttocks were partially exposed. I'm thinking, whatever way this plays itself out, there's no going back to the day-to-day after this calibre of poontang. Like asking a drug dealer or a hold up artist to work as a gas station attendant. Not an option.

"Sure. When push comes to shove, women will hold their children hostage. Use them as bargaining chips."

"Is that what happened to you?"

"Me? Hell, no. Much more basic."

"How so, basic?"

"Well, put it this way. If you marry someone for her tits, and those go, end of story."

Sheba looked at me. I thought I detected some disbelief.

"You Americans are *marrant*."

"Seriously, Sheba. Don't you want your daughter back?"

She shrugged her shoulders.

"*Mère indigne*. Unworthy mother."

"So what. Deadbeat dad. Not the point."

I poured out a coffee. Then, thought, why not, might not like the answer, but what the hell.

"Tell me, Sheba. How old are you?"

"Would you believe twenty-one?"

I looked at her. Enough lights went on in my head to light Times Square.

"I see. How old's that girl of yours?"

"Six."

"Which makes you about ..."

"I was fourteen."

"Should I be asking who the father is?"

"No, you shouldn't."

"I'm going out for a smoke. I want to think about this."

"Be my guest. You're a free man, Franck."

I stepped outside, closed the door behind me, descended the stairwell into the street. I walked several steps down *rue Général du Clerc* towards the gate leading out of the old city. Hearing her voice and looking up. She was perched on the window-sill, holding a bouquet of handpicked azaleas. Casting for another part which would never reach the big screen.

"*Adieu*, Franck."

"*Adieu*."

A slow walk along the ramparts of the old port in the direction of the train station. I arrived at a beach, where we had spent some time just staring at the water while she spun out tales, some true, some manufactured to tit-illate parts of my brain which had never been activated.

I stared up at the twin towers overlooking the old port. *Tour de l'Ecosse* and *Tour de* something or other. Tour de France, maybe. I was alone again, something which had been hovering on the virtual plane for some time, and now was hyper-real, reopening long dormant mental ducts and passageways, kicking parallel lines of thought into gear. Autobahn A of the cerebral turnpike is seeing for the first time that history has a meaning, i.e. if a city looks with fond nostalgia at its sieges and famines, and medieval plots and vendettas, that history is likely to repeat itself, and that an old brick castle or a walled city might look cozy on a postcard, and a three hundred year old accent might provoke an erection that wobbles the frontal lobe, but that to surrender to the forces of history was the wrong move for someone hailing from a contin-ent suffering from collective amnesia. Autobahn B is didactically looking at the case of Franck Robinson, and thinking, Franck, you got way off the beaten track here, the beaten track being the endless labyrinth of asphalt going by the name Paris, which had nothing to do with the surrounding chrysalidic fringe going by the name of *la France profonde*. I stared at Fort Bayard, which she loved to call the Alcatraz of the Southwest. Then *Ile de Ré* and *Ile d'Oléron*. Our islands. *It's the water that draws us together, Franck.*

VII

During the six-hour drive from the South to the country hamlet of Lusignan, I ran a few mental re-runs of trials I'd participated in or witnessed back in the old days when I worked for a living, particularly the Claire Lortie incident. Claire was a fellow defence lawyer. We called her the "ice queen," and oddly enough, one day her neighbours saw her burying her fridge in the backyard. Claire's boyfriend, or what was left of him, was inside the fridge. Claire relied on the O.J. Simpson defence, i.e. that a mysterious invader had killed him, and that she was so traumatised when she discovered the crime, she sawed him into pieces and buried him in the backyard.

If there's one thing you learn in life, it is just how little is random or magical. Lightning strikes, and mysterious invaders kill your spouse, or the hand of God intervenes only when you want to ignore some overwhelming evidence pointing in one direction. So, if a girl is waving her cunt in the direction of middle-aged

Americans while she raves on about death, and an old man is housing her daughter, and the mother is in a cemetery, and nobody's talking about anything, there's a reason for it. You don't have to know what the reason is. You just have to know what you want.

I had brought along a bottle of Pastis just to get through the door. But, after knocking three or four times, I had to walk around and go through the gate to his backyard. He was sitting in the same chair as the last time, in front of the same truncated oak tree, stirring a drink. A bag of Gauloise blonde tobacco in front of him. The little girl sat at a child's fold-up table a few paces away, colouring inside a Tintin comic book. She was dressed up in her Sunday best, blue and white summer dress, hair tied back in a single bow.

He didn't stand up to greet me. He didn't look surprised either. I sat down beside him, pushed the Pastis in front of him.

"I am not marrying your daughter."

"*Ça ne me surprend pas du tout.*"

He poured the remainder of his glass onto the lawn, then rolled a cigarette with his left hand.

"What did she do this time?"

"She didn't do anything. She's just too young."

"That's not why you're here."

"No it isn't. I've come for the girl."

His face darkened, but remained expressionless.

"She doesn't deserve her. She is a *mère indigne.*"

"That's not your call. Nobody is worthy of children. The girl needs her mother."

He remained silent for several moments. Took a deep drag off his rolled cigarette and looked into the ravine behind his property.

"Over my dead body."

I glanced at the girl, intently colouring, registering everything.

"Who dresses her in the morning?"

"What do you mean?"

"Who takes her clothes off at night?"

He slammed down his glass onto the table. His hand was shaking. I briefly debated whether to send the child inside the house, then thought better of it.

"How's the colouring going, *petite*?"

"*Tu veux voir?*"

Within a few years, she'd be an adolescent. Developing her own bag of tricks in life. Maybe she already was.

"You can show me later. In the car."

The old man stared straight ahead. He'd lost everything he'd ever fought for. He was used to it. Defeats were his navigational tools in life.

"Didn't she tell you I'm a lawyer?"

I didn't really care what he'd done or not done. It was a question of energy, of vitality. Nothing more. I still had mine. And this old man was gone, well on his way out. My turn would come.

"There's truths in the combat zone, my friend. And there's truth in the courtroom. Your daughter doesn't strike me as the type who would hold back on the witness stand."

I could see he'd probably killed men. Maybe even quite a few. It's hard to sustain that type of thing in the long run. It was more organic than anything else. The overall energy remaining the same. He slumped over, his head between his legs, buried inside his one remaining hand. I'd seen it in the courtroom. Some of these people, you need winches to get their faces vertical and exposed to the public again.

"C'mon, *petite*. We're going for a car ride."

The girl looked up, clapped her hands.

"*Ouais*! A car ride!"

"Kiss your grandpa goodbye. And promise him you'll be back soon to visit."

It didn't take long to pack her bags and get into the car, but she didn't look too disturbed, one way or the other. More interested in the car.

"*Dis-donc*, we're going fast."

"Ever been in a car before?"

"None of your business. *Mêle-toi de tes oignons*."

"None of my business? Who the hell taught you that? What's your name, kiddo?"

"*Je m'appelle Charlotte*."

Six years old, and already a seasoned pro.

"Okay, Charlotte, know where we're going?"

"Sure, we're going to the moon."

"We're going to see your *maman*."

"In the moon. *Maman*, she lives on the moon!"

"Sure, she lives on the moon. All *mamans* live on the moon."

"Can I have ice cream?"

"Later."

"I want ice cream now! Or else!"

"Keep your mouth shut."

I stopped at a Total gas pump at roadside. A middle-aged bald man wearing orange coveralls approached the car. Charlotte pointed at me.

"*C'est lui, mon nouveau papa! Et je ne connais même pas*! I don't even know him!"

"Kids."

I shrugged my shoulders. The attendant glanced at Charlotte. He filled the tank.

"That'll be 223 Francs."

We rolled out slowly. I checked the rear view mirror, and spotted him noting down something.

"You keep your mouth shut from now on. Hear?"

"I want ice cream."

I stopped at a roadside grocery, purchased a Drumstick for her, returned to the car.

"There, eat that. You and your mother are going to make a great team."

"*Merci, papa.*"

"Cut the *papa* business. What do you want to be when you grow up?"

"Rich."

"What do you want to be, though?"

"A doctor. An astronaut."

"That's good."

"Or a geisha. Or a rabbit. Or a bank robber. Have you met my fairy?"

"No."

"She is always with me. Always. No one can see her but me. But, she is more real than anybody."

"That's good. Everyone can use one of them."

"I know a secret."

"So tell me the secret."

"Only if you promise not to tell anybody."

"Promise."

"No, not just promise. Cross your heart on your mother's neck! *Promis, juré!*"

"Okay, *promis, juré.*"

"On your mother's neck."

"All right. On my mother's neck."

"Everyone else are ghosts. My fairy told me."

"Even me?"

She shrugged her shoulders, cast me a coquettish glance.

"You know any songs?"

"Sure."

"Well, sing me a song."

> *... lundi matin, l'empereur sa femme et le petit prince*
> *sont venu chez moi, pour me serrer le pince*
> *comme j'étais parti, le petit prince a dit*
> *puisque c'est ainsi, nous reviendrons mardi ...*

A couple of hours later, we arrived in the old city of La Rochelle. I parked the car, and we walked inside the walls, Charlotte holding my hand, singing her songs. Somewhere back in the new land, a few other heirs to the Robinson genetic mix were preparing for their kick at the can. Their time would come. And best they navigate that road alone. I picked up a bouquet of Easter lilies. *Muguets.*

We entered the stairwell marked Escalier B, rode the cramped elevator together. I pulled back the wrought iron, grilled gate.

"Okay, Charlotte. The door is at the end of the hallway. When your mother answers, you hand her the flowers."

"That door?"

"That's right. That one."

She walked a few steps down the hallway, turned around.

"That one?"

I waved her forward. As she arrived at the door, I closed the gate. Heard the door open.

"Charlotte, mais qu'est-ce que tu fais là?"

A couple of minutes later, I walked through the gates of the old city, and onto the beach area outlying the old harbour. Looking out at the Atlantic. For no particular reason, I recalled a book written by a German pacifist who fled Germany during the 1920s after being beaten to a pulp by brownshirt Nazis who had mistaken him for a Jew. Towards the end of the book, the hero, a monastic type known as a meister of an obscure game, stares out at the ocean, and walks into it, fully clothed. The water rises gradually, up to his knees, then past his hips and waist. He continues on into the water, as it gradually envelopes him. I never did figure out what that book was about.

I wondered what the hell had got into my mind, dragging an old world whore back to the junk yard of Montreal. Recalled her sitting in the old port, her garter belt and crotchless panties visible from beneath the trenchcoat, as she stared into the waters of the St. Lawrence seaway.

Do you see, Franck? It is what draws us together. The water, Franck.

A cold wind blowing, as the waves lapped onto the shore. We worked on magnetic principles and undercurrents which drew us towards the water, towards each other. I stepped into the water, felt the salty Atlantic water of the inner harbour seeping through my shoes, soaking my feet, lowering my body temperature a notch or two. Some people just walked into oceans or slit their throats, or put the barrels of hunting rifles into their mouths and pulled the trigger, responding to invisible fields of attraction, particles, induction fields. Others show up on time, pay their taxes and expire quietly within the confines of their homes, surrounded by heirs, embalmers and clergymen. Nothing personal. Just attraction and repulsion, inversely proportional to the square root of the mass of the opposite body. Or something like that. Whatever.

The old harbour was losing its charm. Everything around it had lost its charm. Even the word *charm* had lost its charm. I wanted to be free again. Fuck all these neo-templars and medieval whores. I knew some good people back at Wee Willie's. It was over. No more Sheba and Franck. It was more than over. Time to return to Paris. Things would reassume their true proportions there. Paris the most powerful magnetic field of all. And Franck Robinson a free-floating particle, gravitating towards the bistros and bordellos. A neutral principle. Nothing more, nothing less. Fuck 'em. I was Franck Robinson and I came from the New and Improved World. Whiter than white. We nuked people and then taught the survivors how to run franchises and post-holocaust seminars. Then called that democracy.

PART III

I

I tended to gravitate towards *Rue Lepic* from time to time up in the 18th *arrondissement,* because it allowed me to lurk under the shadow of the old *Moulin de la Galette,* and because the 18th still had a bit more of the old Paris than the rest of the city. I'd been back for a few days, and found myself in front of a bar near the Abbesses station watching a twig of lavender blow its way down an awning over the café. It was the music inside the café that had stopped me, a pianist doing a Michel Petrucciani retrospective. Hearing the music reminded me of *Père la Chaise.*

I stopped outside the Frou-Frou club on *rue des Martyrs* to light a cigarette. I was a traditionalist, when you came down to it. Cigarettes, alcohol and whores. A throwback to the past. A mulatto concierge was hosing refuse off the sidewalk in front of the club. She was young, pretty, shapely. And she was hosing down a sidewalk.

"You work at the Frou-Frou?" I asked.

She laughed. There was Dom-Tom intonation to her laugh. It was a laugh without ulterior motives.

"I clean, *m'sieur*. The whole building. Every day. From top to bottom."

"How much does that earn you?"

A primary level schoolgirl walked past us, thoroughly unconscious of our presence. She wore a small leather backpack with gold embroidery displaying the letters CD: a Dior imitation of the apparel worn by her elder counterparts.

> *Je cherche fortune*
> *Autour du Chat Noir*
> *Au Clair de la lune*
> *A Montmartre*

The words came out easily, automatically, as if she used the tune to help her climb the hill on the way to wherever she was going.

"Not much, *m'sieu*r."

"How much, not much?" I pressed, smiling.

"The *SMIC*."

"How much is the *SMIC?*"

"*Une demi-brique. Cinq mille balles.*"

"Tell you what. How would you like to earn a *demi-brique* this afternoon. After taxes?"

Her smile was still there, just a little more wary.

"In exchange for what?"

"Not much. Just suck my cock. An afternoon *pipe*, then you're half a *brique* to the good. Better than the lottery."

"Really?"

"Oh, yeah. Simple as opening your mouth, and whistling Dixie. Even if you're tone deaf."

"Wait just a moment."

"I'm not going anywhere. Take your time."

She reached for her mop, a loose-tendrilled tool whose strands hung like a sea anemone. In one quick motion, she swung the mop around and struck me across the thigh.

"*Salaud! Va te faire foutre*! You think I am for sale?!"

"If you don't like Pigalle, honey, there's nineteen other *arrondissements* in the city."

I looked across the street at a newspaper stand. An Asian man observing the scene from behind page 3 of *Tiercé-Magazine*.

"Robinson! Robinson!"

Tranh crossed the street, approached the concierge.

"Madame."

He executed an obsequious bow.

"I apologize for this gentleman's inexplicable and execrable behaviour. He is clearly suffering from a form of mental distress."

"*Non, mais allez vous faire foutre, tous les deux!*"

Tranh ushered me down the street.

"You are truly incorrigible, Robinson. Come with me. I am inviting you to the *Chat Noir*."

"You see where altruism leads? I was offering her a month's rent!"

"Of course! Of course!"

He examined me, head to toe.

"You look better, Robinson. Less edgy."

We descended *rue des Martyrs* until we landed on the wide pedestrian boulevard separating the two sides of *boulevard Clichy*, then drifted west, past the German tourist buses and a stretch of low-grade shops. Maryelove, Palace Video, Folies Pigalle, porn shops and a streamer of virtual promises — aphrodisiacs, blow-up dolls, gadgets, phalluses, all designed to fill holes and gaps — some of them physical, some psychic.

"I have something to confess to you, Robinson. I have never understood America, and I chose you to be my teacher."

"There's nothing to understand."

"Oh, but there is, there is. You recall Rhanya?"

"Sure, I remember her. The Piaf of the Maghreb, right?"

"How many flowers can she hope to sell in an evening, Robinson? Two? Three? She is in a chronic state of hysteria or drunkenness throughout her waking hours. And look at you, on the other hand. Limitless capability, limitless options. Money, luck, friends, career. Yet you throw it all away. You are the quintessential American. It is something we of the so-called Third World can never understand about you in the West. You have conquered the world. But you throw it all away. Do you know why?"

"Because we get it all through rape and plunder. Booty isn't meant to be saved."

"No, Franck. It is because you have no sense of destiny."

We had arrived at the entrance of the *Chat Noir*. The bartender, a squat man with a walrus moustache, saluted us.

"The usual, monsieur Tranh?"

Tranh nodded. The waiter poured out two cognac glasses with a greenish, foggy liquid.

"Absinthe, Robinson. The drink of the shadow regions. You can still find it here. The founder of the former *Chat Noir*, the original club, was named Georges Salis. He created a marvellous form of theatre. The *théâtre de l'ombre*. Theatre of the netherworld. It produced the greatest occult productions of the end of the nineteenth century. *Carnaval de Venise. Flagrant Délit.* Classics from the underground. And sometimes, imagine Robinson, even religious and mystical themes. In the midst of a sewer of whores. Two of its most celebrated *amateurs* were Zola and Alphonse Daudet. The theatre supposedly died with Salis, but if you read between the lines, you can still see it."

Tranh clinked his glass up against mine.

"I'm very pleased to see you. Where did you disappear to? People have been asking after you down at *Le Tambour.*"

"She's gone, Tranh."

"Of course. You miss her, don't you?"

"Not exactly. It's more like withdrawal."

"It's the warm body, isn't it, Robinson? Love we can do without. But, we all need a warm body, don't we? You just miss the warm body."

"Listen, Tranh, I'm a little short this week. You wouldn't mind fronting a little bridge loan?"

Tranh's rodential laugh darting out of his mouth and into the closest sewer.

"Oh, no, not possible, absolutely not, so sorry, Robinson. But, good luck."

It was about an hour's walk to *rue du Repos. Père Lachaise* cemetery. I was walking towards the mausoleum, picked up a flower from one of the paths. A *Bourse de Pasteur*. She'd asked me to visit the place. *In memory of me, Franck*. I let her talk me into one last meeting. For old times sake. For a moment, she went off on a real tangent.

"You remember how I talked about harems all the time, Franck? Well, they have taken the idea one step further. Obedience schools, Franck. *Des écoles de dressage.* And, once the girls have been prepared ... So we can have enough money forever. *Pour aller jusqu'au bout.*"

Tears were sliding down her cheeks. They looked real. They looked like she might even believe they were real.

"We have to settle down, Franck. Forget all this madness. Find ourselves a place and start up a family together."

Then she had relented, smiled, realized the whole thing was futile. A *brique*'s worth makeup couldn't mask the black eye swelling out of her face. It was just there.

A vaporous mist had descended over the cemetery. As if to provide cover for fugitives preparing a break-out. Then, for the last time: "What are you thinking, Franck?"

"I'm thinking there's a big space between human beings. That in the end we're alone."

"What attracted you to me, Franck?"

"You won't take it personally?"

"Trust me, Franck."

She smiled. We both laughed. I realized that it was one of the things we didn't do too often. Some of the things we did just precluded laughing. Maybe it was that she usually smiled before she destroyed things.

"Your cunt."

"So, it was just like with the others. I was nothing more than your little *pute*, is that it?"

"No, I don't think that at all. You got sidelined, that's all. Your life dream is more traditional. More like, you want a cozy little fireplace, get knocked up again, that sort of thing."

I walked through the bric-à-brac of headstones, flat tombs, and cairns beneath the cenotaphs and shrines ringing the cemetery like contours of a mountain vineyard, the stones overgrown with thistles and vines. As if to mark the occasion, the day had turned dismal. I arrived at the vertical mausoleum and stepped inside.

The same etched inscription on two drawers.

Victor Levy   Estelle Goldstein
Rachel Levy [1950-1970]   "a refuge for men
                                   in need"

An unsuccessful attempt had been made to remove the swastikas scrawled on the wall. The two sets of graffiti still intact. "*Mort aux juifs.*" "*Juden verboten.*" I recalled her words, as she showed me the door.

"In your own way, it cannot end well for someone like me. That would be a betrayal of what I am. Can you see that, Franck?"

"Why does it have to end badly?"

I wasn't trying to stop her from doing anything. That was her business. But, I was curious, particularly since I didn't have to stick around for the aftermath.

"Franck, there are things that are far worse than dying."

It was a stupid question. Who does it end well for? At any rate, I'd done my part. She was free, in the same way that the rest of us were free. Which is to say, for the time being.

II

Dawn. Again. I entered the American bar on Mouffetard, where Sheba and I had spent our first evening together. I ordered a stand-up blackberry brandy and vodka martini. The place was half full or half empty depending on what time you arrived. A group of South American dykes slouched against a billiards table in the far end. Beside me, two couples perched on stools, engaged in a heated discussion while brandishing champagne flutes. She was wearing a fur coat over a rose-tinted blouse and a black miniskirt over black tights. Her left hand curled around three necklaces of lapis lazuli, copal and amber beads. Her right hand held a cigarette, which she was thrusting staccato in the direction of a blonde-haired, foppish boy-toy, in order to assert with considerable vehemence a fact she knew to be wrong. The French are like that. Nubians wearing see-through blouses pontificate blandly about the topography of the Massif Central.

"*Tu vas m'écouter une fois pour tout*, Fabrice. Rodez is not the capital of Aveyron."

She tilted her head to the right, blew some smoke and ashes in the direction of the bartender. Butted out the cigarette. Pulled out another, without lighting it. The boy-toy watched her with an exasperated grimace.

"Rodez. Is. The capital of Aveyron."

"No, it isn't, *espèce de nul*," she rebutted dismissively.

I leaned towards her, pushed a briquet in front of her face, lit her cigarette. Threw in my own two bits.

"Sainte Radegonde. The capital of Aveyron."

"Sainte Radegonde. The capital of Aveyron!" the toy-boy repeated incredulously.

"My uncle, a Jew, was shot at dawn there in 43 by the Nazis. I think there are still shells stuck in the South wall. Just beneath the statue of Our Lady of the Underworld."

"I apologize. *Je suis vraiment navré.*"

He extended his hand. I took it, keeping my eyes on the woman.

"Don't worry about it."

The woman smiled.

"Caroline."

She passed me her card. Caroline Tiberi. Communications Agent. Committee for the Re-election of the President.

"M'*sieur* is a traveller?"

"Dr. Franck Thompson. But you can call me Franck."

"Franck," repeated Caroline, who obviously recognized a fellow philosopher from the school of relative truths.

"A pilgrim of sorts. With many sins to purge."

I turned to the bartender.

"Drinks for my *friends*."

"I think *m'sieur* Franck wants someone to show him around Paris, *non*?"

"Paris," I responded, "the capital of France."

I passed her my business card, wrote down my telephone number, and left the café. I walked up *rue Descartes*, and along an abandoned stretch of *rue Clovis*, against the chalk walls of *Lycée Henri IV*. I stopped for a moment in front of *Église Ste-Geneviève*, recalling my first ride with Sheba, the front-wheel drive spinning out of control, Sheba downshifting into second, the car drifting into the wrought-iron rails surrounding the courtyard of the Pantheon. It was much later that she told me that she had done the whole thing deliberately. To see how I would react.

On Sunday afternoons, Ducastin-Chanel and I usually went out for our Sunday walk. We had just crossed a bridge in the *Bois de Boulogne*, and were now strolling up the *avenue du maréchal Lyautey*, past a string of acne-scarred, Rio de Janeiro pre-op transexuals, parked like Amazons on the asphalt. A storm had uprooted several thousand trees, many of which lay strewn in bric-à-brac piles along the trails of the park. Ducastin-Chanel shook her head disapprovingly as we walked past a six-foot Puerto Rican in a miniskirt.

"Look at this motley collection of she-males. In the middle of a residential district. They should respect the *quartier*. But it proves what I have always believed, Franck. Johns don't like ordering escorts over the phone. You need a sidewalk. Telephone escorts are just a dating service. It has to be a curbside contract, Franck, or it's nothing. *Intuitu personae*. Two parties, vendor and purchaser, cutting a face-to-face, arms-length deal. Value given and received. Over the counter. *De gré à gré*."

Ducastin-Chanel stopped briefly, bent over, coughed up a gob of phlegm and spat it roughly onto the ground.

"That's enough for today, Franck. I can't go a step further."

We continued down the boulevard until I spotted a taxi-stand. I helped her inside the cab.

"You go on ahead. I'm continuing my walk."

"Stay away from those she-males, Franck!" she sputtered.

I descended the *rue des belles feuilles* towards Trocadero, then down to the river. The *bâteau-mouches* moored like floating hives, tourists buzzing into their places beneath the Eiffel Tower. There were a lot of ways to spend your time on the planet. I was a client of the Parisian whore, a sub-stratum of a certain form of perishables. One of the first truly global businesses, and with no risk of going the way of the dot.com and the Edsel. Recession-proof. Immune to the usual caprices of the market. Every group of society had a few members who partook. Bankers, lawyers, plumbers, artisans, the unemployed, politicians, fathers, community leaders, church volunteers, bank robbers, sewer cleaners, cosmetic surgeons. Blacks, whites, greens. Ecologists, stalinists, anarchists, realians, eckankar freaks, speed chess players. All voting with their dicks, so to speak. Dicks as big as genetically modified cucumbers, and dicks as small as a clitoris. Round sticks, limp dicks, dicks as hard as two by fours, circumcised dicks, black dicks, yellow dicks, dicks that wouldn't pass muster at the agricultural fair.

We had no moral qualms about kowtowing during business hours, parking in our stalls and letting society's mechanical milkers hook up to our teats for the day. But once we punch the clock, our thoughts do not turn to the cozy fireplace, or to our spouses and children, or to a prayer of gratitude for god's infinite justice. We just want to get fucked. Fucked royally if possible, and we are willing to pay through the nose for it. And somehow, not enough to do just that, for at heart, the john is not a selfish creature, but an idealist whose dreams have been shattered at some point in time. Shattered by an uncle who wanted to get jacked off. Or by a ball-cutting wife. Or a boss who will make you grovel for a cheque. Or the discovery that a teacher doesn't believe a word of what he is teaching. So, his act requires a sort of communion with the world. At least, that is the way I looked at it. We lived on the assembly line, so we preferred mass, assembly-line sex. We were crushed, so it gave us pleasure to watch our seed squeezed out of us, rather than be wasted on procreation. We were diseased, so it justified our lives to visualize our disease, to witness the sperm, sputum and vomit wash down the St-Denis artery, before stepping up and making our own offering on the altar of waste. We were beyond words; our only way to articulate was to furtively shove our hard-earned cash into the hooker's hands, skulk behind her down a long corridor, or behind a set of washrooms, or inside a car, and getting sucked off, or jacked off, in other words, acting out exactly what is lived day in and out, but at least for once, calling it what it is.

As I entered the apartment, *rue de Mulhouse*, the phone rang.

"Franck," said a female voice as I answered. "Franck," the voice repeated.

I wrenched the receiver away from my mouth and held it at a distance. Covered the mouthpiece. Slowed my breathing down.

"*C'est moi*. Caroline. Committee for the Re-election of the President."

She laughed.

"Caroline," I repeated, still excavating the memory banks for something recognizable.

"Caroline. The girl from Aveyron."

"Sainte Radégonde."

"*Elle-même.*"

During the three or four seconds it took me to place her, I watched the wallpaper change hues, darkening as if the electricity had powered out.

"How are you? That is, how are you, Caroline?" I managed to get out.

"I'm available. That's how I am."

I still had a couple of hours to kill before she arrived. I picked up some Sancerre, champagne, smoked Norwegian salmon and cigarettes. By early evening, I was refilling a daiquiri glass with Triple Sec, cutting off orange wedges for an improvised martini, when I heard the tackety-tack of high heels coming up the stairs. I opened the door, watched her climb the last few steps up to the stairhead.

"*Putain.*"

Her high heels cocked at an awkward angle, inwards. She was pigeon-toed, asthmatic enough to enter a bagpipes competition. I noticed a beauty spot on her cheek. Decided she had put it on for the night. She had the kind of legs which only Parisians have. Thin, but unmarked by exercise. None of the rippling musculature of American women. She wore a black one-sided shoulder dress. A gold chiffon draped over the covered shoulder.

She examined the room, fumbling for something in her purse while she caught her breath.

"Why didn't you tell me you were on the sixth floor?"

"They are hoping to put in an elevator. Drink?"

"Champagne."

She remained standing while I poured out the champagne. I handed her the glass, clinked mine against hers. Placed my arm around her, and kissed her on the mouth. She wriggled away, retreated a step, sat on the bed, drank some of the champagne.

"Take your coat off."

She allowed the coat to fall from her shoulders onto the bed.

"*Tu viens?*"

After she finished the champagne, I offered her one of my own concoctions, a simple boardwalk martini. Vodka, dry vermouth, maraschino liqueur and lemon juice.

She seemed pretty happy with that. I pulled her micro-skirt to her knees, revealing a white panty with a tiny bow in the centre and a black garter belt holding up sheer panty hose. It was like unravelling a Christmas present. The martini glass propped against the head of the bed.

Her facial features had initially reminded me of a burnished rock sculpture of a bird of prey. She had something which was drawn from the same genetic source code as Sheba's. I always watched a woman's face while we fucked. To see where the truth stopped and the simulacra started. Caroline's angular features becoming translucent, like the sheen of her white, lace-top hose now leaning against a half-empty bottle of Vermouth in the corner of the room.

Some time later, we lay in bed, both of us smoking, thinking whatever people think after fucking someone they hardly know. Basking in the zone of relief before the shit begins.

"If you wake up in the middle of the night, I want you to start making love to me before I regain consciousness."

She paused, slowly exhaling.

"And, then, tomorrow, I want to move to a proper hotel. This place is a dump. *Un vrai taudis.*"

We holed up in *Hôtel de Crillon* and were laying in bed in the *Duc de Crillon* suite, a large living room decorated with six metre high, hand-painted, wooden panels, all in an 18th century style. A rectangular, teak coffee table at the foot of our bed was littered with the remains of chilled melon, parma ham, grilled salmon, grapefruit and morellos and pistachio cream, and some champagne. Italian marble bathrooms are all right, and it wasn't my bill, but to me this was the real shite end of the city, who cares if a Duke shat in the same urn three hundred years previous. At any rate, royalty had been replaced with New York Jewesses and wives of dictators, in short people out to prove a point, and pollute the air with their hair dyes and the landscape with the sight of dead animals wrapped round their necks. I was one hundred per cent on the same page as the ecologists on this point. Dead animals were meant to be food, not apparel.

"You know, Franck, there is a copy of this suite in the Metropolitan Museum of New York."

Caroline picked up a *chocolatine*, dabbed it absently with *beurre de Normandie*, considering something.

"Where did you go last night, Franck?"

"For a walk."

"Where?"

"Wee Willie's."

"Wee Willie? Who *eez zat*?"

How could you not like a people whose English-speaking chromosome had been removed at birth.

"Serves the best *Andouillette pommes à l'huile* in Paris."

"I wish you would talk to me the way you talk about Wee Willie's."

I recalled the last good day I had spent there, with a bottle of chilled Chablis on a lazy spring afternoon, to the tune of that second *arrondissement* tart with the pig-tails playing the accordion. Nirvana. For the simple, deal-clinching reason that the only thing you had to pay for at Wee Willie's was the bill, and then it was over and done with and you could move on to the next self-grati-fying piece of sense-titillation, of a particular sub-brand which can only be found in cities like Paris, because they hit you with so much sense-bombardment that any thoughts about the starving children of Africa or social duties, or even paying child support, were safely ex-punged into the netherworld of worthy thoughts, giving hedonism sufficient time and space to run rampant. That wasn't sustainable either, but it sure as hell was enjoyable while running the gamut between cutting the umbilical cord and being kicked into a grave.

"You've never loved anyone, have you, Franck?"

"Depends on your definition of love."

"If you don't feel love, what do you feel, Franck?"

"I just feel what I feel. I don't pretend to know what other people are feeling. Nobody can do that."

She wore her blond hair short, pageboy style. Her skin was fresh, pubescent. Her eyes wide open, a blue that reminded me of robins' eggs. Her cheeks were flush and her skin downy-soft. She wore a white blouse, un-buttoned down the middle, exposing her breasts. It was easy enough to see that Caroline fell into the subset of those with something tainted from the outset, of the kind of depravity that can only be self-taught, rather than learned through abuse, rape, or by a mentor in the sex-trade business.

Below the white blouse, she wore a grey peasant dress, which fell to her ankles. The peasant dress was a wraparound, held around her waist by a cord and covering nothing but a cunt shaved like an apricot. I reached for the cord and pulled it lightly, which peeled away the folds of her skirt. I bent down to one knee, and began suckling her right tit. After a few minutes, she was obviously stoked up. I mounted her from behind, taking my time, torturing her a bit, then thrusting harder and harder. I didn't hear any objections.

The satin sheets beneath us were seeping with blood and menstrual waste. Washing beneath her in a thick, suppurating flow that had dried upon contact, and now was caked to the sheet like a fossilized rock formation that had hardened into tectonic plate. She turned towards me. I noticed that her own face was also covered in a mix of lactation and blood, which reminded me of afterbirth. Somehow, I had pushed her face right into the sheets as I fucked her. She smiled.

"Hold on, Caroline, just have to make a quick phone call."

I dialed Sheba's cell number, but received a recorded message.

"Sheba Goldenstein. *Adieu, tout le monde.* No need to call, Franck. I have departed for the land of no memories."

I waited for the tone.

"Hey, Sheba, sorry you're not there. Listen to this. My new girlfriend, even loopier than you, baby."

I handed Caroline the phone.

"Just say something. Anything."

I wondered whether I knew Caroline's middle name. I thought the initial might be J. If you don't know someone's middle name, you're not interested in them. That's a rule. And, despite all of this, I was thinking, you and me, baby, we are like everyone else on this planet. And no matter how you dress it up, and no matter how good it looks on paper, not even a good piece of cunt tastes better than Wee Willie's *andouillette*. Caroline hung up the phone.

"Who was that?"

"A friend."

"Franck, you know, we don't come from the same place. But, can't you see, Franck, I gave up everything so we could finish our life together?"

"We've known each other for four days. Don't expect commitment from me, baby."

"I can't live without you, Franck. I'll kill myself."

She didn't seem to like what she was seeing on my face, but she was simultaneously reflecting on something, reviewing her options. So to speak. I kept an eye on her, but my mind was doing a fast rewind to the pre-Sheba era, and what followed, thinking because you let yourself listen to this hot little piece of tail and her weird take on destiny, you can say goodbye to Wee Willie's Filet Mignon *sauce tartare maison*, washing it down with Chablis or Sancerre and consulting Omar Sharif's weekly advice on the Friday night race card at Vincennes, just when you're on the verge of retrieving it.

I glanced at Caroline. If Omar Sharif were checking out this filly for afts and raceability, the verdict would be runs like hell, but turns right off the track when she hits the stretch. And if you're riding her, be careful getting off after the race is over, because she might hoof you right in the head.

"Did I ever tell you my first wife killed herself?"

"Non. *Et alors?*"

"I'm not even sure where she's buried. I guess I missed the funeral. Kind of caught me during a busy week."

I lit a cigarette. Didn't offer her one. Looked her straight in her eyes, which were azure that day. Or at least her lenses were.

"Franck, your end is going to be slow and painful."

"It's what precedes the end that interests me, not the end."

"You just don't know how to give."

"That's good. Actually, I think you're just pissed because my world doesn't revolve around you. Every beautiful woman experiences it sooner or later, and career women with looks are the worst of the lot. When men get obsessed with them, they confuse the obsession with them being interesting people. Neither side is sustainable. Count yourself lucky."

"You are a real *minus*, Franck. You'll never amount to anything."

"Hey, that's good. My mother used to say that."

"Really. Tell me, Franck. What did she say?"

"She'd say, Franck, you're too young to understand. But it's a genetic thing. You come from a worthless line of sons of bitches."

She didn't seem amused.

"Franck, you have completely missed what I am about."

"No, I've got a pretty clear read on you."

"Tell me, Franck. I'm intrigued."

"Well, you think you're a fascinating individual, basically because you've relieved a few men of their hard-earned funds in support of the President, who from what I've heard is a bona fide criminal with blood on his hands. You've ridden in some sleek vehicles and attended a few gala evenings. Big fucking deal. You're the nobody, baby, because you think you're somebody."

She's listening, and looking pretty homicidal, but her strongest argument is that pair of tits popping out of the half-cup bra, and I'm starting to think they're watching me as well.

"Franck, have you ever thought of fucking your mother? You want to suck on mommy's tit, Franck? Come to mommy, Francky?"

Bad habits are the hardest ones to kick. She's no longer a face, or a brain, or a set of legs. Just a cunt, speaking via invisible fibre optic cable directly wired to my pituitary gland, taunting me. You're a loser, Franck, you'll amount to anything—can you smell me, Franck? You're a bottom-feeding crustacean, scuttling across the ocean floor, and I'm a sea urchin. And, I'm talking right back to this sea urchin of a cunt, because Sheba has disappeared, nothing left but a fleshy slab oozing more slime which draws me in closer. And, I'm not caring too much about what I just said, or what will happen after, because the two of us, i.e. me and that cunt, have developed our own Esperanto from hell.

I pulled my belt out of its loops, wrapped it around my right hand in a coil, and approached. Two ambulatory human shapes, host organisms for a cock and a cunt, secreting, pulsating, throbbing. We were fulfilling our purpose on planet earth. And maybe it was putting off the inevitable, but it kept us from killing each other for another day.

I was about a step away from her, and could see that she was happy, i.e. in a state of remission, while she waited to get serviced, or beaten or whatever. Then, a knock on the door.

"Who is it?"

"Police."

She crossed the room and disappeared into the bathroom. I opened the door. The man was alone. Dressed in civilian clothes. I stood in front of him.

"Thierry Duboeuf. *Brigade Criminelle.* May I come in?"

"What's the problem?"

"We've had a number of complaints concerning you."

I nodded in the direction of the bathroom.

"Take a seat. Just have to take care of something, and I'll be right with you."

Caroline was busy pasting foundation onto her face.

"You're going to have to leave."

"*Non, mais, tu rigoles.* I'm not moving until I'm fin-ished."

"The police are here."

"I don't care if it's the police. *Non, mais, stop! Tu me fais mal!*"

After I threw her out, I sat down with Duboeuf.

"So, what's this about?"

"The *Société Générale* has contacted us concerning a number of bad cheques."

"The SG? You've got to be kidding. What, have they run out of Jews to spoliate?"

"This is no trifling matter, Mr Robinson. The hotel management is treating this with the gravity it deserves. They are performing their own audit of your accounts as we speak. I understand they are considerable."

"I don't see the connection. I'm an Amex man. Plastic."

"You'll have ample time to present your case. In the meantime, I'm sure you'll understand, the best thing would be for you to leave the hotel."

A sullen girl working the desk at the Clauzel told me Millie had disappeared with six months of back rent owing. I tracked her down on a short stretch of *rue St Honoré* walk-ups which had escaped demolition during the razing of *Les Halles*. Her walk-up squat amounted to a room and a half, equipped with a hot plate and an elephant's foot toilet that wouldn't look out of place on the streets of Sanliurfa. Since I'd last seen her, she had lost a bicuspid, and another one — her eye tooth — had turned a viscous maroon in the interim. She had been pushed down a stretch of St-Denis with the older hook-ers, just off *rue des Lombards*. She poured out a coffee, pulled out a pack of Gauloises.

"Where have you been?"

"My fat mouth, Franck. Some Kosovan girls tried to move in on my clients. I fought back, and they brought in someone. A real motherfucker, Franck. Some kind of Uzbek. Never mind. I'm glad you came by. What can I do you for?"

"Nothing."

"You dropped by to hear more about *la gamine*?"

"No, I'm done with her."

"What, you didn't hear about her?"

"Hear about what?"

She shrugged her shoulders.

"See for yourself."

She threw yesterday's copy of *Le Parisien* onto the table. "Page 17. *Fait Divers*."

There was a picture of her, wearing a beret. I had bought it for her in Biarritz. I felt a gnawing at my stomach. Unidentified girl found mortally wounded in Père Lachaise. Followed by a brief article:

> *Qui est la mystérieuse?*
>
> A group of American schoolchildren touring Père Lachaise was confronted with the discovery of the recently murdered body of a young, unidentified woman in the South end of the cemetery. Inspector Thierry Duboeuf of the *Police Judiciaire* described the young woman as unusually beautiful, "more fit for the catwalk than a cemetery. Not someone who you could forget, even in death." Anyone with information is invited to contact the *Unité de Police de quartier*, rue Gambetta, Paris 20th.

"It doesn't say anything about cause of death."

"She died because her time was up. Franck, I warned you. She was bad news."

I fingered the newspaper, just letting the news sink in.

"She's just a piece of white trash. Good looking piece of white trash with a couple of good angles and a real mean streak in her."

"No, she was more than that."

"Sure, Franck. Did she tell you her father fought in the war? Indochina, Algeria. Et cet-er-a-ba-bla-bla."

"So?"

"So? You know how he lost his arm, Franck? He was an armed security guard for Brinks, and got into a car accident. A fender bender. Five miles an hour. Fell out of the truck. Broke his arm. Broke it, Franck. In France. Like any good drunk, he put off getting it fixed. When he finally went in, the doctor fucked up the operation, and it became gangrenous. So, he and his daughter invented all that shit. End of story. End of the war."

"Whatever. She still deserves a funeral."

"Of course, Franck. You've never followed my advice. I mean, why would you now?"

"You haven't given me any."

She stashed the gauloises into her blouse pocket, pulled a pack of Drum tobacco from the shelf and tossed it onto the table, then spread some of the tobacco onto an old copy of *Midi-Matin* and rolled herself a smoke. She gazed out the window, which looked down on a four-square-metre, inaccessible courtyard. I had seen her only six months previous.

"Not exactly the Clauzel, is it, Franck?"

"Couldn't you make an anonymous phone call? Ask whether a friend can throw a funeral?"

She lit the cigarette. The roots of her hair white, and it didn't look like the hair dye budget was healthy.

"Game, Franck. Life span of an Iguana."

"Out in the wild? Or pet."

"Pet."

"Forty years."

"Twenty. What about a turtle?"

"Fifty."

"Over a century, Franck. Now, human realm. What's the average career span of a player in the National Football League?"

"Easy. Twelve years."

"Four, Franck. Now, getting a little closer to home, let's try a heroin addict."

"Five years. With luck."

"I said averages, Franck. Eighteen months. Now, whore, Franck. How long?"

"Let me put it this way. You look like shit, Millie."

She smiled. Several dozen tricks worth of dental work publicly exposed.

"People over here, they just aren't like us, Franck. I mean, they've got fucking white skin, but shit, man, that's about it. Besides, I'm a Cherokee. But they're not like us, Franck. I mean, you're a scumball, Franck, and I'm a whore. But we both like Stevie Ray Vaughan, and we both ... fuck it, Franck. I have a friend back home, Larry, he's a transvestite dancer, but, I used to babysit his kids. He lives in a trailer camp outside Chicago. I'm thinking of calling it a day."

She shook her head.

"You ever seen a 300-pound linebacker in a tutu? Tell you what; it ain't the Bolshoi, Franck."

"He could always try the *Nutcracker Suite*. Anyway, if you're homesick, that at least solves that."

"Actually, it doesn't at all, Franck. He has no phone, so I somehow have to scrape up enough cash to get back. Fuck, Franck, this would have been a snap six months ago."

"What happened to you, Millie? I mean, nothing personal, but you look like you caught something. You know, like something viral."

"I have no idea. I think it's cancer, or something. Besides, without ovaries, you're not a woman anymore. You get old overnight. Then, these damn teeth problems, Franck. Don't contact the police, Franck. They will fuck you, and they will do it well."

"There's something else at stake."

She shook her head.

"Franck, don't you get it? I thought you were a criminal lawyer. They couldn't care less who killed her! On the other hand, if they nail someone, and I mean anybody, Franck, it's job security for life. You know, like 'I'm the one who caught the prick,' or even better for the grandchildren, 'It took me three days, but, I broke the killer of *la gamine*.' Come to think of it, maybe I should be the one cross-examining you. I mean, who the fuck are you, Franck, when it comes down to it? Some asshole john. Anonymous. Desperate, capable of anything. I should be watching what's left of my own ass for a change."

She looked out the window. Her cigarette had gone out. She wiped her right eye. Maybe, it was just dust.

"What do you want to know, Millie? I'm an open book."

"Well, how about, where were you on the night of ..."

She reached for the paper.

"August 22."

"All right, I see what you mean. Depends on how you look at it."

"On how you look at it!! You've been skulking your way around bordellos asking about her, like some kind of stalker. About 25 girls in and around the street could testify to that. While we're on the topic, what the hell *were* you doing on the Seine the night Alena died?"

"The usual. Out drinking with Tranh."

"Out drinking with Tranh. Damn, I mean, shit, Franck, do you know who this Tranh character is? Has he ever told you what he did, before, Franck? Do you really want to know, or not?"

"Not. Sheba deserves a burial. She was always big on rites."

It was good to get out on the street again. Everybody had their thoughts, and Millie was doing her best, but she was a little too focussed on her return ticket to the States. It seemed like we were both more or less tearing pages out of the same book. And it wasn't the rule book. Little by little, doors seemed to be closing, outside of those leading to the peep-shows. I was probably on my way to becoming some kind of dirty old man. But it was a little late to think about moving onto anything else.

On one level, I felt like I was just getting started on things. If Sheba had shown me anything, she had demonstrated that sex had nothing to do with the appendages hanging from our bodies. Labia, penises, tits and ass, they only had importance *per se* if you were operating in a particular zone which held no interest for me. Fucking was the central goal, but I was more attracted to the self-abasement aspect. I mean, the knowledge that your preferred daily activity involves the unguent, pulsating, pestilent climes of the cunt and other unnameable corners of the body, obviously there was something life itself was offering up that was far worse.

Plus, there were other conclusions that I'd more or less come to. I still hadn't figured out what sex was, but I knew that in its pure form, it could only be a place of desolation or an animal act. The only thing that counts is what you are thinking exactly at the point of orgasm. If you could master that, you became a church of one, without any need for parishioners and collection boxes to keep the operation going.

And then it came to me, and the thought made me angry somehow, not for feeling it, but for taking so long to figure out what it was. I'd only said it to her once, after that incident with the Baron, but the fact was that I loved her. So now, I'm realizing that I was in love with this young French broad who is dead in Père Lachaise, and I know that I'm going to be heading down to the 20th *arrondissement* precinct, and making the day of some 105 IQ type in the Police Judiciaire, and that the odds of him seeing things from my point of view were similar to betting the farm on a syphilitic nag in the fourth race at Vincennes.

But, I still wanted to give her a funeral. I'd never lost a case. Maybe I could talk some sense into the bone-heads down at the precinct.

Dear Hervé,

I was released five days ago, no thanks to you. They've obviously never heard of *habeas corpus* in this country. Preventive detention in La Santé prison is no picnic, and forty-five days is a long time to discover that the State had no case against me.

It might have gone differently if you had answered my one phone call, and hadn't frozen my French bank accounts, friend. It's one thing to kill people around here, but don't get involved in really serious shit like passing bad cheques at five star hotels. Even if you do know the staff.

I've had some time to think about this, Hervé. Just so it's clear, I can smell a man covering his decrepit, poxy backside from ten thousand kilometres away. Trust funds or not, it was my call, and I'm starting to wonder whether you're not giving it to Tillman. Viagra pretty well makes anything possible, doesn't it? What's old Margaret like, Hervé? I can picture her teeth rattling like a player piano, and you sticking that root vegetable of yours up her twat.

So, as long as we're discussing farm products, if you have a *grain* of decency, Hervé, in that seedy old mind of yours, you might free up a couple of thousand dollars *of my own money* and wire it to me, Western Union, Place de l'Odéon, *illico presto*, as I have a few outstanding accounts with some working girls in these parts, and at least *their* accounts should be honoured.

Did I tell you that Sheba died? She left me a note, Hervé, so it must have been suicide, but the boneheads down at the 20th precinct said it was impossible to determine. Because there was only one shot. No reference to six hours per day of sadian sports, no repentance, no nothing. Although she did mention that she had satisfied the criterion to be buried in Père Lachaise, i.e. dying in Paris. And, then, get this, asking me to take care of her daughter. Me, Franck Robinson, whoremonger, man on the run, deadbeat dad.

I was the only person who knew her at the funeral, but I brought along everyone from Number 2, rue de Mulhouse. De Vecchi and I had spent the morning knocking back Pastis, so he was three sheets to the wind. Ducastin-Chanel was in her glory, wearing a floppy hat the size of a direct broadcast satellite. Bazin was impeccable. Even Lafontaine showed up, and render unto Caesar bla-bla-bla, he didn't jack off during the ceremony. This may sound funny coming from me, Hervé, but these people have a core decency about them. You'd be hard pressed to find anyone like them in North America, if you scoured the place for a decade.

The interment itself started out very *pro forma*. Ducastin-Chanel screeched out a few lines of the Ave Maria and then went into full drift. At one point, she lifted up her dress, and for a good five minutes fixated on scratching a corn off her thigh. The officer of the 20th *arrondissement* stuck to his job. It was routine, which was fine, but when he paused at her name, something got to me. It was a fill in the blank rite, pure boiler plate, Hervé, but still. I tore the sheet out of his hands, and started my own oration. Argued my best trial ever. Talked about a handful of scumbags taking over the planet, thinning out populations, twelve year old children being buried to their waist in excrement and stoned to death, Presidents getting their cocks sucked in sub-basements. I really went off on a tangent, Hervé. Admittedly, I'd had a few drinks that morning, but I was still ranting when the police arrived and dragged me down to the station. As a material witness.

So, that's about it, until I receive some more funds from you. And, with nothing to go back to, and nothing to look forward to, do you think old Franck is going to buy a few months' reprieve by reforming?

You know me better than that.

III

The day after my release, I returned to the section of Père Lachaise where the funeral ceremony had been held, but saw no tombstone. I recognized the scattered remnants of a bouquet of white roses that Ducastin-Chanel had brought with her, but no other sign of our presence. I stood for a moment in the drizzle, then left the cemetery, and headed for the 20th *arrondissment Mairie* on *rue Gambetta, Service de l'Etat Civil.* I took a ticket number, sat down, waited til my number came up, told the clerk I wanted to see the Officer of the Civil Registry. Waited some more. A security guard walked up to me. Pointed at a poster on the wall, depicting a cigarette. The cigarette was covered by a large red X.

"*Défense de fumer.*"

"You have got to be kidding. This is Paris. What are the ashtrays for?"

"To put them out. *Nouveau règlement.*"

A man emerged from the rear offices. Smiled, friendly enough. Come with me. I followed him into an office
looking out over the *rue Gambetta*. He offered me a seat.

"So, what can I do for you?"

"You remember me? You presided over the funeral of
a friend. Sheba Rosenstein."

"Of course I remember you. You created quite a
scene. Very unworthy of your office."

"I just returned from the cemetery. I can't find her
grave."

He shrugged his shoulders.

"*C'est normal.* It's not there."

"Listen, friend, I'm not here to pull teeth. What's the
story?"

"No arrangements had been made. In these cases,
and since no arrangements had been made, it is no longer in my jurisdiction. *Ce n'est plus dans mon rayon.* Wait a
moment."

He stood up, walked across the room to a grey metal
3-door vertical filing cabinet. Opened the second drawer,
and pulled out two sheets of paper, sat down again and
passed one of them across to me. It was titled Decree of
13 July 1948 concerning the interment of human remains.

"Look at article L-2235. Right there. 'For entitlement to
burial, the deceased must hold a reserved *titre de concession.*'"

"So, what does that mean?"

"It means that without a plot of land, no burial. And,
now look at article L-2276. Where, after 45 days, the
remains of the deceased are unclaimed, the *Mairie* may
dispose of the remains as it sees fit."

"Hold on. It's only been 43 days."

"That is correct."

"So, where the hell is she!?"

"In the morgue. For two more days."

"Christ, that's great! So, we can still do this thing!"

I punched the air upwards. He watched me, as they say, impassively.

"So, where do we start? I want to bury her."

He stood up again, back to the same drawer, another form, back to the desk.

"**Form B**—*Claims pursuant to the Decree of 12 July 1948.*"

"What's this for?"

"Mr Robinson. You stated that you would like to bury Ms Rosenstein. This is France. We have laws. Usually there are fees to pay. In this case, interment is subject to a fee of 2400 francs."

"All right, fine. I'll take it."

"That's fine. If you wish, I can prepare the paper work. Take this *bordereau* out to the Caisse, and then come back here. Either cheque, or Carte Bleu."

"I don't have either."

"I am sorry. We no longer do death on the instalment plan."

"Look. She deserves a proper burial. Isn't there some way of discounting this?"

"I'll be back in a moment."

He left the room. Several minutes later he returned.

"What's that for?"

"A *pêle*."

"I know it's a goddam shovel. What's it for?"

"It's our self-service option. At the price you are willing to pay, only one person is qualified for the job. Take it or leave it."

"I'll take it."

"*Bien*. Go to the South entrance of the cemetery. The concierge is Monsieur Paul. I will phone him in the meantime. If you dig the hole yourself, I will take care of the rest."

By four in the afternoon, I had made good progress, but it was starting to rain. At the edge of the cemetery, I noticed an Asian man pointing in my direction, accompanied by an old woman, their faces barely visible through the rain, under an oversized umbrella.

"Robinson! *Mais, c'est formidable*!!"

Ducastin-Chanel shook her head.

"*Un scandale*! You don't make a man dig his own wife's tomb! *Mais, c'est dégueulasse*! They're treating him like a dog! *Choquant*."

"We heard you were in prison, Robinson! When did you get out?"

Ducastin-Chanel interrupted.

"Franck, I am going right now to buy a *messe* for your girlfriend. And some flowers for you. Don't you worry a bit."

Tranh clapped his hands.

"Absolutely right, *madame*. We must console the poor man. May I buy you a drink, Robinson? Come, come!"

IV

"*Je vous emmène, chéri?*"

Collette watched the first *arrondissement* pedestrian traffic move past through those unblinking gimlet-green eyes, as if she were a teller at the *quinte* window, selling tickets down at the Vincennes track, croaking out the same invitation with reptilian patience. Collette was a great-grandmother who worked the *rue de la Grande Truanderie*. Her features displayed nothing. Neither kindness, nor pity. Particularly not entreaty.

She smiled invitingly at nobody in particular, that is if you are inclined to call a desert gila monster grinning in three directions at once from the edge of a scalding boulder an invitation. Whatever she hadn't already hawked on *rue St-Denis* over the previous four decades peered out through her turret face, a makeshift construction of day creams, foundation, mascara, lipstick and rouge, shrouding half a century of fellatio, and marking half century of cataclysms and upheavals—the Indochina and Algeria conflicts, attempted coups against de Gaulle, the May '68 revolution, the all-night concerts and parties with Chet Baker, the destruction of *les Halles*.

"*Je vous emmène?*" she cawed again, and I realized the hoarse lilt of the question was asking a question behind the question. *Un train peut en cacher un autre.* The lizardskin epidermis collapsed into an atavistic grin. She rubbed her thumb and forefinger together as if starting a fire with flint.

"*Je vous emmène?*"

Then, in an undertone.

"You've brought it with you?"

I nodded. If she belonged anywhere, it was in Marvel Comics. The Incredible Hulkette. I followed her upstairs. She removed her shoes. She had a club foot and limped heavily. We entered a second-floor flat overlooking the pedestrian street. On the table beside the bed, a set of knitting needles in a plastic cup. Beside the cup, a partially darned set of stockings for an infant. On the wall behind, a photo of a young woman, wearing a bridal gown, accompanied by a dark, curly-haired man wearing a tuxedo. Cherubic looks.

"Did you bring the money?"

"It's arriving on Tuesday. Western Union."

"*Écoutez, mon mec*, you said you had the six hundred francs! To think I believed you were a lawyer. *Putain. Quel con!*"

I lit a cigarette.

"Who's that in the photo, Collette?"

"*Mêle-toi de tes oignons.* I want my money, or I call my pimp."

"Tell you what, Collette. Ever been to America?"

"*Quel intérêt?*"

"*Quel intérêt?* It's every French girl's dream! Pacific ocean. *La forêt canadienne.* Niagara Falls. A chance to begin everything."

Two tears streamed down her caulked face. Rivulets dripping through a chasm of broken dreams.

"*Conard*! *C'est le fric qu'il me faut, pauvre con! Fou-moi la paix.*"

"You know the *gamine*?"

"*Écoute, tu me fous la paix, tu m'entends!*"

Sometimes when, as the French put it, your butt is between two chairs, you end up, like I was, staring at a rhomboid-shaped lump of sugar on a table in an empty couscous restaurant in the early afternoon. As if it were auditioning for a Delaunay canvas. I don't suppose too many Hollywood scripts will be snapped up about guys spinning sugar cubes on table tops, but that is what I was engaged in. The label was a Euro production, approved by all the requisite Euro sugar *Appellation d'origine contrôlée* bodies in four languages. Zuiker. Sucre. Zucchero. Sugar. A coagulated lump of approved soluble glucose.

A heavy smog had descended over the city. I lit a cigarette, stubbed out the one still burning, caught sight of the pink neon sign overhanging the entrance to the *Brasserie Guignotte*. Lobster was on special. The banner in the window announced *Homard du Canada — fraîchement importée!!* I recalled the last time I had made love to her, and it suddenly didn't seem like a beautiful thing anymore. More like a couple of lobsters, beady, stalking eyes, oversized pincers; fighting for space on a stone-bed in an aquarium, oozing trails of lime-green unguent too vile to name.

Just about noon. Tranh would be arriving soon. I had enticed him with the image of Canadian lobster and *vin de Bourgogne*. Bourgogne. Dijon, capital of Bourgogne. Any place principally known for its mustard to be avoided at all costs. The pinnacle of municipal achievement a tripartite concoction of rape seed, vinegar and water. On the other hand, *Bourgogne Aligoté* was a nice base mix for a Kir. After a few of those, and lunch with Tranh, if I could squeeze a few hundred francs from him, I could pay an afternoon visit to Galicia and persuade her to give me a half hour of her time down in the former leprosarium. For old times sake. It wasn't perfection, but it was a hell of a lot better than living in Dijon.

Tranh entered the *Brasserie Guignotte* just as I waved the waiter back for a refill of my Kir.

"Cancel the order," Tranh called out, "a bottle of Veuve Cliquot and two flutes."

"What's the occasion?" I asked as he took a seat.

"The most remarkable occurrence, Robinson. My wife has died!"

"She died, or you killed her?"

"Incredible, Robinson. *Inoubliable.* Now, I can tell you everything. But, first promise me. Will you come to the funeral?"

"I don't know, Tranh. Not too big on ceremonial rites. We'll see."

"All right, fine, that's fine, we can discuss that over the champagne. Waiter, oh good, he is coming. My wife had made a last request. Victor, she had said to me before her decline, no matter how difficult, I want you to make love to me before we go to the Netherlands. It will bring me good luck. Of course, I agreed, despite the obvious logistical difficulties. And, yesterday was the big day. I will not bore you with the mechanics of the event, Robinson, but I will say that from my standpoint, it could not have been better. And, in mid-thrust, she expired, Robinson! Have you ever heard anything like it? Sudden cardiac death. I shall either be imprisoned, or go down in medical history. Or both!"

I had seen Tranh overexcited before, but it was the first time I saw him happy. We caught up on some other news in and around the quarter, when the topic of Alena came up.

"Robinson. Speaking of funerals, did I mention to you that I attended Alena's?"

"Our Alena? The one who jumped into the Seine?"

"One and the same. There were only three of us at the burial. Alena excluded, of course. Her mother was in attendance. A short, fat, non-descript woman from the Vienne region. She worked as a Monoprix cashier. Have you ever noticed those throw-away nail files the girls use on the street?"

"As a matter of fact, I have."

"They all come from the same Carrefour. A *grande surface* in Poitiers. A competitor!"

"So, who was the third person at her funeral?"

"You'll never believe it. Yannick, the doorman."

"What was he doing there?"

"It turns out he was madly in love with her, Robinson. During the ceremony, he threw himself into the open grave. During a rainstorm in Père Lachaise, *imagine-toi*. Alena's mother and I spent over half an hour just dragging him out of the hole. In the end, we were all covered in mud. So, other than that, nothing much. How are things with you?"

"Couple of residual issues. Nothing serious."

"The Vietnam veteran is still after you, I presume."

"Actually, Tranh, just between you and me, I don't think he'll be a problem."

Tranh sipped his champagne for a moment in silence. He was watching me, trying to figure something out. It didn't really bother me. He was far enough outside the loop. No dangers of the *téléphone arabe* being accessed.

"I mean, he's not quite as dangerous as I made out."

"But what about the wanted poster, Robinson? And the threats against your person."

"Actually, uhh, I sort of had something to do with that."

"Is it possible?"

"Oh yeah, it's possible all right. More than possible."

Tranh's attic mouse titter was activating, and continued like a low decibel scuttle for a good minute.

"Truly, truly, I have underestimated you. It was a ploy to rid yourself of this woman. Don't answer, I do not need the answer. May I ask you a favour?"

"Sure. You can ask."

"May I call you Franck?"

"Sure."

"Franck, I no longer know what to think. Only that there are no clear lines in life. Things are out of our hands, ultimately. And, I don't really care. Now, let's have some lunch!"

V

September 11. I'd been skulking up *rue St-Denis* towards *Porte St-Denis* and back to my starting point for two years. Djana, Verena and the African girls were out on afternoon shift. I spotted Galicia, standing in a doorway. She was wearing scarlet pumps, a dull pink t-shirt, and a set of canary pedal pushers so tight, her legs resembled a sulphurous yolk oozing out into the grate of a sewer right outside the door. Ready for a day at the beach. A Monoprix throw-away nail file propped negligently upwards between her thumb and index of her left hand, as she examined her lips in a compact mirror held in her right. She spotted me just as I crossed *Pas de Caire* in front of the leprosarium housing the Thai massage parlor.

"*Franck, tu viens?*"

I shook my head and burrowed forward. The sky was darkening. A grey rain dripping down for three days running.

"*Franck, tu viens?*"

Water sluicing through the gutters, a gastric acid of the previous day's waste.

"*Tu viens, Franck?*"

The street cleaners were on strike again. The shit, garbage and sputum caked to the asphalt. The work of a scatological schizophrenic with artistic pretensions.

"*Franck, tu viens? Allez, viens, je t'emmène, Franck ...*"

The African girls joined in Galicia's taunts. They formed a loose semi-circle. A Salvation Army choral group, offering cunt instead of eternal redemption. Galicia balancing a powder pack in her left hand. She couldn't have held a robin's eggshell with more delicacy, her lips puckered in mock pity.

"*Franck, tu viens pas?*"

At *boulevard de Bonne Nouvelle*, I turned left, and found myself in front of a bookstore of historical erotica. The thing about sex is you are just in it. All activity is reduced to the emission of fluids — the secretion of saliva, sweat and grunts. I lit a cigarette, and surveyed a string of photos, showing a Prussian nobleman of the nineteenth century flagellating three servile blondes on leashes.

The St-Denis whores had woven a web of their own making, stretching end to end along the seedy thoroughfare of human refuse. The pimps, flics, barmen and johns were nothing more than *figurants*, bit-players, and anyone who inhabited the realm knew it. We were the drones buzzing around in concentric circles, and the circles spiralled around chakra-like nexa, located in each and every cunt along that forsaken road.

Our own movements were without focus or direction, except as a function of the cunt. Their immobility was apparent only. It was the presiding of queens overlooking their domains. And St-Denis was the heart of it. Sex was for sale everywhere in the city of Paris. In respectable quarters and less respectable, but St-Denis was the temple of sleaze, and the crypt of the temple was down on the street. On the street, not even the cops or the pimps could compete with the girls. Any display of masculine power was sporadic, ineffective and purely ornamental. In theory, a pimp could beat the shit out of his girls, but if he did, word would get out and his stock-in-trade would decline overnight. An eager young pup of the *Brigade Judiciaire* could theoretically intervene, at the risk of discovering he had arrested the Deputy Mayor, or a Cardinal, or the bastard son of the Justice Minister. Or that he was screwing with his colleagues' side pay and commissions. The girls on the other hand knew that *as long as they put out*, they were basically untouchable.

I continued up *rue du Faubourg Poissonnière* towards the *Gare du Nord*.

I walked into the *Gare du Nord*. It too had been bombed, and somehow survived. Nazis had the run of the place for awhile. I walked back to *Brasserie la Guignotte*, and sat down. At Platform 9, the Customs police had teamed up with the CRS, and held three blacks handcuffed to the ground. I took a seat and ordered a Meteor beer. Across the way, a digital neon screen flashed a message:

> Discount fare: *on bouge?*
> Fantasia voyages

A tour guide leading a group of dowdy Brits in town for a shrinks convention. They walked into a QUICK fastfood and timidly took their seats.

Franck, tu viens?

I continued right out of the district, and up *Réaumur* until it turned into the *rue du 4 septembre*, and back to the

American Express office. There were two letters waiting for me. I exited the *rue Scribe* offices, and stopped in at the *Café de la Paix*. I ordered a coffee, and opened the first, from the Law Society:

> Dear Mr Robinson,
> **RE: Reichman vs Masbourian et al**
> Please be informed that your disciplinary hearing has been cancelled due to the disappearance of the complainant. We shall keep you apprised of any further developments in this matter.
> Yours truly,
> Margaret Tillman

The second letter was postmarked Boca Raton, Florida.

> Dear Franck,
> Laraine here. I'm down recuperating from another bout with Dr Cooper, Franck. Is it worth it? Who knows? But, Franck, I need some company, and while you're drinking Bacardi in my million dollar flat, have I got a deal for you, Franck? Take a break, Franck. You're a prick, but you make me laugh.
> Love,
> Laraine

I stared out the window of the *Café de la Paix*, right at the spot where Oscar Wilde couldn't sponge a centime from the patrons who had idolized him a year previous. That's the problem with literature. No contingency funds. Then, staring into the window, I recalled Sheba looking through the plexiglass of the Montreal airport about thirty lifetimes previous. Pushing the index of her left hand up against the glass, drawing a vertical line on it, then peering through it at the whiteness outside. Then uttering my name, sending a small trace of vapour into the window.

"Franck."

Where had we fucked each other in the city? Père Lachaise. The catacombs. The crypt of the Madeleine. If she were only a whore, why can't you get her out of your mind, Franck? The answer is simple. You just don't. It was like Tranh said. The lines weren't really clear in life. Whether Spike found me or not wouldn't resolve anything one way or the other. As for Sheba, she would stick around for awhile in my brain. Then, the storm would pass. But the overall energy would remain the same.

Then, the thought of that yard-ape Charlotte came to mind. I reached into my pocket, pulled out my wallet. The old man's phone number in Lusignan. It was a long shot, 9-1 at best, and even if it panned out, it was another crapshoot having a nine-year-old version of Sheba to deal with. But, hell, she still couldn't handle firearms, and, what were the options — Margaret Tillman? I walked up to the counter.

"Give me a *jeton* for the telephone."

On the other hand, Millie had offered me a freebie for the afternoon. I walked down the stairwell curling downwards, towards the toilets and telephone. As they say in the New World, heads I win, tails you lose.

David MacKinnon is a lawyer by training, member of both the British Columbia and Quebec law societies. He has five university degrees, including two law degrees and two degrees from *Université de Paris IV-Sorbonne*. He studied history, law, languages and philosophy at the universities of British Columbia, Louvain (Belgium), Sorbonne (Paris), Laval (Québec) and Ottawa. He has worked in oilfields, factories and warehouses, morgues and operating rooms, lumberyards, shipyards, construction sites and in the courtroom as a trial lawyer. For the better part of twenty-five years, he lived and worked in France and Quebec. He has written eight novels.

About *Leper Tango*

Leper Tango recounts the lunar trajectory of Franck Robinson — a self-confessed member of "the despised and despicable sub-species of skirt-chaser known as the john." During one of Franck's regular free-falls into the Parisian night, he meets Sheba, who moves from being Franck's favourite hooker to being Franck's obsession. *Leper Tango* is a confession of an unrepentant man whose stated life aim is to screw an entire city. The author, presumably the alter ego of Franck, is also a jack-of-all-trades and vagabond spirit.

— *FNAC Book Review*

Franck Robinson, forty-something, chaser of skirts, usually the low-end sidewalk variety, combs the streets of Paris in search of Sheba, whom he imagines to be the ultimate Parisian whore. Franck drifts from bordello to bar, and ultimately finds himself trapped by his own demons of alcohol and a fatal attraction. With this hilarious novel, the Canadian MacKinnon showcases a talent for the absurd and a mastery of language reminiscent of Henry Miller.

— *Glamour Magazine*